'What a ride but somehow also brilliantly funny'
Jesse Sutanto, author of *Vera Wong's Unsolicited Advice for Murderers*

'Cracking . . . it's funny, outrageous, gruesome and thoroughly entertaining!'
Charlotte Levin, author of *If I Can't Have You*

'A whip-smart whodunnit, this will keep you guessing'
Red

'*Made in Chelsea* if it got seriously dark'
Heat

'A compelling and incredibly important novel'
My Weekly

'Funny, touching, horrifying and surprising almost in equal measure'
Catherine Cooper, author of *The Chalet*

'A fast-paced thriller with clever twists'
Bella

'A must-read'
Erica James, *Sunday Times* bestselling author

'Razor-sharp and immensely funny'
Jessica Moor, author of *Keeper*

KATY BRENT is the author of three novels. Previously an award-winning journalist, she always dreamed of writing a book and lockdown finally gave her the excuse to do it.

Also by Katy Brent
How to Kill Men and Get Away With It
The Murder After the Night Before

I BET YOU'D LOOK GOOD IN A COFFIN

KATY BRENT

ONE PLACE. MANY STORIES

HQ
An imprint of HarperCollins*Publishers* Ltd
1 London Bridge Street
London SE1 9GF

www.harpercollins.co.uk

HarperCollins*Publishers*
Macken House, 39/40 Mayor Street Upper,
Dublin 1 D01 C9W8, Ireland

This edition 2025

25 26 27 28 29 LBC 11 10 9 8 7
First published in Great Britain by
HQ, an imprint of HarperCollins*Publishers* Ltd 2025

ISBN: 9780008656737

Set in Sabon LT Pro by HarperCollins*Publishers* India

Printed and bound in the United States

For my Sophia,
Fuck the patriarchy, baby girl

'Whoever fights monsters should see to it that in the process he does not become a monster.'

—FRIEDRICH NIETZSCHE

Prologue

I've missed this.

I don't care how far I've come in my recovery or how 'good' I've been for so long. The truth is, I've really fucking missed this.

I feel powerful again.

I feel like me again.

I feel like I can finally breathe after . . . well, a long period of not being able to.

I look at him. The man whose blood is making my skin clammy and my Comme des Garçons dress unwearable. The man who's looking back at me wondering what my next move is going to be. Wondering what I'm going to do to him. Wondering if these are going to be his last moments of life.

That's the million-dollar question.

Are they?

If I do this, if I kill him, there's no going back. I'll know I can never really stop. And I'll know I don't want to.

The monster inside me is unfurling, pushing its way out. I feel it flex its claws and take in a deep breath, getting ready to roar.

I

And it feels so fucking good.

I lean forward and softly press my lips against the man's blood-smeared cheek.

'Thank you,' I whisper into his ear. 'Thank you for bringing me back.'

1

@BlazeBundy Here's a joke for you.
Q. Why are so many women murdered?
A. Because they deserve it.

I know I shouldn't be doing this.

It very much isn't part of my agreed recovery plan. The one I agreed with myself: to give up killing men, no matter how much they deserve it. Also my other plan to step away from social media, both influencing – which is what I used to do – and scrolling. Because I don't need a therapist to tell me that, for me, murder and social media are inextricably linked. The scrolling is where I find accounts like this. Accounts that promote misogyny, shame women and reduce them to nothing but body parts. They give me rage and the rage makes me murderous. And I don't want to murder anymore. I don't want to be a killer. A body count of eleven – and I mean actual bodies, not sexual partners – really should be more than enough for one woman. Not to mention the mental

3

breakdown I had after accidentally killing the wrong guy last year when I was actually trying to kill his toxic brother. Oops. I have a life now, things to stay out of jail for. One of these 'things' is currently in the loo while I furtively sneak looks at Instagram: my boyfriend, Charlie.

I'm doing super well actually, being murder-sober, even if I do say so myself. If there were some sort of step programme for not unaliving terrible men, I'd definitely have a few of those coin things by now. I haven't killed anyone since last year. Not since I took out a high-profile serial abuser and his mad, treacherous daughter, who also happened to be Hen Pemberton, one of my best friends. Anyway, it's all been going brilliantly and I've been able to channel my energy into my life, into living rather than killing. Isn't that poetic? And right now, I can honestly say I've never been happier. Things with Charlie are going perfectly and I feel like I'm connecting on even deeper levels with my best friends – the two that didn't turn out to be psychopaths – Tor and Maisie.

Life is good.

It's really good.

Except.

There's this one thing. This one *man* who is a huge, filthy fly jizzing into my beautiful, happy ointment.

This dick.

Blaze Bundy.

Ugh, even his name gives me the massive ick.

He's a relatively new Insta, TikTok and YouTube influencer. I use that term in the loosest possible way. He's only been posting for a few months but he's already built up a following of several million across his platforms. But Blaze Bundy is *not* the sort of person you want influencing anyone. He shouldn't even be allowed a platform at all. Because all he does is fill it with this kind of rampant misogyny. I don't know how many times I've reported his hate speech to Meta et al., but he's still here, still spitting his poison out and into the eyes of disillusioned young men who make up the majority of his followers, who are also victims of the patriarchy even if they don't realise it. So, even though I know I shouldn't be looking at Insta, even though it feels wrong and seedy sneakily doing it at my birthday meal, while Charlie is away from the table, I have to.

Somebody needs to keep an eye on this mother fucker.

There's a problem though; I can't keep as close an eye on him as I'd like to because I don't have a clue who he actually is. Blaze Bundy is a pseudonym and he uses one of those sound modification devices so no one can recognise his voice. He's also clearly subscribed to some Starter Pack For Incels newsletter because he hides his face behind a black bandana – where do you even *get* bandanas these days? – aviator sunglasses and a black baseball cap. He's a prolific poster, uploading his disturbing brand of content several times a day, every day. And cross-platform too, just in case any of his followers miss anything. I used to judge people purely by their social media following and, let's just say, if I was still that person, I would be extremely impressed. He's got 3.9 million. It took me well over a year to hit the magic one-mill mark and he's only been posting for a few months. And his count goes up by the hour. Imagine 3.9 million people hanging on to your every word. It would be intoxicating. It would make you feel so seen, so special.

It would make you feel like a god.

No wonder he's such a narcissist.

And if the posts weren't bad enough, the comments are an absolute bin-fire in hell. Thousands and thousands of men posting about how right he is. How terrible women are. Spreading Bundy's fucked-up views like an antibiotic-resistant strain of gonorrhoea.

I'm snapped out of my reverie of fury by the sound of glass smashing and I'm surprised to see broken shards on our table when I look down. There's also a tiny puddle of blood pooling on the tablecloth. Pain registers in my little finger and I realise that I've been squeezing the stem of my wine glass so tightly that I've actually snapped it, the bulb of the glass shattering as it hit the table. I pop my pinkie into my mouth and suck the droplets of blood away just as a waiter and Charlie hurry over.

'Kits? Are you okay?' Charlie asks, a look of deep concern on his handsome face. 'What happened?'

'Nothing. I'm fine,' I reply, smiling to show just how fine I am. 'I'm so sorry,' I say to the waiter who is frantically clearing up the broken glass. 'I don't know how that happened.'

'It's okay,' the waiter assures me in a soothing voice. 'Happens all the time.'

'You're bleeding,' Charlie says, taking my hand and turning it over to see the wound. 'Do you need a plaster or something?'

'No.' I pull my hand away and inspect my finger again. A tiny droplet of blood glistening like a red diamond. 'It's just a scratch. Nothing to worry about.'

'But it's your birthday,' Charlie says. 'You shouldn't be bleeding on your birthday.' Hmm. It doesn't *feel* like a particularly good omen so I'm pleased I don't believe in things like that.

I pull him towards me and kiss him on his gorgeous, stubbly cheek. 'Really, it's tiny. I'm fine.'

'I'll bring you a fresh glass and an antiseptic wipe,' the waiter says. 'Can't be too careful.' Feels like there's a lawsuit behind *that* comment.

Charlie untangles himself from my grip and sits back down opposite me, reaching for my hands. 'Are you having a nice night?' he asks. 'Apart from the bleeding.'

He's brought me out to one of my favourite local restaurants to celebrate my birthday. Not just any birthday either. Today I'm thirty. The big three-oh. Halfway to sixty. The age where women hit The Wall, according to Blaze Bundy. I'd very much like *him* to hit a wall actually. A brick one, preferably travelling at a very high speed in a vehicle without brakes.

Fuck's sake. I need to stop thinking about him and focus on this lovely evening with my equally lovely and extremely hot boyfriend.

'I'm having a gorgeous night,' I say, even though the shard of icy anger from Blaze Bundy's latest post is wedged firmly in my heart, making everything else seem slightly less beautiful, less perfect. Even the vegan chocolate dessert which is now being brought out to me with a single candle stuck into it. I cringe as the waiter starts singing 'Happy Birthday' and the other diners join in one by painful one. I specifically told Charlie I didn't want any fuss. I shoot him a withering look and he mouths 'it wasn't me' even though it clearly was because *I* certainly haven't told anyone that it's my birthday. The last thing I want to do is draw attention to myself. Even though I rarely post anything online anymore, there are still people who recognise me from my Instagram days and I *really*

7

don't want anyone asking for a selfie or worse – a *video* – tonight. The waiter places the pudding down in front of me with a flourish while around me everyone claps and whoops before turning back to their own meals and lives.

'Compliments of the chef,' he says, before giving a little bow and disappearing into the kitchen.

'Ah, that's nice of them,' Charlie says.

'They probably don't want me to sue over my injury.' I hold up my little finger, wiggle it and Charlie chuckles.

'Happy birthday, Kitty,' he says. 'How does it feel being thirty?'

'Honestly, it's fine. Absolutely no different.' I've been having a mid-size existential crisis for the past two months, terrified about being old. But actually, it's nothing. Poor Charlie though. I've made him check my head almost every day for greys. I suppose he knows roughly what it would be like to have a kid with lice now. 'How does it feel dating someone who's no longer in her twenties?'

'Hideous,' he says with a little smile that makes his dimple pop and my crotch pulsate. 'Might have to trade you in for a newer model.'

'All right, Leonardo DiCaprio,' I say. 'Shall we get this to take away?' I suddenly just want to be at home, away from people and eyes that might recognise me, curled up on the sofa with my sexy boyfriend.

'I couldn't think of anything I'd like more,' Charlie says and disappears off to settle the bill and get the dessert boxed up.

2

'It's pretty late for the hard stuff,' Charlie says from the kitchen. 'Do you want decaf?'

'Yes, please,' I say.

While Charlie is busy making us Irish coffees, I open Blaze Bundy's Instagram one more time. There's another post. It feels like there's *always* another post. Whoever he is, he could never be accused of not being dedicated to his cause.

This one's a reel. As it plays I sit back, ready to hear whatever new poison he's about to spill.

'Hi, disciples.'

Yes, he really calls his followers 'disciples'. I wish I was making this up.

'I hope you've all had a great day. I hope you're all keeping your eyes open and staying awake to everything that is going on around you.' Part of his spiel is that *everything* is a conspiracy theory and men are being lied to by everyone, from the government to their gym instructors. Blaze Bundy is the only person they should trust.

'So I want to talk to you now about a date I went on last

night. As most of you know, I'll only date a woman until I have sex with her. After that she's of no interest to me. And I don't date anyone more than three times. If she hasn't given herself to me by the third date then I have to assume she's gay and hasn't come to terms with it yet.'

I cringe at his words.

'Sometimes I think there's nothing wrong with taking it anyway if she hasn't given it to me. You know what I mean, men. You've paid for the dates, you've taken the time out of your busy lives to wine her and dine her or whatever. And then she thinks she can just say, "It was nice to meet you but I'm not feeling this"? Well. I don't think that's okay. I think she owes me. It's the reason I make sure I take my dates to the most expensive places. It's why I insist on paying. Because then she *feels* like she owes me, you know?'

Is he for fucking real? I frantically click on the three dots in the corner and hit report. He's promoting sexual assault. This has to be taken down. I tap the 'violence or dangerous organisations' option; his horrible distorted voice drones on in the background.

'Last night's date was date three. I'll call her Ruby. Ruby's hot. Of course she's hot, I wouldn't waste my time on a dog. No matter what anyone tells you about ugly women being better in bed, ignore it. It's not true. And you don't want to be seen out with an ugly female; it reflects badly on you. If someone sees you out with an ugly woman, they will assume you can't get anything better. You don't want that. You want people looking at your date with envy. You want them to think that this stunning woman is with you because you're *the man*. No one will think that if you're with some ugly girl, right? I've gone off on a tangent; I was telling you about last night with Ruby. So yeah, it's our third date and time to pull out the stops so I took her to the most expensive, exclusive restaurant around here. You know I can't tell you where I am because The Feds, but, let me assure you, this place is everything. It's the sort of place where the wait list has a wait list. So when I told her that's where we were going, I knew she was wet for me already. I knew I'd be getting it.'

I feel the lovely food and wine I had earlier this evening curdle in my belly, threatening to come back up. But I can't stop listening.

'And I wasn't wrong. You guys have never seen a woman so blatantly gagging for it. But I kept teasing her. Kept telling her exactly what I planned to do to her when we got to mine. She didn't even want to see the dessert menu. That's how desperate she was for me. Saved me some coin.

'We got back to mine and I still didn't even kiss her. Poured her a wine, took her shoes off, massaged her feet. She was practically whinnying with want when I put my hands on her. In the end I made her plead with me to fuck her. And she was so wet I didn't even need to bother with foreplay. Slipped right in. When I'd finished I called her a car. She was so grateful she didn't even ask to stay the night. Just kept saying thank you and looking at me with tears in her eyes and went home like a good girl. Obviously I blocked her the minute the door was closed behind her. If you're watching this, Ruby, thanks for the orgasm. Don't call me.

'If any of you want to learn my secrets of seduction, click the link in my bio and sign up to my Masters in Sex class. You'll soon be beating *them* off instead of yourself.'

He laughs like a demon before adding, 'Oh, I almost forgot. Before I sign out for the night and pick which female I'm going to sleep with, I want to wish someone a very happy birthday. I know you watch my stories, Kacey, I hope you're enjoying them. Happy birthday, doll. There's a present on its way to you soon. I'm sure you're gonna love it.' He laughs again and the screen goes blank.

I sit staring at my phone screen for a few minutes, my brain desperately trying to process what I've just seen. Whoever this Kacey person is, it sounds like there's something pretty horrible heading her way. If I was still in the business of making this my business, I'd try to track her down and warn her. No woman, especially not a birthday twin of mine, deserves anything from that cretin. If there was anyone who could make me end my murder-sobriety it's this guy. I should block him and get on with my life. But I just can't bring myself to do it. Like I said, he needs eyes on him.

Charlie is at my side with our drinks. 'What was that you were watching? Birthday message from a friend?'

'Absolutely not,' I say. I hold my phone up to him. 'Have you heard of this Blaze Bundy person?'

Charlie rolls his eyes. 'That misogynistic piece of crap? Yes. Unfortunately. Harry's a follower and has been banging on about him for weeks. He keeps sending me links like "How To Discipline Your Girlfriend" or something equally gross.' Harry is Charlie's brother and this revelation doesn't surprise me one bit, which tells you all you need to know about Harry. 'I checked out his accounts. He's disgusting. Needs shutting down,' Charlie's saying now. 'Why are you watching his shit? He makes *me* fucking angry and I have a nice spot within the patriarchy so I don't even know how furious it would make a woman.' My Charlie, the ally.

'Pretty fucking furious,' I say through gritted teeth. 'It's just so backward and gross. I can't believe anyone actually listens to him, let alone laps it up like his *three point whatever million* followers do.' Charlie sits down next to me, handing me my coffee and sliding my phone out of my hand.

'Yep. He's a total tool. But anyway, don't think about him. Not now. Don't let him put you in a bad mood and ruin your birthday night.' He leans over and kisses me on the neck. 'You look very beautiful, by the way. Did I mention that?' I turn to face him and kiss him on the mouth, gently, slowly. Yes. Distraction. This is what I need.

'You did not,' I say. 'Why don't you tell me now?'

'You look very beautiful tonight, Kitty Collins.' He kisses my neck again, takes my coffee out of my hand and puts it on the floor.

'Even for a thirty-year-old?' I say as his lips make their way down my throat.

'Hottest thirty-year-old I've ever seen.' He's unbuttoning my shirt now, slipping it over my shoulders. 'Now be quiet. I've got work to do here.'

I sigh as his mouth dips down even lower and soon I'm not thinking about Blaze Bundy and his fucked-up video. I'm not thinking about anything other than how very lucky I am to have Charlie. And Charlie's very skilful tongue.

3

KITTY AND CHARLIE'S APARTMENT, CHELSEA

'Oh, I almost forgot,' Charlie says a little bit later after he's distracted me on the sofa, in the shower and in the bedroom. Twice. 'There's a package for you in the lounge. It came earlier. Shall I get it?' I make a move to untangle myself from the sheets we've managed to twist into sweaty knots but Charlie shakes his head. 'You stay exactly where you are. I'm not done with you yet.'

I watch as he gets out of bed, naked, and wanders through to get my post, thinking again how lucky I am to have him in my life. I've never had a love like this. A love where I feel safe and secure, no leaking anxiety slowly poisoning everything. It's like Charlie sees me, sees my scars, but instead of recoiling from them, he runs his fingers along them, kisses them. He doesn't want to make me better, but he does. He has his own scars too, a broken relationship with his father, a bone-deep wound left by the death of his mother, his own addiction – drugs – that he will always be in the shadow of. And I kiss them too, hoping that I also make him better but without wanting to change him at all.

Charlie returns about ten minutes later with a fruit platter, two glasses of champagne, a small parcel and an envelope.

'Oh,' I say. I don't get a lot of unexpected post these days. Since I took a step back from Instagram, the freebies that used to arrive by the truckload have more or less stopped coming. Charlie hands me the envelope. It's thick and white and has a postmark from France. It's from my mother. It must be. She's been living on the French Riviera for the best part of fifteen years. Ever since the night my world came crashing down and I walked in on my father trying to rape her. I lashed out, smashing his head in with an antique vase. It turns out antique vases are pretty sturdy and the blow killed him instantly. I can't imagine anything from Next at Home causing such damage to a human skull. Anyway, I saved my mother and then she saved me back by getting rid of the body. In one of my father's own abattoirs. Being an heiress to a meat-processing business has its perks, even for a vegan like me. Things were never the same between my mother and me after that night though. I think we both saw something in each other that scared us. Still, she's the only person I know in France who would send me something for my birthday. Not that I was expecting anything. It's more her style to transfer an obscene amount of money from my father's fortune into my bank account. But I won't look a gift card in the mouth or whatever the saying is. I take the package from Charlie, the envelope forgotten for the moment. Who's interested in cards when there are presents? I tear off the paper and find a deep red jewellery box inside.

'Gosh,' I say to Charlie. 'This is from Cartier. She's really pushed the boat out this year.' Charlie leans over my shoulder, keen to get a close-up of whatever my mother has sent me. I open the box and inside is one of the most beautiful necklaces I've ever seen. A small cylindric pendant made of white gold and encrusted in dozens of tiny diamonds which twinkle up at me. I pull the necklace out of the box, gently, because the chain is as thin as spider thread. 'Wow,' I say. 'This is beautiful.' I turn the little pendant over in my fingers a few times. It's gorgeous. There's a card in the package too. I take it out.

My darling Kitty,
Happy thirtieth birthday, beautiful girl.
Please wear this necklace always so part of me is forever
with you.
I love you.
Your mother x

Christ, she makes it sound like she's implanted some of her DNA in it or something. Ew. I hope she hasn't. It's very pretty though. No one can say Carmella Collins doesn't have taste.

'Shall I?' Charlie asks, holding his hand out for the necklace. I nod and stand up, pulling my hair out of the way so he can fasten it around my neck. Then I look at my reflection in the mirror. The pendant sparkles back, a tiny galaxy sitting at my throat. 'It looks beautiful on you.'

He's absolutely correct. I can barely tear my eyes away from my reflection, but then I remember the envelope. My mother hasn't sent me a birthday card in years. Certainly not in my adult life. She ostensibly doesn't believe in cards, thinks it's a waste of paper and time, but I actually think it's just because she never usually remembers until it's too late. The envelope is luxuriously thick and white and the card inside feels expensive too. But when I pull the contents out, I realise it's not a birthday card at all. It's an invitation.

A wedding invitation.

To my mother's wedding.

> *Kitty Collins and Charlie Chambers are cordially*
> *invited to join Carmella and Gabriel as they*
> *celebrate their wedding.*

What?

Who the hell is Gabriel?

Can my mother even *get* married? As far as the rest of the world knows my dad's a missing person. No one apart from the two of us knows for sure that he's never coming back. My head swims and I need to sit back down on the bed as I read the rest of the invitation.

The wedding is in ten days.

'What you got, Collins?' Charlie asks, looking at the invitation in my hands.

'My mother's getting married. Soon. In France. She wants us to go,' I say miserably.

'Sounds fun,' Charlie says, popping a grape into his mouth and bursting it with his teeth. It's something I'd usually find achingly sexy, but right now it just irritates me. I need some time to process this news. There's a lot to unpack. Not just the fact that my mother is marrying someone I've never met, never had the chance to vet, her track record with men isn't the best, let's be honest. But also, why didn't she tell me sooner? Is our relationship so fractured that she couldn't share this news with her only child? I suppose it is. Something shattered between us the day my dad died, something irreparable. There's a reason we've barely spent more than an hour in the same country since then, a reason we can't look at each other. I won't be going to this wedding.

'I'll start looking for flights,' Charlie is saying. 'What's the date?'

'We're not going,' I tell him. 'No. Nope. No way.'

He looks at me, confused.

'Why not? It's your mum. You can't miss her wedding.'

'I've barely seen her in the past fifteen years,' I say, aware my voice is getting hysterically high-pitched. 'I've never even met *Gabriel*.' I say the name in an exaggerated French accent. 'Why would I want to go to the wedding? And why would I ask you to endure it too?'

Charlie looks at me, a little crease appears between his eyebrows.

'But I want to meet your mum,' he says. *His* voice is all calm and even and in its usual key which makes me even angrier. I feel my jaw tense. I'm sure I read about a Botox treatment that stops this. I need to look into it before I grind my teeth to powder. 'I want her to get out the Kitty baby photos,' Charlie is saying. 'I want to know everything about you when you were little. I bet you were super cute.'

'But I want us to go on holiday together this summer,' I whine. 'Somewhere really hot and exotic. Like Mexico. Or the Seychelles. Lots of sun. Floating breakfasts. Couples massages. Lazy, holiday sex.'

'We can do all of that in the South of France,' he says.

I don't want to go to fucking France and face my mother.

Not after everything that happened. It's a whole level of

family dysfunctionality that I'd really like to keep hidden from my shiny, new live-in boyfriend.

'It's not the same,' I grumble.

Charlie leans over and takes my hands in his, stroking my fingers with his thumbs. 'It's your mum, Kits,' he says, still in his sensible voice. 'I know things are weird between you and all that, but it's your *mum*. I'd give anything to get something like this in the post from my mum.' He'd have a fucking Olympic-sized shock considering his mum has been dead for almost twenty years. I don't say this even though the words are dancing on my tongue.

'You're emotionally blackmailing me,' I say instead. Charlie's mum died when he was a teenager, leaving him with his emotionally constipated father and brown-nosing, money-loving brother. Her death and his grief sent him spiralling into a pretty severe cocaine addiction that almost ruined his life. It was only when he founded The Refugee Charity that he got clean and started healing.

Charlie thinks for a moment. 'A little bit,' he concedes. 'And I'm sorry for that. But it's more that I'm asking you to remember that we don't get the luxury of knowing how long people are going to be in our lives for. I don't want you to regret anything.' He lifts my hands to his lips and kisses them. 'Your mum obviously wants you there for her special day. Why not use it as a chance to repair your relationship? She must really mean it. That necklace isn't nothing.'

'About ten grand,' I say. 'Loose change to my mother.'

'Kitty, I wish you'd tell me what happened with the two of you,' he says. 'I wish you'd let me in.'

'You know everything,' I say even though it's not true.

Charlie doesn't know what really happened to my dad, Michael 'Captain' Collins. Like the rest of the world, Charlie thinks he mysteriously vanished one night, never to be heard of again. 'She took off to France the moment she was sure I'd be able to survive by myself and didn't look back.' It's not exactly a lie. There's also the fact that I despise myself for failing to protect her. I wasn't there for her when I was younger, when she really needed me. I was in my father's thrall like so many other people. A daddy's girl while he hurt and humiliated my mother. It turned out *that* night was just the tip of the domestic - abuse iceberg. She went through so much at his hands and I should've realised it sooner. It's something I can never forgive myself for. It's why I find it so hard to be near her.

Guilt.

It's a fucking killer.

'Will you at least think about it?' Charlie asks.

'No,' I say firmly with a shake of my head. 'We're not going. And I'm actually furious that she's sprung this on me like this. On my fucking birthday.' I grab one of the flutes of champagne from the tray and down it in one even though my head is starting to thump.

Charlie looks at me. All sad face and puppy eyes which would usually make me melt. I don't care. He won't change my mind about this. 'Do you want some more champagne?' he asks eventually.

'No, thank you,' I say. 'I'm done celebrating my birthday now.' I pull the sheets over me and close my eyes feeling like a horrible bitch. Charlie and I have never gone to sleep on an argument before.

Trust my mother to make it happen for the first time.

4

KITTY AND CHARLIE'S APARTMENT, CHELSEA

When I wake up, I reach for Charlie. My heart sinks a little when I realise he's not next to me and I remember our argument the night before.

This is the start of it then. The start of him seeing me for who I really am and pulling away.

I can't really blame him, I suppose. He lost his mother, who he adored, and he can't understand why I wouldn't leap at the chance to have mine back in my life. I gently touch the pendant around my neck. He is probably realising right now that I'm not as good as he is. Not good enough for him.

You don't have a dad but you don't try to push Charlie into a relationship with his.

I shake the thought away, even though it's actually a very good point. But, just as I'm about to crawl out of bed and find Charlie probably getting ready to move back into his own flat, the bedroom door swings open and he comes in with a tray loaded with breakfast paraphernalia.

'Breakfast in bed for your birthday Boxing Day,' he says. 'And to say sorry. I shouldn't have pushed things last night.'

I watch, just delighted that he isn't leaving me, as he places the tray down next to the bed and hands me a coffee. 'There's something I haven't told you,' Charlie says, fixing my eyes with his. My heart sinks. No conversation in the entire history of conversations has gone well after opening with that line.

'What is it?' I pull my hands away from his, crossing my arms over my chest. He suddenly looks so dejected I want to pull him into my arms again but I can't. I've drawn a line between us.

'My mum and me weren't speaking when she died,' he says, dropping his gaze to his hands which are now in his lap.

'Why not?'

'She knew about the drugs,' he says miserably.

'What do you mean?' Charlie had always let me think that he'd turned to drugs *after* his mum died, using them to bury his grief and fill his hollows. I didn't know he was already taking them before her death.

'I started when she got ill,' he says, still not meeting my eyes. 'I couldn't cope. Seeing her so sick and helpless and knowing there was nothing I could do. Anyway, she knew. She knew me better than anyone, she could tell that I wasn't okay. Obviously she didn't approve.' He gives a bark of dark laughter before finally lifting his gaze up to mine. 'I was so angry with her, Kits. For getting cancer. Which is really fucking stupid because it wasn't her fault. She needed me and I was too selfish to see it. I don't think I'll ever forgive myself.'

Now.

Now would be the perfect time to tell him about what happened with my father. How I feel the same way about letting my own mother down for all those years. He's confessed something so painful to me and I could use this opportunity to let him in, to bring us even closer.

But I don't.

Because I cannot tell this kind, beautiful man that I'm a killer.

Instead, I say, 'You were just a kid.'

We sit in silence for a few moments before he says, 'I'm sorry I didn't tell you the truth. I'm ashamed.'

I understand that particular shame.

'It's okay,' I say, reaching for his hands again. He lets me take them. 'It doesn't matter.'

'It does. And I wanted to explain to you why I was so pushy about your mum's wedding last night. But I can't use your life to put right my mistakes.'

I nod. 'We are not in *Quantum Leap*.'

Charlie smiles at my reference to one of the many geeky TV shows I've sat through with him, for him. 'No,' he says. 'We are not.'

I pull him to me now. 'I'm sorry,' I say. 'I'm sorry about your mum.'

'Thank you.'

'You loved her so much, Charlie, she would've known that.'

'I hope so.'

'I know so.'

'Will you forgive me?'

'There's nothing to forgive,' I say. 'Thank you for sharing that with me. It's just, things with Carmella are—'

'Complicated, I know,' he says, handing me a glass of freshly pressed orange juice. 'I just want you to be happy forever. I want you to have everything.'

'I already do,' I say, leaning in and kissing him which I don't usually do in the mornings because, ugh, morning breath . . . but, ahh, make-up sex.

Later, we're still in bed, limbs entwined and lazily half-watching TV when my phone buzzes. It's a WhatsApp message from Tor in our group chat with Maisie.

Tor: OMG! Loooooooook!

She's attached a video which shows a number of police vehicles and a forensic tent set up alongside the river, just a few minutes' walk from where I live.

Tor: There's a body in the water! It's all over socials. All the police are here. It's a woman's body!

I gasp.

'What's wrong?' Charlie asks. 'Are you okay?'

'Tor's just messaged. She says a woman's body has been found in the river. The police are there now.'

'Oh my God,' says Charlie.

'I know,' I say, my mind already several miles ahead of me wondering who she is, who she won't be going home to tonight and which man is responsible for her death. Because it's always a man, isn't it? My hands tingle, the nerve endings alive with the beginnings of the white-hot fury.

Maisie: Omg! Tor! Are you there right now? What's happening?

Tor: I was just walking past and noticed something was going on. I can't really see anything though, just know what people are saying. Apparently a dog walker spotted something in the water this morning! Hang on, I'll FaceTime you.

My phone buzzes with an incoming call from Tor.

'Look,' she says, pointing her camera towards the action.

I immediately recognise the location; it's just down the road from my apartment. I can see a bustle of activity, police cordons are going up and there's one of those white forensic tents that only mean one thing.

A body.

'I can't get anyone official to tell me what's happening,' Tor is saying now. 'It was someone doing a TikTok Live who told me it's a woman's body.'

'Fuck,' says Charlie who is leaning over my shoulder watching. 'That's literally down the road.'

'I know,' I say. 'I wonder who she is. That poor woman.' I think of the family somewhere who will be expecting their daughter, sister, friend to come home today. Who, instead, will open the door to a brace of police officers delivering the worst news imaginable. My heart breaks for them.

There's a sudden exclamation of surprise from Tor, and I squint at the screen.

'What was that? What's happened?'

'I think they've pulled someone out,' Tor says. 'Hang on, I'll see if I can get closer.'

There's a commotion as Tor tries to get a better view of what's going on.

'Yeah, someone is definitely being pulled out,' she's saying as Charlie and I stare at the little screen in horror. Tor's managed to zoom in on a diver climbing out of the water, with something in their arms. The picture isn't great, but I can make out long, water-darkened hair, plastered to a pink face. I squint even harder, trying to make more out, my blood running simultaneously hot and cold in my veins.

'Stop fucking filming!' someone off-screen shouts. 'I said turn that fucking thing off.' A uniformed police officer is approaching Tor now. The image jostles and the screen goes blank. But not before I catch a closer glimpse of the body, the face. Wide staring eyes and a mouth permanently locked into a perfectly round O. The perfectly round mouth of a blow-up doll. Which is exactly what has just been recovered from the river. Not a body at all.

'Did you see that?' I turn to Charlie. 'Did you see what that was?' He's watching the screen with a shocked expression that must mirror mine.

'Looked like it was a sex doll,' he says. 'The police will *not* be happy about that. All those resources over something someone probably threw into the water on a night out. Obviously that's better than it being a body though.'

'Yeah,' I say, distracted as my phone begins to buzz with WhatsApps.

Tor: Omg. It's not a body. It's just a sex doll dressed in a brunette wig and woman's clothes. The dress looks like your pink Dior, Kits. What a waste! There is chaos here.

Maisie: Wow. I mean, so pleased it's not an actual dead body but that is wild.

Tor: Right?? They're moving everyone on now, but I've taken some pics. See you both at brunch??

Maisie: Yes! See you soon!

There's another notification. This time from Instagram.

I open it.

It's a message request from Blaze Bundy. The disgusting misogynist-slash-conspiracy-theorist.

Why in God's name is he messaging *me?*

What I *should* do is ignore it. I should block him and forget about him and move on with my life. Of course I don't do that though. Of course I accept the message request. I need to know what he wants.

It's a picture of a blow-up doll, clearly made up to look like me, in a pink dress and dark brown wig. It's the same doll that was just pulled out of the Thames right by my home. The letters BB are scrawled on its arm in black marker. My stomach rolls with nausea and apprehension which is about as fun a combination as champagne and shit.

There's just one sentence alongside the image.

Hope you enjoyed your birthday surprise, KC.

Then it hits me. KC, not Kacey. My initials, Kitty Collins. He was talking to me on his reel last night too.

But why?

What could the King of the Incels possibly want with me?

5

BLUEBIRD CAFÉ, CHELSEA

I'm half an hour late to meet Tor and Maisie for my birthday brunch because I ended up scrolling through Blaze Bundy's entire social media history to see if I could spot any clues as to why he might be targeting me. But there was nothing. How would he even know it was my birthday? I haven't put anything online and I don't think I've been tagged in anything. How does he even know I exist? I've never even so much as commented on any of his toxic-masculinity videos. I mean, he can see that I've viewed his shitty content but so what? Sending me a photo of a sex doll dressed up as me, just as one is pulled out of the river, is a bit of an overreaction to just *looking* at his shit. He's lucky I'm embracing murder-sobriety or I'd be tracking him down at this very moment.

There must be something else behind it. But what? I feel uneasy and wrong-footed. He clearly knows who I am but I have no idea who he is. It all feels so disgustingly familiar. Like when Hen was stalking me last year. I'd suspect she was up to her old tricks again if I didn't know with absolute certainty that there is no way Hen is making Instagram reels.

It would be quite a hard thing to do when your body has been dismembered and fed through the mincers at an abattoir. Fuck's sake. It's probably nothing. Some kind of misogynistic 'joke' because I'm a woman looking at his page. I need to stop thinking about it. Nothing good will come of thinking about it.

'Sorry,' I say when I reach our usual table in the courtyard outside. It's a beautiful day. The sun is shining and everyone is happy, sporting light tans. May is my favourite time of year and not just because it's my birthday month. The girls are sharing a bottle of sparkling water and Maisie is nibbling on a bread roll. 'Got caught up with something.'

Maisie gives me a naughty look from over the top of her glass. 'Yes. I often got "caught up with something" when Roo and I first started living together too.' The pair of them cackle and Tor makes kissing noises. This is the level of maturity I'm dealing with.

'Stop it, children,' I say. 'How fucked up was that doll in the river?'

Tor shrugs. 'Probably just something from a stag that ended up in the water. Weird that it looked a bit like you though.'

I'm about to tell them about Blaze Bundy and the strange message he sent me but Tor starts fussing around me before I get a chance to.

'Sit,' she instructs me. 'We have things for you!' She stands up and wraps me in a hug. 'Happy birthday for yesterday, beautiful. Did you have a wonderful day?'

'It was great,' I say, squeezing her back before pulling out my seat and sinking into it. I don't mention the message, the argument with Charlie or my mother's shotgun wedding.

'What did Charlie get you?' Maisie asks and I pull my hair back so they can see the princess-cut diamonds he gave me sparkling in my lobes. 'Ooh. They are gorgeous.' She sighs. 'I was sort of expecting him to give you a different sort of diamond though.'

I let out a snort of laughter that really isn't very attractive. 'God, no. We've barely been together a year. And Charlie knows how I feel about marriage and all that crap. It's not on our radar. Not at all.' I'm a feminist and think that marriage is nothing but fancy ownership. Still, some nice dresses though.

Maisie makes a *that's what you say now* face which I ignore. She's watched too many Disney films and read too many romance novels and thinks that everyone will eventually succumb to their inner desire to be wifed.

'And this bag,' I say holding up my monogrammed Louis Vuitton Neverfull tote which illicits the correct amount of 'oohs' and 'ahhs' from my friends.

'And what's this?' Tor gives the necklace from my mother a little tug. 'Is this from lover boy too?'

'No,' I say. 'It's actually from Carmella. I guess she wanted to mark my thirtieth. Pretty, isn't it?'

Maisie leans in and coos, twisting the pendant around in her fingers.

'That's gorgeous, Kits,' she says just as the server comes over to take our drinks order.

'What are we having?' Tor asks. 'Mimosas?'

'Actually, I think I might just have the OJ,' I say and her eyes almost pop out of her head. She looks at my stomach. 'No. I'm not pregnant. I just want to keep a clear head today.' I've actually got to drive later, but they don't need to know about that.

'Me too,' Maisie says. 'I'm trying to be sensible with booze now I'm *thirty*. Falling down drunk just isn't cute when you reach a certain age.'

Tor stares at us both as if she has never seen us before in her life. 'I might need to get some new friends,' she mutters before she asks the server for a round of orange juices. We come here and drink our way through the cocktail and wine menus so often that even the server looks a little bit unsettled. They visibly relax when Tor asks to make hers a Bloody Mary instead.

'Open your presents!' Maisie says, clapping her hands together, and Tor pushes two beautifully wrapped packages towards me. 'It's really hard to know what to get the woman who literally has everything, so keep your expectations low. This one's from me.'

I giggle as I unwrap Maisie's gift and gasp when I pull out a stunning pale-blue silk scarf from the box. 'It's gorgeous,' I say. 'Thank you.'

'Scarves are a wardrobe staple now we're old,' she says. 'So you can cover up your saggy neck and not offend anyone.'

I laugh. 'A gift to me and to everyone around me.'

'Exactly. Someone called Nora Ephron wrote a whole book about how disturbing necks are. Is she Zac Efron's mum?'

I lean across the table and kiss Maisie's cheek.

'Different Ephrons, darling,' I say. 'Different spellings.'

'My turn!' Tor squeals and pushes the other present towards me. It's a medium-sized gift and I pull out a flat, velvety jewellery box. 'Open it!' Tor can barely contain her excitement and she knows what's in there. I give her a smile and snap the box open. Inside is a beautiful white-gold bangle with four tiny diamonds embedded into it. It's stunning. 'I know Audrey Hepburn said diamonds are tacky for women under forty, but Marilyn had a whole song about them being a girl's best friend, and I'm with her on this. Do you like it?'

I take the bracelet out of the box and slide it onto my wrist. 'I love it, it's beautiful.'

'The diamonds are us,' she says. 'Me, you, Maisie and Hen.'

Oh good, a permanent reminder of the treacherous best friend I killed. I want to rip it off my arm. But I smile instead.

'That's such a touching gesture,' I say.

'So she's always with us, wherever she is.' We sit in silence for a moment, Maisie and Tor no doubt wondering where our missing friend is, me clenching my jaw so hard I'm worried I might crack one of my veneers. 'There's something else in there too,' Tor says as the server comes over with our drinks. I smile as I reach into the box, wondering what other horrors she has packed in there for me. Maybe one of my dead dad's teeth set in a nice pendant. Or the screaming souls of all the damned men I've killed melted down and moulded into a scented soy candle. I pull out two pink oval keyrings. They look a bit like vulvas.

'They're personal alarms,' Tor says. 'There's one for each of you. They're a prototype that a startup has kindly donated to the centre. Look, they have a laser as well as the alarm so you can temporarily blind your attacker if you're somewhere remote or the alarm fails. Clever aren't they?'

'Is that legal?' I say, turning it over in my fingers.

Tor shrugs. 'Don't know. But that sure as hell wouldn't have bothered me if I'd had one of these little baddies in Mykonos.'

Maisie's eyes tear up as she reaches across and picks up one of the little pink alarms. 'Thank you, darling.' She places her hand over Tor's and gives it a squeeze as I tuck it into my new bag.

'I'm giving one to every woman that comes into the centre,' Tor says. 'Although it's too little too late by the time I see them.' She squeezes Maisie's hand back and picks up her glass. Tor volunteers at a rape crisis centre in Brixton three days a week. I was so worried when she told me about her plan to work there, but it seems to have given her a sense of purpose since her own horrific attack while we were in Mykonos last summer.

'Are you sure this is a good idea?' I'd asked her when she told me. 'Don't you think it could be hugely triggering and upsetting for you?'

'Kits, I love you for caring about me but really, this is something I want to do. I want to help other women the same way someone helped me.'

Tor's attackers – there were three of them – were reported missing and presumed dead days after they'd drugged and raped her onboard a yacht. While I know exactly what happened to them – and trust me, they won't be drugging and raping anyone else any time soon, what with being dead as fuck – Tor preferred to see it as something karmic and spiritual. And helping other survivors really has given her a sense of purpose and something to work for. Although it's also made her bloody earnest.

'I was so scared when I was watching those police divers around the river earlier,' Tor is saying now. 'So scared that it was going to be someone I knew.'

'You know I kind of thought it might be Hen,' Maisie muses.

'Why did you think that?' I ask. Maisie doesn't usually bring up the subject of our missing fourth wheel, although I can tell how deeply she misses her. But she didn't know what Hen was really like. A stalker, blackmailer and psychopath to name her top three qualities.

'I don't know, it's just so weird that she dropped all contact with us the way she has. I know she's off finding herself or whatever but it's just so strange. I've messaged her a few times on Insta as well as WhatsApp and stuff. She doesn't even read them.'

Not for the first time, I grit my teeth, wishing that I'd kept Hen's phone after I killed her and used it to update her Insta, telling everyone she was going away for a while. It would be useful to log into her socials every now and again to stop people wondering where she is. I could kick myself.

It's such a basic rule of murder.

'We just need to give her time,' Tor says, signalling to the server that we're ready to order food. 'She's dealing with some pretty gruesome shit. If it was *my* dad who'd been outed as a massive predator then I'd probably go into hiding too. You know Hen. She'll pop back up when we least expect it.' I take a long gulp of juice.

I really hope she doesn't.

'Antoinette has been talking about reporting her missing,' Maisie says and I almost spit the juice back out. Antoinette is Hen's younger sister. Fuck. I didn't even consider that she might start freaking out when her big sis went completely off-grid. 'I think she might have a point,' Maisie continues. 'Not

34

wanting to talk to us is one thing but having zero contact with her family is something else. Nets, Ben and their mum must be going out of their minds with worry. I mean, it *is* weird that she hasn't been in touch with *any* of us for months and months. Even on her birthday. Her thirtieth. That's really concerning. This is *Hen*. Hen loves her birthday.' She's right. Hen was always such a birthday princess. The celebrations would last the whole month and we'd all spend a small fortune jetting off to various destinations to celebrate her being alive for another year. There's absolutely no way she *wouldn't* make a grand re-entrance into society just in time for her thirtieth. That's if she genuinely was off finding herself.

I sigh inwardly. 'I think if Hen wanted us to know where she is, she'd have told us,' I say, trying to sound authoritative. 'She's probably hooked up with a hot guy and is working out all her trauma with some A-grade dick.' I have to admit, that *does* sound very much like something Hen would do too. You know. If she wasn't literal mincemeat. Even so, I mentally kick myself again. I should've really planned for this probability. While having Hen go 'travelling' in the aftermath of her dad's scandal and death has worked for a short time, obviously her remaining family would start to worry at some point. I can't have the police getting involved in Hen's disappearance which is what will happen if she's reported as a missing person. I'll need to think about this properly later. 'Shall we talk about something a bit less depressing,' I say. 'This *is* supposed to be my birthday celebration, after all.'

Tor gives me a small smile. 'Yes, please,' she says. 'Oh, I almost forgot. Sylvie and I had a wedding invitation yesterday, Kits. From your mother. You kept that quiet.' Tor's adopted mother, Sylvie, is a singer who was massively famous in the Eighties and Nineties, but really should consider hanging up her mic and taking up crochet or something at this point. She definitely shouldn't still be touring. Or wearing leotards while she does.

'I didn't know,' I say. 'The first *I* heard of it was the invite I also got yesterday.'

Maisie stares at me, her mouth open. 'Wow. What a way to break the news to you. I'm sorry, Kits.' She reaches over and touches my arm gently. 'She invited us too. Well, the invite was for "Maisie and Richard", but I assume she means Rupert.' Rupert, or Roo as Maisie sickeningly calls him, is her long-term partner. They actually seem very happy together even though I will only ever see him as a pair of red trousers with a blow dry.

'Are you going?' I ask.

Maisie shrugs absently. 'Not sure. It's quite short notice.'

'Sylvie's still on tour, so she said she'll try to drop in if she can. I'm up for it though. We haven't been to Cannes for soooo long together. It'll be fun!' says Tor.

When we were kids and our families were super close, we all used to summer in the Riviera. I have glorious memories of us as tanned, skinny children splashing around in the Med, while our mothers sat on the beach sipping cocktails and bemoaning letting the nannies have the summer off. Happy, halcyon days. Before my fuck-brained father shagged Hen's mother and the whole commune vibe went to crap. I mean, surely an expert philanderer like my dad would know not to shit where you eat. Anyway, that was the end of the group summer holidays. It also made play dates at Hen's super awkward.

'I'm not going,' I say firmly. 'And don't even try to convince me otherwise. Charlie's already tried and it's not happening.' I smile at them both. 'Save your words.'

They exchange the tiniest of looks and I know they'll be talking about me in their private WhatsApp group later. All WhatsApp group chats have splinter chats for talking about the other participants. I have one with Maisie *and* one with Tor.

'Okaaaaay.' Tor drags the word out so it lasts several seconds. 'Tell us about Charlie then. How is cohabitation going? Do you want to kill him yet?' She leans across the table and eyeballs me. I've always wondered if Tor knows it was me who made sure her attackers could never hurt anyone ever again. I don't think she does. But every now and then she acts like *this* and I question it.

'No urge to kill here!' I say. 'He's an absolute delight to live with.' This is mostly true although, after spending all my adult life living alone, there have been a few teething troubles.

'Tell us!' says Maisie, leaning across the table too, all thoughts of Hen and weddings forgotten for the moment.

And so I do. I tell them all about how every day feels like it's suddenly filled with Charlie and it's mostly perfect. Mostly. But now I've turned thirty I'm worried the fun part of my life is behind me. I tell them about how I've gained ten pounds and have watched almost everything on Netflix and that, while it was lovely and still is, I'm starting to miss my old life. Just a bit. A tiny bit. The teeniest of tiny bits. I don't mention that it's the killing bit of my old life that I miss the most.

'So what you're saying,' Tor says when I've finished, 'is that you're bored with domestic life?'

'Not *bored* as such,' I say, aware of how much of an ungrateful, whiny little bitch I sound. 'Just . . . unfulfilled . . . maybe.'

'Is it because you're not really doing Insta anymore?' Maisie asks. 'Like, that was such a huge part of your life. Maybe you're missing it?'

Insta. Or murder.

'It could be that,' I say, taking a big gulp of juice. 'I don't think I'm cut out to be a Stay At Home.'

'It sounds to me like you need a hobby,' Tor says, before tearing up a bread roll and shoving it in her mouth.

'I'm thirty,' I say. 'Not seventy.'

'Ooh, project!' Maisie excitedly squeals. 'Let's choose something for you. What do you like doing? What gives you purpose? What gives you joy?'

Hunting deviant men and murderising them in the cruellest and most unusual ways possible.

No. Stop that.

'Um . . . interiors?'

Maisie claps her hands together in glee. 'See. That was super easy. Let's find you an interior design course. You can do evening classes or online classes. Or day classes actually now you don't do anything. You could even set up your own business and become the next Instagram sensation.'

'She's quit Instagram.' Tor sighs. 'That's the whole point. Ugh, I'm getting a wine. Are you bores really not drinking?'

Maisie and I both shake our heads.

As Tor disappears off to the bar inside, Maisie ducks her head down to look at her phone as she frantically tries to find something that could give my life some meaning. I hate to be mean to her but I really don't think choosing between various shades of identical grey for other people's walls is going to cut it.

I miss cutting.

Seriously, stop it.

'There are tons of courses you could take,' Maisie's saying now. 'I really like this for you, Kitty. You could totally reinvent yourself.'

'I don't want to totally reinvent myself,' I snap, slightly offended. 'I just want something to fill the gaping void in my life that is becoming bigger and more encompassing every single fucking day.' *Now that I'm not killing.*

Maisie sucks in a breath, presses her lips together and puts her phone down. I feel horrible. I'm never mean to Maisie.

Tor returns to the table with her wine just at that moment and looks at Maisie, then me, then Maisie again, clearly sensing the tension.

'Kitty just shouted at me,' Maisie says like a snitch who doesn't know what snitches get. 'She never shouts at me.'

'It wasn't a shout,' I say, petulantly. 'It was a slight raise in my usual speaking volume. And I'm sorry.'

'Well, you should be. And apology accepted,' she says primly, nursing her glass like a mother at a school coffee morning.

Tor is still eye-scolding me. 'You're not yourself, Kits,' she says eventually. 'I don't think it would be a terrible idea to take something up.'

'What about getting more involved with The Refugee Charity? Helping people who really need it has honestly made me grow so much as a person. It's so rewarding and life-affirming. I definitely recommend it.' Tor again. See? Earnest as fuck.

The Refugee Charity is Charlie's baby though. His way of sticking two fingers up to his miserable dad who wanted him to have a career in finance like him. Only Charlie could rebel by becoming a philanthropist. And, as much as I love Charlie, I don't think I could bear him being the boss of me. Well, nowhere apart from in bed.

'I think, what I really need is something away from Charlie,' I say. 'Something that's just mine.'

Like killing men.

Men like Blaze Bundy.

Stop it, stop it, stop it! I don't *do* that anymore.

I sip my orange juice under Tor's disapproving glare.

'Definitely think about a hobby,' Tor says, draining her wine.

6

What neither Tor nor Maisie knows is that I actually already have a hobby. And while it doesn't quite fill the hole in my life that ridding the world of bad men does, it *does* help me manage my lingering feminist rage quite well. I mean it should. It's a literal anger management group.

I've been coming to Angry Women Anonymous for about four months now and, honestly, it's just so great to know that I'm not the only absolutely livid woman out here. Who'd have guessed?

We meet in a little church hall in a village in Surrey once a week. We drink very bad coffee – I have to bring my own oat milk because the budget doesn't stretch to 'fancy vegan stuff' – sit on little plastic chairs and share our stories of how men have angered us this week. I have my favourites here. There is Linda who is in her seventies and absolutely loathes her husband. They've been married for over forty years and I cannot blame her. From what she's told me about him, Dennis Nilsen would be a preferable housemate.

41

Linda fantasises about her husband dying, although she hasn't quite got to the point where she fantasises about him dying at her own hand. Well, not that she's admitted. I have though. In quite a lot of detail. He's diabetic and I've had quite a few thoughts about offing him with his insulin. But I wouldn't. That's not the point of the meetings. There's also Keira, a transwoman, who was horrifically beaten by a group of cishet men last year, men who were supposed to be her friends. Despite knowing who the men are and going to the police, nothing was ever done. My fantasies about these men are a lot more violent and bloody than insulin – but – again, I'm not going to act on it. Keira isn't here to get vengeance, she's here to come to terms with – and move on from – an event that has impacted every corner of her life. Then there's Melinda, she runs the group and is a rape survivor. Melinda is one of the lucky ones in that her attacker was actually brought to justice and convicted. Melinda is only too aware that she's classed as 'lucky' because justice did what it is supposed to do for once. Lucky because she got the bare minimum from the system. She is extremely aware of the unfairness of this. That's why she started the group. Because there are so many women who justice turns its back on. Closes its eyes and pretends not to see.

When I arrive tonight, Linda is handing out biscuits she's baked for us. I won't eat them because I strongly suspect she won't have used non-dairy products but I take one anyway as I pour myself a cup of weak tea. Linda is a vegan denier despite me explaining it to her several times.

'There's no meat in it, Kate,' she says. I obviously don't go by my real name here. 'So it's perfectly safe for you to eat.'

'Thanks, Linda,' I say, already wondering where I can hide the remnants once I've furtively crumbled it up in my hands.

'They're chocolate chip, Freddie's favourite.' She smiles. 'I had such a nice time thinking about how I could replace the chocolate chips with ricin.' Linda watched *Breaking Bad* recently after Keira recommended it to her. Their friendship got off to a bit of a wobbly start as Linda had never met a transperson before. Well, not that she was aware of. But after Keira patiently explained things to her and brought her in lots of reading material, Linda studied hard and now the pair of them are best friends. Just goes to show. Old dogs can indeed be taught new tricks if they have a willingness to actually learn. Except when it comes to veganism, apparently.

'I didn't hear that!' I say as I take my usual seat in the circle just as Melinda swoops in. She's incredible. She's got this long swishy blonde hair that sort of floats around her like a perfectly styled cloud. She's fierce and she's sexy and refuses to either be a victim or let her rape define her. I want to be her when I grow up.

'Hello, everyone,' she says, taking a biscuit from Linda before she sits down. 'So glad to see you all here tonight. So this evening, we're going to begin with a burning visualisation ritual,' Melinda says and we all close our eyes like good angry women. 'We're going to take our feelings of rage and burn them away in a spiritual fire.'

I'd rather burn Blaze Bundy in an actual fire.

Stop that.

I've already decided the best thing to do is to ignore him. Breathe in and rise above, as Melinda would say. If he wants to play games with me, he can play with himself. Or something.

'Now imagine yourself in a little cottage, somewhere rural, deep in a forest. You spot a fire burning away in a hearth. Next to it is a basket of firewood. Head over to it and pick up one of the logs.'

I open one of my eyes, suddenly paranoid that this is some sort of joke and everyone else is watching me. But they're all sitting with their eyes closed and their hands resting softly in their laps.

'As you hold the log, you can feel your anger and your rage transfer into the wood. Let it flow. Let it go,' Melinda continues. 'It could be generic anger, or it could be your rage about a particular injustice or situation in your life.'

Well, that's not hard. I try to concentrate on visualising how angry Blaze Bundy makes me feel, on transferring the rage into the wood. But all I can see in my mind's eye is Blaze himself burning in the fire. That ridiculous bandana – which will surely be made from something cheap and highly flammable – going up in flames. His screams as the fire catches his clothes, his skin and he burns, burns, burns.

'Now, throw the wood into the fire. Watch as it catches. Watch as the smoke spirals up into the chimney, taking your anger and rage along with it.'

Argh. There's no wood on my fire at all. Just burning body parts and that fucking bandana. I furtively open my eyes again but everyone is still looking peaceful and serene as their rage-absorbent wood magically burns their fury away, while my own fire is hissing and spitting at me with increasing venom. What's wrong with me? Even my imaginary fire is livid.

Once everyone's anger has burned away and floated out of their spiritual chimneys, Melinda tells us to open our eyes and come back to the room.

'Well done, everyone. I hope that helped you all find your centres and dispel any lingering rage. And I hope you're all having extremely calm weeks. Is there anything anyone would like to get off their chest?'

The sessions always start like this; after a visualisation exercise there's a chance for us to share our anger with the group. We are free to confess any instances where we've acted on the anger so we can think about how we might've handled it from a calm headspace. A woman called Beatrice raises her hand. She divorced her husband a few years ago after he relentlessly bullied and controlled her at home. She left him and took their two daughters with her. But her husband wasn't going to let her get away with leaving him and damaging that delicate male ego of his quite so easily. He punished Bea by taking the kids back and then taking her through the family court. He accused her of having an alcohol problem as well as serious mental health issues. By the time social services had completed their investigations, the judge decided that the kids were already settled with her ex and gave him full custody. Poor Bea only sees her daughters every other weekend now and has to live her life knowing they're being raised by a narcissistic dickhead who lives to fuck her life up.

'Yes, Bea,' Melinda gently encourages her.

Beatrice stands up. 'My name is Bea and I'm an angry woman,' she says.

'Hello, Bea,' we all chant in unison.

'This week I'm angry because it was my youngest daughter's fifth birthday and I am supposed to be allowed two hours with her. This is what the court decided at our final hearing. But my ex-husband was forty minutes late dropping her off

45

to me. He said the traffic was bad but this was a lie. He was then ten minutes early collecting her. We'd already arranged this because he said he had booked to take her and her sister to the cinema. So I only actually got an hour and ten minutes with her. With my baby. With the child I grew in my body and pushed out into the world. She was in tears when she had to go; she said she didn't even want to go to the cinema and wanted to stay with me, but he wasn't having any of it. And it's all to punish me for leaving him. When will he realise that hurting me hurts them as well? Or why doesn't he care?' Bea looks heartbroken as she wipes tears away from her eyes. 'I can't stop thinking about it and crying,' she says. 'But I'm not sad. Well, I'm not *just* sad. I'm so angry. Just so absolutely fucking livid that men are able to do this. He doesn't care about the children. Not really. He's just using them as another way to stay in my life and make it awful. I can't bear it anymore. I wish he was dead. I'm not even kidding. I literally fall asleep fantasising about horrible ways in which he can die. Hoping he gets cancer or something.'

'Cancer's too good for him,' Linda mutters murderously. There's a soft ripple of dark laughter around the circle.

'I'm sorry you're going through this, Bea,' says Melinda. 'And we see you. Your anger is completely valid. How are you managing it?'

Bea shakes her head miserably. 'Not well,' she says. 'I've started a boxing class at the gym and that helps. I don't need to tell you who I'm picturing when I'm dishing out a tasty right hook.' She gives a sad, lopsided smile and I want to know more about this arsehole who has tried to drag her down into the gutter. I can't stop thinking about Bea saying she wishes her ex-husband was dead. How would I do it if I were her? Slowly and painfully would be best. Maybe I wouldn't even kill him before I started taking him apart. Seems fitting for the way he's pulled Bea to pieces. I want to sink my hands into his chest and rip his heart out. So he knows exactly what it feels like. I'm so angry that I don't realise how hard I'm gripping the little polythene cup of tea I'm holding until it breaks and tea spills all over my hand and the floor.

Melinda turns to me.

'Kate,' she says. 'You seem to be holding onto some anger of your own. Is there anything you'd like to share with the group?'

'Just all of it,' I say. 'It just all makes me so angry. Every time I turn on the news. Every time I go on social media. Every time I speak to a woman. There's just so much that makes me angry. Bea, I am literally sat here wanting to kill your ex-husband. But not just him, I also want to murder the judge that handed your babies over to him. I want to punch the people who made the judicial system so fucking anti-women in the face over and over again until their brains explode out of their ears. I want to hunt down the men who hurt Keira. I want to give Linda's husband a too-much shot of insulin. I just hate it all. I want to hurt them all.' I do. I do.

The women in the group stare at me as I rant. It's the most they've ever heard from me. I've never shared 'my story'.

'What happened to you?' Keira asks almost in a whisper. Almost as if she might break the spell of me opening up if she speaks too loudly.

I shrug. 'It's not even about what happened to me. It's what is happening to us always. All the fucking time. It's not fun to be a woman. No matter how much we think the world has changed, it really hasn't. And it won't while there are still men like Bea's ex-husband and the men who hurt you walking around with no consequences. I just feel powerless. And it makes me so fucking angry and so fucking tired.' And it's true. At least when I was killing men I felt like I had some control over all of this. At least I felt like I was doing something. 'There's this influencer guy at the moment who is making me just absolutely incandescent with rage,' I continue. 'I don't know if you've all heard of him.' I know for a fact that Linda will not have. She still thinks the internet is something dark and dangerous and not to be trusted. She may have a point actually. 'He calls himself Blaze Bundy.'

Keira pulls a face. 'Well, anyone who calls themselves that is clearly not a great person. And probably a total narc.'

'What does it mean?' Linda asks.

'It's probably some nod to Ted Bundy,' Keira tells her gently. 'You remember him?'

Linda nods. 'Yes. He was one of them who killed all those women.' Keira reaches over and gives the older woman's hand a squeeze.

'I've heard of Blaze Bundy,' Melinda says. 'Unfortunately.'

'Well, I haven't.' Linda is getting impatient. 'Tell me who he is Kate, and what he does that's making you so angry.'

'He's this social media influencer.' I pause, half expecting to have to explain to Linda what an influencer is, but to my surprise she's nodding along. 'His whole spiel is about promoting traditional masculinity and gender roles. He believes that women should be in the home and having children while men should be doing, basically anything they want to.'

'Toxic masculinity,' Linda is saying, still nodding. 'I've read about it in the papers. Always struck me as funny to be honest with you.' She quickly glances around the circle. 'Not funny haha, funny like not right. From my experience most masculinity is already toxic.' Her comment is depressingly correct.

'What I hate the most,' Bea says, 'is that we have to have this group to be angry in a safe space. Men are just allowed to be angry, aren't they? But not us. Somehow female rage is something we have to suppress.'

'It's like the one emotion men are actually allowed to have,' says Keira. 'They have to tone down every single other emotion or they're "weak" or somehow not a proper man. And all that does is lead to anger. More anger.'

'The patriarchy doesn't serve anybody apart from the rich, straight, white men who created it,' says Melinda.

'When I was going through the courts, I remember saying to my solicitor that the system is broken,' says Bea. She read this quote to me, I can't remember who said it now, but it was basically that the system isn't broken at all. It's working exactly how it was designed to work, by the men who designed it.'

'It's true,' says Melinda and we all sip our tea miserably.

Just as Melinda calls the meeting to an end, my phone vibrates in my pocket. It's Maisie messaging the group chat.

Guys. Can we do lunch tomorrow? There's something I need to tell you. I should've done it today but chickened out. Love you xxxx

Oh what *now?*

7

BLUEBIRD CAFÉ, CHELSEA

When I arrive – on time today – Maisie is already here and I can tell this is serious. Which is something of a surprise because this is the woman who called an emergency meeting one time because her facialist was relocating. She looks exhausted and her usually glowing skin looks grey and somehow both dry and greasy at the same time. Did she look like this yesterday? I can't remember. But then I *was* a little bit distracted with the whole sex doll/mother's surprise wedding dramas. Tor is already sitting down next to her.

'Is this about Rupert?' Tor asks as I slide into a chair opposite her.

'We'd never pass the Bechdel test, you know,' Maisie says.

'Are you okay, Maze?' I say. She looks paler than I've ever seen her and there are huge black rings under her eyes. Maybe this *is* another facialist catastrophe

'I'm okay, Kits,' she says. 'Thank you for asking. And Roo is absolutely fine too, Tor.' I want to ask why she looks like utter shit but manage to keep my mouth shut. 'I've actually got some news for you. I really wanted to tell you yesterday, but it was your day, Kits. I didn't want to step on your toes.'

'Christ,' says Tor. 'Are you sick? Tell us you're not sick!' She takes a bottle of wine out of the cooler and moves to pour Maisie a glass. Maisie stops her by putting her hand over the top of her glass.

'Not for me, thank you,' she says and I immediately know what the news she has for us is. And why she looks like she moisturised with chip fat this morning.

'Maisie! Are you pregnant?'

She blushes, which adds some colour to her spectre-like complexion, and looks down as she nods shyly. 'I am,' she says, proudly. 'But that's not all.' She leaves a dramatic pause while Tor and I nearly fall off our chairs. 'I'm having twins!'

'Oh my God!' Tor screams, her hands shooting up to her mouth. 'Twins! I thought it was cancer!' She realises she's shouting and lowers her voice. 'But it's twins! Maisie! This is amazing.'

I squeal with delight and give Maisie a gentle hug. Are you meant to hug pregnant people? Can it hurt the baby? Babies? I literally have zero idea. 'That's amazing,' I echo. 'Congratulations. You must be so happy.'

Maisie has always wanted a family. Out of our friendship group, she is the only one who hasn't had a massively dysfunctional childhood which resulted in a morbid fear of procreation. She grew up happy as a clam with her mother, father and sister, Savannah. She's the only one of us who I'd trust to reproduce without passing down an entire juggernaut of generational trauma.

'I am.' She smiles beatifically, and I just know she's been

practising that serene mother-to-be look in her mirror with photos of Kate Middleton as inspo. 'I really am. We had the twelve-week scan the day before yesterday. Absolutely blown away to find out there's two of them in here!' She gives her barely-there bump a loving rub.

'That's just so great,' I say. 'The best news.'

'Do you mind if we toast to you?' Tor asks and Maisie laughs.

'You go right ahead. I'll need you guys to drink all the wine I can't for the next few months.' Tor pours a glass of wine for herself and me and some water into Maisie's wine glass so she can still join in the toast.

'Congratulations to Maisie,' Tor says. 'You're going to be the absolute best mama in the world. I just know it.'

'Seconded,' I say. 'I didn't even know you were trying?'

'Well,' Maisie says, 'it wasn't entirely planned. But once we got our heads around it, we decided that we're delighted and want nothing more than to be a family. Of course, Mummy has lost her shit and is insisting we get married before I start to show. Obviously I've told her that will *not* be happening and this is not the 1950s.' We all laugh.

'So, tell us, what's it like being pregnant?' I say. 'How does it feel having *two* brand-new people growing inside you?'

She laughs again. 'Full disclosure?'

Tor and I nod eagerly, hungry for the gruesome details. Because this girl clearly isn't glowing.

'Fucking horrible. I'm tired all the time. Literally all the time. I need about five naps a day. And it's not easy to fit that around the constant puking.' She shudders. 'My hormones are all over the place, I can't stop eating and hello, breakouts.'

She points to a cluster of angry-looking spots on her chin that she's tried and mostly failed to conceal. 'And then there's the anxiety. Every single twinge or spasm sends me spiralling into a huge panic that something awful is happening. So, yeah, I'm having an absolute ball.' We make soothing noises at her. 'But now we're past the twelve-week mark, things should start being a bit easier. My midwife says the second trimester is when women really start to glow. I think she is a fucking liar, but I live in hope.'

'Is Roo happy?' I ask, which I'm sure is a ridiculous question because Roo is exactly the kind of man who will be sickeningly delighted that he's managed to impregnate a woman with his manly seed and continue his bloodline. He's probably smoking cigars with all his red-trousered friends as we speak.

'He's so happy,' she says, beaming. 'He's going to be a great daddy.'

Tor visibly shudders. 'Please don't start calling him Daddy in public. It makes me feel a bit queasy.'

'I'll save that for the bedroom then.' Maisie winks, but then looks like she will throw up herself. 'Well, I would but our sex life died a death as soon as Roo knocked me up and I started projectile barfing all day every day.' She drifts into a little reverie for a micro-second, presumably grieving for her late sex life. 'Anyway, Roo and I have been chatting and we want you both to be the babies' godmothers. Please say yes!'

Tor and I shriek at the exact same moment. 'Yes!'

'Of course we will!'

'As if you even need to ask!' I say. I might not be interested in having any children of my own but when it comes to being a moral guardian for Maisie's babies, I really can't think of anyone better.

We have a few more drinks to celebrate Maisie's news, and then she tells us she needs to go home before she falls asleep at the table.

'I can't believe most people *work* through the first trimester.' She yawns. 'They're superheroes.'

When she's gone, Tor turns to me.

'Well, fancy that,' she says. 'A bit of a surprise?'

I think about this for a couple of moments. 'No, not really. I'm surprised she waited until the grand old age of thirty to be honest.' We sit in silence for a couple of beats.

'Actually,' Tor says and I don't like the tone of her voice at all. 'I'm glad I've got you on your own, there's something I want to talk to you about.'

'Right? Don't tell me you're knocked up too?'

She laughs. 'God no. Happy to let Maisie road test that one for us.' She's playing with the stem of her wine glass, looking very shifty.

'Come on then,' I say. 'I'm not getting any younger here.' Tor is looking into her glass. Something is up. She hasn't made a sassy remark about my recently deceased twenties. 'What is it? Are you okay?' I reach across the table and squeeze Tor's hand but she shakes me away, then looks up, smiling.

'I've been seeing my therapist,' she says, a big stupid grin on her face.

'Yes, I know you've been seeing a therapist, Tor.' Jesus, old news or what. Is she losing her mind? Is it early onset dementia? 'And you're doing really well.' I give her an encouraging smile. 'You're very brave.'

'No, Kitty,' she says, that smile getting wider. 'I mean, I've been *seeing* my therapist.'

What? '*Seeing* seeing?'

She nods. 'Yes.'

'*Seeing* as in romantically involved with?'

Tor nods again, still smiling like she's literally just told me she *wasn't* an idiot. Like she hasn't just told me something she surely would know would make my insides boil like they are right now.

'Wow. Okay.' I don't know what else to say so I take a sip of wine while I process this news, hoping it might dampen the fire in my gut. But alcohol is an accelerant.

Tor's face falls.

'You don't approve? I knew you wouldn't. This is why I haven't said anything sooner.' She is missing the point completely.

'Tor, it isn't that I don't approve,' I say. 'Although, for the record, I really fucking don't. It's that, I'm pretty sure, it's actually illegal. Or something.'

She's shaking her head though, *no, no, no,* like a spoiled fucking kid.

'It's not illegal,' Tor says. 'It's frowned upon but it's not against the law. And I'm not seeing him in a professional capacity anymore anyway.' She has absolutely taken leave of her senses.

'Oh, well, that's okay then,' I say.

Tor looks up at me. 'You understand?' She's beaming and clearly dickmatised beyond all recognition as she's completely missed my sarcasm.

'No!' I hiss. 'I do not fucking understand. I think you need to report this creep to whoever deals with creepy fucking predatory therapists who prey on vulnerable young women.'

Tor rolls her eyes again. 'Oh here we go with the dramatics. Look,' she leans across the table, 'it's not a big deal. Loads of people meet someone at work.'

What? Just what?

'Yes, but *you* didn't meet him at *work*, did you? When did you get a job? You met him while you were recovering from probably the most traumatic thing that can happen to a woman. While *he* was at work. And he should know better.' I sigh heavily. It sounds aggressive. Good. I feel aggressive. 'Seriously, Tor, what the fucking fuck? Can you hear yourself? This isn't some guy you met in a bar. He is your *therapist.*'

'*Was* my therapist.' She's looking intently at her nails. They're a nice colour actually. A sort of deep coral. I must remember to ask her where she had them done when I've sorted out this shitting fuck show. 'I've transferred my care to someone else. Although Aidan doesn't think I need to see anyone at all anymore. He says I've come so far since I started seeing him.'

I bet Aidan *does.*

'It doesn't matter,' I say slowly, like I'm talking to someone of limited intelligence instead of, up until five minutes ago, someone I would've counted as the smartest woman I know. 'It's still an imbalance of power. He's still breached a fuck load of therapist ethics or whatever. *Aidan* is a professional and he's abused his position.'

But she's not listening to me. She's found her stride.

'So, what? You think that I should only date people who can't get it up like Ben fucking Pemberton? Do I not deserve to be with someone that makes me happy? After everything I've been through?' Tor briefly dated Hen's brother – Ben – when we were in our early twenties and told us his erection was as dysfunctional as his family. Obviously I do not wish that on her.

'I absolutely did not say that and absolutely do not think that.'

Fuck this.

I need a drink.

I mumble to Tor that I'm going to the bar where I order a bottle of Sancerre and some edamame. I need to have something in my stomach to carry on with this conversation. The bartender tells me he'll bring it over and I head back to the table where Tor is tapping away on her phone. Texting *Aidan* no doubt.

'He said you'd be like this,' she says, not looking up. 'I said you wouldn't. I said you'd be cool once I explained to you that we're in love.'

I almost choke.

'*Love?*' I say, the disbelief audible. 'Tor, you don't think you're actually in love with this man, do you?' It's a rhetorical question. But she answers anyway.

'I do, Kits, I really do.' Then she turns her eyes to me and they're big and imploring and she really, genuinely believes she loves him. 'Please can you just be happy for me? Like you're happy for Maisie and Roo?'

'Maisie and Roo aren't in a morally dubious relationship where one of them has overstepped their professional responsibilities and boundaries!' I say. 'I don't know how you can't see this. Seriously, Tor. You work with vulnerable and traumatised women all the time. What would you say if a woman who comes to your centre told you she was having a sexual relationship with her therapist?'

The bartender comes over at this point with the Sancerre in a cooler and the edamame. Tor's voice drops to a whisper. So she *does* know it's wrong.

'Of course I'd tell her that she was too vulnerable to engage in that sort of relationship,' she says. 'But this isn't the same, Kitty.' She pauses and I wait with an impending sense of dread as she says exactly what I knew she was going to say. 'I'm not like them.'

'I've heard enough,' I tell her, grabbing my bag. 'Enjoy your wine.'

'Kits, listen . . .'

I don't wait to hear what she wants to say.

I storm home at a pace that would impress Usain Bolt, totally powered by fury. I'm angry at Tor for being unable to see what a massive breach of trust is going on here. But I'm much, much angrier at this therapist, this Dr Aidan. He needs to be stopped. He needs to be struck off and thrown in a cell.

He needs to be killed.

No, no, no. Stop that. That's just the rage speaking.

I take some deep breaths and try to focus on a grounding exercise Melinda taught us a few weeks ago.

'Think of things you are grateful for,' she'd said in her hypnotic calm-person voice. 'It's impossible to feel anger at the same time as gratitude.'

'Charlie, my friends, Veuve Clicquot.'

Kill him, kill him, kill him.

Stop it.

'Maisie's babies, Net-a-Porter, abattoirs.'

Kill him in an abattoir, kill him in an abattoir.

No!

Fuck, this isn't working. I quicken my pace even more, which is pretty impressive – maybe I should take up sprinting – focusing on the rhythm of my feet hitting the ground. I just need to get home. Charlie will calm me. Charlie will be my peace.

8

Charlie isn't there when I get home so I do the next best thing and take a bottle of Chablis from the wine fridge and pour myself a giant glass. After a few heavenly sips, I feel the bubbling anger begin to subside and I can think clearly again. Who needs grounding exercises when wine exists? What I need to do is find this man and do my own research on him. Then I can come to a sensible and measured decision about whether I need to do anything about him or not. And by 'do anything', I mean *report* him to the proper body.

Or make him a dead *body.*

No. Not that.

I take out my laptop and start furiously googling therapists called Aidan in the SW3 area. I don't have much to go on. All I know is that he's based in one of the clinics near here and his first name. But I have absolute faith in my detective skills.

And rightly so.

After just twenty minutes and one glass of wine, I'm pretty sure I've found him. There are only two private psychologists called Aidan in the area and one of them has got to be at least sixty. Unlike myself and poor dead Hen, Tor doesn't have daddy issues. The other Dr Aidan is closer to our age and he's based three streets away from me.

I'm pleased that I've found him but, honestly, what am I going to do with this information? Obviously, if this was a year ago, I'd have been straight round there with my vial of GHB and my freshly sharpened Shun knife. But I'm not that person anymore. So what do I do now? Put in a complaint about him? How long would that take? And surely he'd just deny it anyway. As Tor says, she's technically no longer his patient so I strongly doubt it would be a high-priority investigation. Who would I even report him to anyway? No. This calls for a face-to-face meeting. I can't find out what I need to know about him through a webpage.

I need to know, for Tor's sake, if he's genuine or just another predator.

Dr Aidan's photo on his website is either really flattering or the guy is hella hot. He's all come to bed eyes and curly bed hair. I can see why Tor would be attracted to him, even if he wasn't privy to all the goings-on in her head and therefore able to manipulate her into fancying him. I do what any decent friend would do and call the number on his page.

'Hello, Dr Ward's office, how may I help you?' A young woman answers the phone. I wonder if he's shagging her too.

'Hi, I hope you can help,' I say, making my voice sound shaky and nasal, like I've been crying. 'I . . . I would like to make an appointment. Please. As soon as possible.'

'Okay. I do need to let you know that we have a bit of a waitlist at the moment though. You're looking at about three months for an initial appointment.'

Three months? What's that about? I'm having a mental health crisis here. Well, obviously I'm not really, but the gatekeeper doesn't need to know that.

'Don't you have anything sooner?' I say, all quivery. 'I really need to see someone now.' I hear some tapping.

'I'm sorry but there just isn't anything available. He's a very busy man. If you're having an urgent mental health crisis we advise calling an ambulance. Are you having an urgent mental health crisis?'

If I *was* having an urgent mental health crisis, would I know I was having one? I'm so confused.

'I don't think so,' I say. 'Not an urgent one. But I can't wait three months. It might end up being an urgent mental health crisis by then.' In all honesty, it's likely to be urgent by the time I hang up the phone at this rate.

'I'm sorry, but as I said, we just don't have anything sooner. If you like, I can take your details and put you on a wait—'

'I can pay!' I say. 'Double the usual fee.'

'One moment please.' There's music as I'm put on hold. Three minutes forty-five seconds and she's back on the line. 'Right. I've checked in with Dr Ward and he has agreed to see you for an initial assessment as a gesture of goodwill. Can you be here for 6pm tomorrow?'

Gesture of goodwill, my tits. As always, it's the money that talks.

9

What does one wear for a reccy meeting with a psychologist who has crossed professional boundaries and is boning one of his patients? It's a tricky one. I need to look wholesome and damaged enough that Dr Aidan sees me as a genuine client but also hot enough that he sees me as a sexual possibility. I'm putting him to the test. I need to know if he is the exact sort of sleaze I think he is. The kind who will try to make a move on any attractive and vulnerable young woman he gets on his couch. If I catch his eyes wandering, if they slip even for a second to my legs or my cleavage, he fails. And then I'll decide what I'm going to do about him, i.e. report him.

Kill him.

No.

In the end I choose a white maxi sundress by The Row that I've had for a year or so but I don't think a dusty shrink will be judging me on last season's clothes. It's got an almost obscene slit in the skirt. It's enough to tempt a priest. Although, I'm not sure that's a great metaphor. I've

63

seen *Fleabag*. I keep my make-up natural and leave my hair down. I check myself in the mirror and approve of what I see. Then I give myself a squirt of Baccarat Rouge aka instant nose-gasm.

'You look nice,' Charlie says as I walk into the living room. 'Are you off out again? You didn't mention.'

'Just going to grab a quick supper with Maisie,' I say, pulling a face. 'Girl stuff or I'd invite you along.'

He pulls a face back. 'Nah, you're okay. I'll stay in and do boy stuff.' For Charlie this means reading long and boring articles about proposed parliamentary bills. He really goes wild when I'm out.

'Oh my God, I haven't told you, have I?'

He looks at me, suspicious. 'Told me what?'

'Maisie's pregnant! She told us yesterday. And get this, it's twins! Tor and I are going to be godparents.'

'That's cool,' Charlie says. 'Twins. Christ. Rather them than us.'

'I know, right? Anyway, enjoy your snooze-fest,' I say, kissing him on the cheek. 'Maybe we can go for a drink when I get back?'

'That would be nice,' he says. 'Have fun. Say hi and commiserations to Maisie for me.'

It's not that I enjoy lying to him. I really don't. He's so sweet and trusting and it absolutely stabs me in the heart when he just swallows up the lies like he does. But I have to remember that I'm doing this for the greater good. Tor is in danger. She's being manipulated by someone who should know better. That girl went through absolute hell last summer and I'd thought I'd done enough to protect her. But it's never enough, is it? As long as men exist, I'm going to have to be out there protecting women. I'm sure Charlie would understand if I actually sat down and explained it to him.

Okay. Maybe not.

Dr Ward's practice is based in a normal-looking house. As I arrive, I see a woman leaving. She's tall and willowy and I wonder if she is a patient or the woman I was talking to on the phone yesterday. Am I going to be alone with Dr Aidan?

I press the buzzer and a male voice answers. 'Yes?'

'Oh hi, it's Kitty. Kitty Collins? I have an appointment at 6pm.'

'Right, yes. Come in, Kitty.' Even through the intercom his voice sounds as smooth and buttery as silk. Well. Of course it would.

I walk in and am greeted by the man I recognise from the website. Dr Aidan is dressed down in grey joggers. He's not wearing any shoes, just socks on his feet in, what I would guess is, an attempt to make me feel comfortable and at home. Like *hey, mi casa, tu casa* vibes. He's probably expecting me to take my own shoes off but this will not be happening. I'm not stupid. I know that I will need them on should I have to suddenly run. He's wearing a T-shirt with some obscure band I've never heard of emblazoned on the front. The Byrds. Who? He's got three-day stubble and black-rimmed specs. He looks like a cool uni professor. Well, like how I imagine one would look. I bet both his male and female clients all have crushes on him. He must be completely socially inept though. How could an attractive man with a career and a house not be able to get a girlfriend through the usual avenues?

He smiles at me. It's a hot smile. And it's pretty obvious he knows it. This must be the point where vulnerable women know they're a hopeless case and think they may as well just hand their knickers over to him on a plate.

'Hi, Kitty, it's great to meet you.' He almost has me believing him as he holds out his hand, oozing charm. He's professional. If he recognises me or my name, he doesn't let on. Not for a second. And Tor said they'd talked about me together.

'Thanks for seeing me at such short notice,' I say and I can tell by the way he's tilted his head and is looking at me with big *sympathetic* eyes that he's buying my performance too. 'I really appreciate it.'

'No problem at all,' he says, his accent is Home Counties. 'I talk to my clients in here,' he tells me, indicating a door to the left. He opens it and leads me into a room that's part shrink's office and part Ikea-sitting-room display. It smells like lavender and depression. 'Take a seat.' He points to an oversized yellow wingback armchair. I do as I'm told. He sits opposite me on a brown leather Chesterfield. I wonder if he and Tor have fucked on it. I wonder how many more of his clients he's fucked on it. Bodily fluids wipe off leather easily.

Like blood.

No. Stop it. I'm not here to kill him. I'm here to find out if his intentions with my friend are honourable, or if he screws every pretty, messed-up woman who comes his way.

'There's some blankets next to you,' he's saying. 'Some people like to have them for comfort, especially for the first few sessions.' I look at the pile of blankets to the right of me. They look like they might have fleas.

'Thanks but I'm fine.'

He smiles and nods. Adjusts his glasses. There's a large dark wood coffee table between us with a jug of water and a box of tissues. I wonder if he and Tor have used those tissues to clean up after fucking on the leather Chesterfield.

'So what do you need from me today, Kitty?' he asks. 'Magdalena said that you were eager to see me as soon as possible.'

I've already got my answer prepared for this. 'I'm struggling with a break-up,' I say.

'Right, well, that's perfectly normal. Many people find it hard to bounce back in these situations. But the good news is that it's definitely something I can help you process and move on from in a healthy way. Can I ask how long it's been? Since the break-up?'

'About six months,' I say. 'I just can't seem to move on. It's like I'm stuck.'

'Was it a mutual separation? Tell me about it.'

I hesitate. 'It was more of a forced separation. It's like I had to give up something I loved. For my own good. But it's still so hard.'

Dr Aidan is nodding. 'I understand. Very few break-ups are actually mutual and it can feel like it's something that's been forced upon you. Something you didn't necessarily want. Would I be right in thinking it was something of a toxic relationship?'

He's good.

'Very toxic,' I say. 'But it didn't feel like that when I was in it. When I was in the thick of it, it felt magical and special and like I was the most amazing person in the world. It gave me validation. It filled a hole inside me.' I watch for a reaction as I talk about my hole being filled. I don't see one.

'Toxic relationships often feel like that. That's what makes them so addictive. Studies have shown that some relationships can be as addictive as drugs or alcohol. That's why you feel so awful when they end. Your brain reacts in the same way as an addict would react to withdrawal. It's very common.'

'So do you think you can help me?'

Dr Aidan peers at me over his specs. 'I would say so. Six months is quite a long time to still be in the denial stage. Did you know that break-ups make you go through the same cycle of emotions as grief?'

An image pops into my brain uninvited. It's me, several years ago, shortly after finding out Adam, my then-boyfriend, had been cheating on me. Just after I'd bashed him round the head with a fibreglass trophy he'd won for his novel leaving him unable to speak or move. I'm lying listlessly on my bed while my friends try to encourage me to come out. They tempt me with shopping, alcohol, drugs, boys but I don't want any of it. I'm skinny, but not in the good way. In the very unwell way. My hair is unwashed. For some reason the scene is in black and white. Like a Jean-Luc Godard film. Then, later, I'm screaming and throwing things and collapsing into myself, crying. Yes, I know very well how break-ups can mirror the grief cycle. And it's something I never ever want to go through again. I don't think I could survive it another time.

'Do you feel comfortable telling me their name?' Dr Aidan's soporific voice breaks through my thoughts.

'Sorry?'

'Your former partner. The person you're struggling to move on from?'

'Oh. No. It's not a person,' I say. 'I'm struggling to break up with social media.' Really, I mean killing, of course.

'I see,' says Dr Aidan, his brow furrowing. 'Well, in that case we'd be looking at addiction treatment and ways to break your crave cycle.' He starts going on about identifying my triggers (seeing violence against women), my addiction-related thoughts (how I want to find the perpetrator and inflict some violence of my own) and the craving itself (kill, kill, kill). 'In the end,' he says, 'it all comes down to choice. You make the choice whether you're going to open the app or not. The difference between addiction and non-addiction is being able to make that choice. If you can easily stop, then you're not an addict.'

Well, that's fabulous news, isn't it? I haven't killed anyone in ages. So I can't be an addict because I made the choice to stop.

I can stop whenever I want.

He talks to me a bit more about addictive personalities, hands me some leaflets and tells me to make another appointment tomorrow if I think therapy is something I want to pursue.

'I have to say,' he says as he shows me out. 'I've never worked with someone addicted to social media before.'

Oh Dr Aidan, you don't even know the half of it.

10

I leave Dr Aidan's office with plenty to think about, although none of it is exactly what I hoped to come out with. I didn't find out anything about him and Tor at all. He sidetracked me into an actual therapy session somehow and now I'm thinking about myself. I'm not sure if this makes him a master manipulator or just a very good therapist. I have to admit that he doesn't come across like an evil predator abusing his patients. He seems like a very nice and very gentle man. I often forget that there are some out there. Charlie is living proof of that. Maybe I am being too overprotective of Tor. But it's hardly surprising, is it? Maybe I should just let her get on with it. Okay, I don't approve of how they met, like *at all*, but there are worse things in the world, aren't there? And he didn't even *look* at me in a way I'd consider inappropriate.

Maybe it really isn't any of my business.

Or maybe I *do* need to make that follow-up appointment. Just to be sure.

I'm so in my head about Tor and Dr Aidan that I don't

even realise I've collided with someone until I hear a squeal and bring myself back to the moment.

'You really need to watch where you're going,' I snap before I see that the person I've crashed into is Antoinette Pemberton aka the younger sister of my former-best-friend-now-sausage-roll-filling Hen.

Well, this is awkward.

'Kitty!' Antoinette says with a big smile that makes me feel just horrible. I guess that's going to happen when you wipe out two-fifths of someone's family in one evening. For reference, as well as unaliving Antoinette's psycho sister, I also had to kill her dad, James, for being a horrendous sexual predator. Personally, I think the whole family needs some fucking intensive therapy.

'Hi, Antoinette,' I say, trying to match her smile. 'Sorry, I didn't realise it was you.'

She chuckles. 'It's fine. I wasn't looking where I was going. Totally my fault. How are you?'

What is the appropriate response here?

'I'm really good,' I say. *Okay, it's probably not that.* 'Well, you know. Missing Hen of course. Have you heard from her?' As far as Antoinette and the remaining members of her family are concerned, Hen is off finding herself somewhere after the death of her father and big reveal of him being a rapist with a special interest in very young women.

'No.' Antoinette shakes her head. 'Mum is beside herself and thinks we should go to the police but I don't know.' She wrinkles her nose and looks almost identical to her sister for a second. I mean her sister when she was alive obviously. No one would want to look identical to how Hen probably looks right now. 'She's a thirty-year-old woman who posted on

71

Instagram that she needed some time away. I don't think it's a police matter. What do you think?' Am I imagining that she's peering at me a little bit *too* hard?

'I think you're right,' I say. I really don't want the police looking into Hen's disappearance. 'You know Hen. She'll turn up when she's ready. Probably with an inappropriate man carrying her bags for her.'

'Yeah.' Antoinette smiles. 'You're right. I'll convince Mum to hold off. For a while anyway.'

Fucking phew. A while is enough time to figure out what to do next.

'How's everything else . . . ?' I obviously mean her dad but it feels rude to address it directly. There was a media shitstorm when James Pemberton, a highly accoladed music mogul, was found dead, choked to death by a stocking and wearing a corset and suspenders. I thought that was a nice touch for when he was found.

Antoinette shrugs. 'Confusing. Ben is devastated, you know how much of a daddy's boy he is. I'm firmly lodged in the angry stage. Mum is living on a diet of gin and diazepam. She's struggling.'

I pull what I hope is a sympathetic face but I couldn't care less about Laurelle Pemberton having some sort of breakdown. An image of her bent over a pool table in my childhood home, my dad grunting away behind her pops into my head like a twisted flashcard. I really wish there was some sort of deep cleansing treatment for the brain.

'I'm sorry to hear that,' I lie. I touch her arm gently. 'I need to get going but it was nice to see you. Let me know if you need anything okay?'

'Thank you,' she says. I give her arm a little squeeze before I start walking again, keen to get home to a glass of something cold. 'I'll see you at your mum's wedding!' I turn back and Antoinette is smiling at me again.

'Sorry?' I say.

'Carmella's wedding? Ben and I are coming so I'll see you in France.'

I smile back weakly. Has my mother invited everybody in SW3 to this wedding?

11

When I got home yesterday, after recovering from my Antoinette encounter with a glass of Chablis, I decided that I *will* go back to Dr Aidan. He totally sidetracked me with his therapist talk and, while he seemed like a nice enough guy, the dangerous ones often do, don't they? That's exactly how they manage to worm their way into the lives of the women they go on to hurt. I'll go back, *prepared* this time, and ask him about Tor.

So here I am, sitting in that yellow wingback again, determined to stay on track.

Tell me more about how Instagram makes you feel, Kitty,' Dr Aidan says after pouring me a glass of water. He's got another band T-shirt on. It's The Beatles today. At least I've heard of them.

'Good,' I say. 'Most of the time. At first. Posting photos made me feel powerful. Follows and likes made me feel like I really existed.'

'You didn't feel like you existed before Instagram?'

'I did. But a different sort of existence. Kind of like I was here but I was hollow. Like an empty shell or something.'

74

Damn, he's good.

'So it made you feel validated?'

'Yes, that's it. It felt like, if all these people were telling me I was great, then I must be. I had over a million followers.' I'm embarrassed at how proud I still feel about this. 'A million people can't be wrong, can they?'

Why can't I stop talking about myself? I'm supposed to be here for Tor.

'And when did it start to feel toxic? Why did it stop feeling good?'

'I made a mistake,' I say. We sit in silence for a moment as he waits for me to elaborate. I don't. I'm not talking about Instagram anymore, I realise. I'm talking about Ruben Reynolds. The innocent man I put in a grave last year because I didn't do my research properly. It was supposed to be his brother I killed. Raphael Reynolds was the bad man, the famous footballer and serial rapist. Ruben's only crime was looking far too much like him.

'Do you want to tell me about it? The mistake?'

I shake my head. Shake myself into action.

'I'm not actually here to talk about myself,' I say, finally getting a grip.

He tilts his head in that therapist way which must be taught at therapist school. 'That's kind of the point of therapy though. Isn't it, Kitty?'

'I know, you know,' I say.

He doesn't say anything, just waits for me to keep talking. Something else I'm sure is one of the very first lessons in therapist school.

'About Tor,' I continue, 'I know you're sleeping with her.

And I want to know why. It's not right, is it? You know what she's been through.'

'Ah. Kitty. Right, yes. I wondered if that was what your visits were really about,' he says. 'I can imagine what you're thinking and I know it doesn't look great, but it's not like that. It's really not. Tor is incredibly special to me. I have very deep feelings for her. And the moment I realised that, I stopped seeing her in a professional capacity. I've handed her care over to a fellow psychologist who I trust implicitly.' He sighs. 'I know it's not the most ideal of situations, but I, *we*, really hoped you'd understand.'

I shake my head. 'She was raped. Drugged and raped by three men. She came to you because she was traumatised. And all you've done is show her that men *can't* be trusted. You've used her vulnerability to sleep with her. Honestly? I want to kill you.'

He smiles at me like he's being very patient with a particularly difficult client. 'No, Kitty. You've got it all wrong. We haven't slept together. Not yet. Not ever if that's not what she wants. I'm not in it for that. And she can trust me. She *does* trust me.'

'You haven't slept with her? And you won't if she doesn't want to? Do you expect me to believe that?'

He sighs again. Is that a hint of exasperation I detect? 'It doesn't matter what you believe or what you don't believe. It's the truth. For God's sake. Neither of us chose to feel like this. I'm more than aware that it could torpedo my entire career.' I keep staring at him. 'I'm being honest with you. Tor means a lot to me. This isn't something that either of us have gone into lightly, especially with everything she's been through.

I'm painfully aware how bad it might look to anyone on the outside, but I would never do anything to hurt her. She's so special and strong and I'm just honoured that she trusts me enough to love her. She's a remarkable woman.'

'She is. I suppose that's something we agree on.'

'Look Kitty, Tor and I both would like your blessing. I know it means a lot to her and she was so worried about telling you. And I completely understand why. But you have to know that I would never do anything to hurt her.' He stands and makes his way over to the door. 'I think you should probably leave now though. This isn't the right place for this conversation. I won't charge you for the session. If you'd like to continue exploring addiction therapy then I can recommend one of my colleagues but it's a conflict of interest if we work together.'

I leave feeling confused. He seems genuine about his feelings for Tor. And he hasn't given me so much as a sleazy side eye. But predators don't announce it, do they? I guess I'll have to wait and see whether Aidan can be trusted or not.

And believe me, I'll be watching.

12

'I'm still livid,' I say to the other women when I arrive at tonight's AWA meeting. 'Even though he seems to have done everything properly, I'm still fucking livid. I just don't see how a relationship that starts with such a huge imbalance of power can ever work. Am I the arsehole?'

'You're not,' Keira says. 'You're just worried about your friend. And rightly so. It sounds like a massively toxic situation. Especially after everything she's been through.'

Melinda is nodding. 'She's obviously very vulnerable, even if she doesn't see herself that way. How did you feel after visiting him?'

'A little better,' I admit. 'But of course I would, he's *trained* to make people feel better. That's why it's so dangerous.'

'You could look into reporting him to the professional body?'

I shake my head. 'I don't know. He says that they haven't actually had sex so I don't know what the crime is. I mean, obviously he's groomed her emotionally but . . . I don't know.

She'd kill me if she found out too. That would be it for our friendship.'

'Even though you're just looking out for her, pet?' Linda says.

'She thinks she's found love,' I tell her. 'She'd never forgive me for ruining it.'

'Could you forgive yourself if you turn out to be right though?' Melinda asks.

I'm mulling this over when the door to the church hall swings open and makes us all jump when it hits the wall with a loud crash. A woman has walked in and she's looking a bit embarrassed about her noisy entrance.

'Sorry,' she says, her eyes flicking over each one of us. She looks super nervous. 'I'm here for the meeting? My counsellor gave me the address?'

Melinda stands up and opens her arms in greeting. 'Yes, yes. Come in and take a seat. Grab yourself a tea or something first if you'd like. We're just having a chat about toxic masculinity. Or just masculinity if you'd prefer.' She gives Linda a warm smile.

'I'll get you a tea,' says Keira. 'Or coffee if you'd like? You sit down. Don't be shy. We're a really nice group. No one here bites.'

Well, I do. But only men.

'What's your name, lovely?' Linda asks as the new woman perches on the edge of the plastic chair next to me.

'Cassie,' she says. 'My name's Cassie. And I would love a tea. Thank you so much. Just milk please. Thank you.'

'Do you want normal milk from a cow or some of the fancy stuff our Kate here brings?' Linda indicates me. 'You won't mind sharing will you, Kate?'

Cassie turns to look at me. 'Kate?' she says in a soft voice. She stares at me for just slightly longer than feels comfortable before she shakes her head as if getting rid of an intrusive thought. 'Just regular milk is fine. Thank you.'

Melinda is smiling at Cassie now. 'Do you want to tell us why you're here?' she prompts. 'You don't need to if you don't feel ready just yet. There's no pressure. Some women like to offload immediately at their first meeting. A lot of us have been sitting on our rage for so long that we find it deeply cathartic just to dive straight in. Others take a bit longer until they feel comfortable.' She gives me a soft smile. 'But it's totally up to you.'

I steal a glance at Cassie. She doesn't look like someone who is boiling over with rage. She just looks very broken, almost like her insides have been scooped out. I can see it's taking all her strength to hold herself upright and put one foot in front of another, day after day.

She gives Melinda a nod and begins to talk. 'My name is Cassie and I'm an angry woman.' Her voice is brittle but surprisingly strong. 'I'm angry because, two months ago, my daughter was sexually assaulted by someone she works with.' She pauses, takes a breath, then pulls herself up into a taller sitting position. 'She's only eighteen. And it's not even a proper job, she's just been doing work experience at a TV station before she starts uni. But that's not happening now. She doesn't want to leave home. She barely leaves her bedroom.' Cassie's voice trails off slightly but she gives herself an internal shake and starts again. This time she looks each of us in the eye as she speaks. 'This man, more than twice her age, asked her to go for a drink to talk about how her placement was going. My daughter trusted him. She didn't think she was in any danger. She *shouldn't* have been in any danger. He paid for two drinks and some chips while they chatted. She was having a nice time. She says he was charming and funny and she was obviously a bit in awe that this man was paying attention to her, just a work experience girl. She hadn't noticed that when she got up to go to the toilets, he followed her. She didn't know until he grabbed her when she was on her way back out and tried to kiss her. When she refused and asked him to stop, he didn't. He put his hands in her trousers. He told her to relax and enjoy it. When he'd finished with her, he led her back to the table, finished his pint, winked at her and said he'd see her tomorrow. And that it was their little secret. She didn't tell me for a week. She was so ashamed. She couldn't understand why it had happened. She thought she'd done something to lead him on. She didn't go back to the placement. And he had the nerve to contact her and tell her that he was disappointed not to see her the next day as they'd had such a fun time the night before. Can you even believe that? A fun time? He assaulted my child and described it as a fun time?' She shakes her head in sheer disbelief. 'When she eventually told me what had happened, I wanted her to go to the police. But she refused. She said no one would believe her. It was her word against his. That even if it did go as far as him being charged, she'd be dragged through a horrible trial, her actions would be scrutinised. She'd be the one under a microscope. She cried and pleaded with me not to make her go. Of course, I wanted her to report him, but making her do something she wasn't comfortable with was not the right thing. And, after I'd calmed down, I realised that she was right. And because of this, he'd get away with it. And that made me angry all over again. I haven't really managed to calm myself down at all. It's eating away at me all the time. I have to remain calm and supportive for my daughter, but it's like I'm acting all the time. I want to hurt this man. I want to destroy him.'

As Cassie speaks she becomes more animated. Her fury is evident in every fibre of her being. She loathes this man. She would do anything in her power to pull his life apart. To make him pay for how he treated her daughter. It's a feeling that resonates with me. I can feel it in my actual bones, the way I'm sure Cassie does.

'Thank you for sharing your story,' Melinda says. 'I think we can all understand how you feel. I'm sorry this happened to your daughter. But I'm also sorry it happened to you. How is she doing?'

Cassie gives a small shrug, a microscopic movement of her right shoulder, as if her speech drained the very last of her energy. 'She's just not the same,' she says eventually. 'She's not the woman she was. Not at all. At first she was so, so angry but the rage has gone now and she's just a shell. She won't talk about it anymore, just pretends everything is fine, but I know it's not. How can it be? She's always been this beautiful, trusting soul and it's been swiped away by this monster. And he's still on our TVs every night. I wish she'd go to the police.'

Melinda is nodding kindly, her head in the tilt of sympathy she does whenever one of us speaks about our rage. 'But you understand why she doesn't want to?' she asks, her voice so light it pretty much floats across the circle to Cassie. 'Why it's so hard for any woman to go up against someone in a position of power?'

'Yes,' Cassie whispers. 'I do. And I understand why she's scared and why she feels powerless. I really do. But I just keep asking myself, *what if he does it again*?'

I dig my nails into the palms of my hands. These men. They're everywhere. They're still everywhere. They're TV stars, they're influencers, they're fucking *therapists*. They're calling themselves Blaze Bundy and posting misogyny on social media, luring disillusioned young men into their toxic ideology.

As we file out of the hall when the meeting has ended, I feel a hand on my arm. When I turn around, Cassie is there – a nervous smile on her face.

'I hope you don't mind me asking,' she says in a low voice. 'I know this is supposed to be anonymous and everything. But aren't you Kitty Collins?' It's been a while since I've heard those words. When I was influencing, I used to hear them pretty much every day. You'd be amazed at how quickly you can get bored of hearing your own name. But it hasn't happened for ages. One of the good things about influencer culture is that you can be quickly forgotten about. If you're not uploading new and relevant content every single day, several times a day, people move on. There is always a queue of younger, more tech-savvy girls waiting behind you, waiting for their turn to flog diet drinks.

'I am,' I say, matching Cassie's whisper as we get outside and the other women start heading off on their journeys home.

'I'm sorry to out you,' she says shyly, 'but I wondered if it would be possible to get a photo of you?'

A weird request from a woman in her forties.

'It's not for me,' she adds quickly. 'It's for Scarlett. She used to love your videos and was really upset when you stopped posting. It's only a little thing but it might cheer her up a bit.' She sighs. 'So few things bring her joy anymore.'

How can I say no to that?

'Of course,' I say and Cassie snaps a selfie of us both.

'Thanks so much,' she says. 'I'd better dash, don't want to miss the bus. Hopefully I'll see you next week? And don't worry, your secret is safe with me.' She turns to go.

'Wait,' I say. 'I'm driving. Let me give you a lift home?'

'Oh no, really, I couldn't ask you to do that. I live about half an hour away.'

'Honestly, it's no problem at all.'

'Okay . . . well, if you're sure.'

'Totally sure, I'm over here.'

Cassie follows me to my car and climbs into the passenger seat. I smile at her as I start the engine and the doors lock.

'I didn't mean to put you on the spot just then,' Cassie says as we pull onto the main road. I wonder if any of the other women know who I really am. Linda's probably too old but Keira is definitely social media savvy and Bea looks like she knows her way around a smartphone. Melinda knows who I am as I had to fill in a load of forms when I signed up for the course. I feel momentarily touched for no one calling me out. 'Don't worry, I won't blow your cover,' Cassie is saying now. 'But I couldn't not mention it. I won't say anything to Scarlett either, I'll pretend I ran into you in town or something.' Cassie talking about her daughter so openly makes it easy for me to segue into the conversation I really want to be having.

'Do you only have one daughter?' I ask.

'Yes.' Cassie nods.

'How is she doing?' I say. 'I mean, you don't have to tell me, but what you were saying, your story, it really got to me.' Not a lie.

Cassie sighs. 'We were supposed to be coming together today.' She gives me a sad smile. 'But she couldn't. Got as far as the doorstep and had a panic attack. She'd have loved to have seen you. It probably would have made her year.'

'God, I'm so sorry. Does she have them a lot? The panic attacks?'

'Yes and they seem to be getting more frequent. Poor girl. I need to sort out some therapy for her but it's hard when she won't even leave the house. She just doesn't feel safe anymore. And I feel like I've failed her. It's like the one job you have as a mother, keep your child safe, and I couldn't do it. I fail to do it every day. God, not to make this about me but that fucking bastard just doesn't realise how deeply the consequences of his actions are felt.'

I reach over and put my hand on top of hers. 'I'm so sorry, Cassie. I'm so sorry for Scarlett but for you as well. I can't imagine how hard it is for you.'

'She doesn't even walk around the house in her pyjamas anymore. I know she's not scared of her dad but that fucker has made her scared of men. He's made even her own home feel dirty and unsafe. And then you've got people like those so-called masculinity influencers making her virtual world feel unsafe too. And you know how much kids live their lives online.'

'Your husband must want to kill him,' I say.

Cassie's eyes ignite with rage. '*I* want to kill him,' she hisses.

Me too.

'I want to tear his throat out with my bare hands. I want to make him absolutely fucking cry and piss himself with fear. I want to know that he will never make another girl, another family suffer like mine.'

'You know,' I say. 'With men like that. Scarlett probably isn't the first.'

'And she won't be the last,' Cassie says sadly.

She's right. This *creature* will get away with it. And then he'll do it again. And again. And again. Unless . . . no, I can't think like that. This isn't my problem. They need to go to the police. Get justice the proper way.

'Who was it?' I ask, my mouth several miles ahead of my brain.

'Between you and me?' Cassie says.

'Yes,' I say. 'Strictly between the two of us.'

'It was Max Macintyre.'

I nod. I know Max Macintyre. Everyone in the UK probably knows Max Macintyre. He's the weeknight TV host with a megawatt smile and year-round tan. He flirts with his female guests, is BFFs with his male guests and could probably charm the knickers off a nun. He's many things and I'm not surprised that sexual deviant is one of them. I just can't trust someone whose teeth are that white.

'Not a huge surprise,' I say. 'Exactly the sort of entitled white man I would have expected. Probably was never told no as a child. Doesn't think the word applies to him.' I'm talking but my mind is already a hundred miles away at the headquarters of the channel Max Macintyre works for. It's already following him out of the building and holding a syringe of Rohypnol in its pocket. It's already sliding bits of his horrible body into a mincer.

Stop it.

Stop. It.

'Men like that think "no" is a negotiation,' Cassie says. 'And if that doesn't work, they just take what they want anyway.' She's practically grinding her teeth with rage. Then, suddenly, her body goes slack. I literally see the moment the fight is sucked out of her. The moment she remembers that Max Macintyre is a powerful man and she and Scarlett are just two powerless women.

But they're not.

They have me.

No. They *had* me. I don't do that anymore.

They have me.

'I'm so sorry, Kitty,' Cassie is saying now, apologetic instead of rageful. How women are supposed to be. 'You don't need to hear all this when you've obviously got your own stuff going on. I mean, I'm guessing you're at Angry Women Anonymous for a reason. Is it something to do with why you went offline?'

'Kind of,' I say. 'And look, please don't apologise. I'm happy to listen.'

But that's not all I want to do, is it?

We drive on in silence for a bit before our conversation moves onto safer topics like the weather and my satnav tells us we've arrived at Cassie's house. Cassie says she'll see me next week and I watch as she walks up the little cobbled pathway to the door of her cottage. I see her put her key in the lock, open the door and catch a glimpse of someone waiting behind the door for her to come home. A willowy blonde ghost-girl with a gaunt face and haunted eyes. She falls into Cassie's arms, a broken doll, before the door closes again.

Scarlett.

By the time I'm on the move again, I've already made my mind up. I'm going to kill Max Macintyre. I have to. Because someone needs to get justice for that girl. And someone needs to stop him breaking another young woman. And it's just this one. Just this one terrible human.

And I can stop any time I like.

13

The good thing about someone doing a live show at the exact same time in the exact same place every weeknight is that I know exactly where to find Max Macintyre. God, if only they all presented themselves to me on a plate like this one. And, thanks to Cassie, I already know he's got a predilection for pretty young women who look up to him. All I need to do is put myself in the right place at the right time and, well, this really should be like taking candy from a baby.

I just hope I'm still young enough.

It's two days after my conversation with Cassie at AWA and I'm just about ready to meet Max Macintyre. I look at myself closely in the mirror in my en suite. Are those lines around my eyes? My mother pushed a skincare routine onto me the exact moment I hit puberty like she was some kind of product queenpin. I remember coming home from school one day and finding an array of cleansers, toners, masks, serums and moisturisers stocked in my bathroom.

'You need to look after your face,' she'd told me. 'It's the only one you'll ever have.' This is kind of ironic now as I'm fairly sure Carmella is on her fourth nose now. She wasn't wrong though and an extensive skincare regime is something I've always invested in. Along with regular facials involving gross things like my own blood platelets and salmon semen, I think I can pass for early twenties. I frown at my reflection.

I just hope this is young enough for him.

Of course, I've had a good snoop of Max Macintyre's Instagram as part of my research. I had to make sure he wasn't away on holiday or something. He's one of those presenters that seems to need hot holidays every few weeks because reading words that someone else has written off a screen in front of you is super hard work. Anyway, he's not on holiday.

And his wife, Lauren, has just had a baby.

Their first child.

His Insta is a sickening slide show of Max Macintyre Family Man Extraordinaire. There are photos of Max changing the baby's nappy. Of Max with Lauren in hospital, presumably just moments after the baby's birth as Lauren looks traumatised and the baby still has flecks of blood in its hair. Of Max proudly holding a tiny pair of booties with a fucking huge grin plastered across his overexposed fucking face. There are photos of Max bathing the baby and – the pièce de résistance – a shirtless Max holding the naked baby against his chest like one of those old black-and-white posters. It's this shot that has the most comments; they literally go into the thousands. They're mostly from middle-aged women who get wet knickers over him cooing about what a wonderful man and father he is. They wouldn't be saying that if he was ever left alone with one of their daughters. This family man act is beyond gross. He's beyond gross. Cuddling babies with the same hands he used to touch up a teenage girl in some scruffy pub loos. He makes me feel physically and emotionally sick.

I can't wait to kill him.

Oh, another thing I found out while forensically combing through Max Macintyre's Insta is that he and Blaze Bundy are mutuals. Which surprised me a little as it's not really in keeping with Max's carefully curated family man image. But it also didn't surprise me at all because, well, they're cut from the same cloth, aren't they?

And the cloth is a dirty old cum rag.

I check my reflection in the full-length mirror in my hallway before I leave the house.

I look good.

I always like to look good for nights as special as this one.

'Are you off out with Maisie?' Charlie asks me as I step into the lounge where he's watching politicians argue with each other on TV. That's weird. Maisie *did* message earlier asking to meet me for supper but how would Charlie know that? I must've mentioned it and forgotten.

'Um . . . yes,' I say. 'Her morning sickness has finally stopped and it's like she wants to eat the world now.' I laugh awkwardly.

'So you'll be a few hours?'

'Yes,' I say. 'At least. I wouldn't wait up.' If everything goes to plan, it could be a very late night for me indeed.

'Cool,' Charlie says. 'Have a fun time.'

Oh. I absolutely intend to.

14

I'm wearing a short Comme des Garçons dress and some kitten-heeled Louboutins when I arrive at the studios at 7.30pm. I look cute, but not too sexy; I need an innocent vibe about me if I want to convince Max Macintyre that I'm interested in an internship with him. I've never had a job interview before so I had to get some tips on what to wear from TikTok. But I think I've nailed it. I've got my sensible handbag with me – a D&G leather tote. I've even packed a (fake) CV in there. Alongside some cable ties and a syringe full of Rohypnol.

Max Macintyre's nightly chat show is a mix of celebrity guests and members of the public who have done remarkable things and it goes out at 8pm. All I need to do is get inside that building. And all that is stopping me is a security guard so burly he is practically round. But it's fine. I've sweet-talked much scarier men than this one. Obviously I can't just kill him although I have that lovely syringe in my bag and it would be so easy. But no, it's one of my rules, only very bad guys.

Shame.

Instead I walk up to the gate, with my Best Smile plastered across my face.

'Yes?' he says gruffly, barely looking at me. At first I think this is bad. He needs to be looking at me so I can charm him. But then I realise he's actually looking at my legs. Okay, that makes it easier. Why are men so predictable? At least challenge me a bit, guys.

'I'm here to see Max Macintyre,' I say.

'Yeah, you and half the female population. Sorry, love, permits only.'

'But he's interviewing me,' I say. My voice is all perky excitement.

The guard looks at the tablet he's holding. 'What's your name?'

Oh fuck.

Fuck fuck fuck.

Why can't I think of a single fucking name.

'Harriet!' *What?* Where did that come from?

'Harriet what, honey? What's your last name?'

'Styles.' *Seriously? Wtf is wrong with me?*

The security guard looks at me with narrowed eyes which is exactly how I'd be looking at me if our roles were reversed.

'Your name is Harriet Styles?'

I smile feebly. 'Yes?'

We stand in silence for a few moments as he assesses me. Then a big smile breaks out over his face. 'In that case, you're obviously here for the *Help! I've Got the Same Name as a Celeb and It's Making My Life Hell* feature.' He opens the gate.

The what?

I stare at him.

'Come on in then. Harriet. You just need to sign for a pass.' He pushes an A4 book towards me where I sign my name. Two seconds later he hands me a paper pass in a plastic envelop with Harriet Styles written on it. 'There you go, Harriet. Take a seat. Sophie will be down to collect you in a moment.'

Sophie? Who the fuck is Sophie? I give him a smile and take a seat. Of course there's a Sophie. There's always a Sophie. Did I really expect Max Macintyre would just come to the front desk and introduce himself? What an idiot. The barrel-shaped security guard has picked up the phone and called to let this Sophie person know that I've arrived. I can feel my heart beating aggressively in my chest. Why did it have to be a woman? Women are so much smarter than men. She won't fall for my incredibly basic tricks that get men doing what I want them to do.

'Yes,' the security guard is saying. 'That's what she's saying her name is. Okay. Thanks.' He puts the receiver down and stares at me, puzzled. 'She's on her way. Harriet.' Why does he keep saying my (fake) name like that?

Two minutes later, a blonde woman bounces into the waiting area. She gives me a huge smile but it's about as genuine as the name on my permit.

'Hi, Harriet, is it?'

I nod enthusiastically. 'Yes, that's right. Hi. You must be Sophie? I think we've spoken over email!' I'm massively lying but hoping she might think she's the problem if I'm convincing enough. 'I'm here for Max Macintyre!'

'Okay,' she saying, nodding slowly. 'So you're here for our

Help! I've Got the Same Name as a Celeb and It's Making My Life Hell feature?' She's frowning at me.

'I think so?' I say, letting my voice inflect at the end.

Sophie's face remains expressionless as she stares at me for a moment. Then she looks at her own tablet and frowns at that. 'There's definitely some confusion,' she says finally. 'Because I'm expecting a Millie Bobby Brown, a Gillian Anderson and, remarkably, a Kim Kardashian. But not a Harriet Styles. That's not even right, is it? Do people call you Harry?'

'Um . . . yes?'

'Yeah, this isn't going to work. Sorry. But send your travel receipts to me and I'll make sure you get reimbursed. Could you see her out, Micky?'

'This way, please,' says the security guard.

I nod and follow him.

'I'm going to need that back, Harriet.' He points at my lanyard. I take it off and hand it to him. 'It was really low to lie to try and get on *Help! I've Got the Same Name as a Celeb and It's Making My Life Hell.*' He shakes his head in disappointment before holding the door open for me and watching as I leave the building and walk away from it.

Well.

That went brilliantly.

15

I'm feeling more than a little bit embarrassed when I spot a pub on the corner of the street. It looks like a standard Central London place, aimed typically at tourists. So there's a lot of Union Jack bunting and pictures of red phone boxes. I need something to take the sting of humiliation off and help me think of a new plan. A proper plan. Because, really, that was totally fucking lame. What was I thinking? I walk into the pub and am greeted by a bartender whose beard is probably his entire personality. I order a large Marlborough Sauvignon Blanc and take it to a table near the window. The pub is reasonably busy and reminds me a bit of the place Charlie and I went on our first date which was about a year ago. I take my phone out of my bag and open Instagram. I scroll through some notifications before I see something that chills me to my absolute core.

Blaze Bundy has posted another story.

This time there's no sound, just a visual of him throwing darts at a blow-up doll. Again, it's been made to look like me. He's not that good at darts but to be fair to him, trying to aim when your face is obscured by a bandana and sunglasses can't

96

be easy. After about five attempts, he manages to hit the doll which deflates into a pool of rubber and clothing. It's only then that I notice the doll is wearing a Hello Kitty T-shirt.

What the fuck?

With my plan to kill Max Macintyre and my mission to find out what sort of a man Tor's new boyfriend slash therapist is, I'd almost forgotten about Blaze Bundy and his weird fascination with me. This video is absolutely grotesque and very definitely a threat. I mean, he's literally throwing darts at an effigy of me. And he's already thrown another one in the Thames. Is Blaze Bundy actually threatening to kill me? There's no question about it now. I can't ignore him any longer. I need to find out who this nutjob is and why he's going to this much effort to scare me. What have I done to attract his creepy attention?

I have another glass of wine and watch the story over and over, unable to believe what I'm seeing. I just don't understand. My head is feeling more than a little bit fuzzy when a notification pops up, alerting me to a direct message that's come into my inbox.

It's him. It's Blaze Bundy.

Like what you see, KC? You'll be seeing much more real soon 😌

I almost choke on my wine and push the phone away from me with such force that it skids across the table I'm sitting at and clatters onto the floor, landing at the shiny black loafers of a man. I watch as he reaches down and lifts it up, placing it on the table just in front of me.

'I think you dropped this,' he says. It's a voice I know. A

voice I recognise because it's the same voice that's on the TV at 8pm every weekday evening. It's the voice of Max Macintyre. I look up and, through my slightly wine-blurry eyes, I see the face of the man loved by women up and down this country. The face of evil. Maybe tonight isn't such a write-off after all. Maybe things are just about to get interesting.

'Oh,' I say. 'Thank you very much.'

'My pleasure.' He gives me a wide smile before turning away. He barely even looked at me. Maybe I am too old to appeal to him. I need to do something to get his attention back.

'Let me buy you a drink to say thank you,' I say, knowing this is a little bit over the top. All he did was pick up my fucking phone. No wonder men think they're such heroes. I stamp down the thought, reminding myself I'm doing this for the greater good.

He turns back to face me and looks at me properly this time. I swallow down a shudder as I feel his eyes travel over my body. Up, then down, then back up. Lingering on parts that his eyes, and certainly no other part of him, have any business lingering on, before he settles on my eyes. He obviously likes what he sees because he smiles again at me. But this time it's not the wide TV- and family-friendly grin he gave me before. This is something deadly. He just doesn't know quite how fitting this is.

'There's really no need,' he says, but he's being polite. I already know he's going to accept my offer before he pulls out one of the chairs opposite me. 'But let me buy you one instead. You shouldn't be drinking alone.'

I briefly consider asking him exactly why I shouldn't be drinking alone. What might his answer be? Is it because I could accidentally attract a sexual predator? Instead I return his smile, but mine is smaller, quieter, less certain than his.

'Thank you,' I say. 'Could I have a white wine, please?' I wish I could make myself blush. That would really be great right now.

He places his own drink, a pint of something, on the table and gives me a little salute before he turns back to the bar.

Having a face that launched a thousand (well, six) primetime shows seems to give an instant queue-jump in pubs and it's not even two minutes until he's back and plonking a ridiculously massive glass of wine in front of me and another pint of whatever watered-down piss he's drinking on the table too. Then he pulls out a chair and sits.

'So why are you here, drinking alone and throwing your—' he looks at my phone, 'rather expensive iPhone across the place?'

'Well, I'd heard that it was a local hangout for famous television presenters,' I say, coyly. 'I was hoping that throwing my phone across the place might attract the attention of one.' I run my forefinger around the rim of my glass before moving it between my lips. I don't take my eyes off Max Macintyre as I do this. He doesn't take his eyes off my finger, shuffling in his seat slightly.

'I think you've achieved your goal,' he says and I can see him sort of puff up a little. Fuck's sake, men. They're putty if you're stroking either their ego or their dick. 'You haven't told me your name.'

'It's Kitty,' I say. 'Kitty Collins.'

'I'm very pleased to meet you, Kitty. And I'm very pleased to have saved your phone.' He looks around, squints his eyes a little as if he's making judgements about the various people in the bar. 'It looks to me like there are some rather unsavoury characters in this establishment. It could've clattered to the feet of anyone. I would say you are very lucky it was me.'

Very lucky indeed.

'You're my hero.' I giggle. 'I can't wait to tell everyone that my iPhone was saved by Max Macintyre. And then he bought me a drink! I was actually trying to see you tonight. I wanted to ask you about doing some work experience with you. I think you're so great!'

I see a little dark cloud pass over his eyes. It looks like danger. 'Yeah,' he says. He brightens up again. 'I know a little place nearby. Why don't we go there and talk about it a bit more? If you'd like?'

Of course I'd fucking like.

'Yes, please,' I say. 'What is it? Like another bar or something?'

'It's actually a place I have near the studios. My family live outside London so sometimes I stay here during the week. Would you like to see it?'

It doesn't escape me that he says 'family' rather than 'wife and child'. I wonder exactly how many young women he's used this exact line on while Lauren and their baby are asleep at home, not knowing what Max is up to.

'It's not far,' he says. 'We can have some drinks there too.'

I feel excitement ripple through my veins.

I'm going to kill him.

I'm going to kill him tonight.

Fuck sobriety.

16

I giggle and link arms with Max as we walk to his 'place nearby'. It's actually a small complex of apartments practically next door to the Orion Studios. How convenient. They've made it so easy for him to cheat on his wife. He barely even needs to lie to her when he tells her he's working late at the office. It's so close that my phone connects to the Orion guest wifi when we're inside.

'Well, this is my humble abode,' Max says, gesturing around the flat. Humble is an understatement. It's painfully unimpressive, clear that no one lives here full time. Like a bachelor pad Pinterest board. Open-plan and colourless with white walls, floors and kitchen units. He has a dark brown leather sofa in the living area with a matching armchair shoved in one corner. There are some shelves and a large floor lamp in the corner too. I make a note to check which books are on his shelves when he goes for his shower. There's also a big TV on the wall. Probably big so he can watch himself on it. He doesn't show me the bedroom.

'Take a seat,' he says. 'What can I get you to drink? I've

got wine. Or something stronger if you fancy? I've got a rather nice Macallan?'

'Wine will be fine, thank you.' I've no intention of drinking it anyway.

I've probably already had a little bit too much at the pub and I need my head to be as clear as possible for the next bit. I put my hand in my pocket and let my fingers trail across the syringe.

I already know I'm going to enjoy this.

Max pours me a glass of wine and brings it over to where I'm sitting. 'So, tell me about yourself, Kitty. What do you do?'

'At the moment, nothing,' I say. 'But I'm really interested in having a career in TV.'

He scoffs. 'I think we've said enough about work. Tell me what you do for fun. For pleasure.' He growls the last word in a way I know he thinks is sexy and seductive. It isn't. It sounds like he needs to cough some phlegm up.

'I kill bad men,' I say with a smile and take a pretend sip of my wine.

He laughs. Loudly. Like I've cracked the joke of the century. 'Good one. And what do you do to good boys?' He's closer now and his hand is on my thigh, just above my knee.

'I'm not sure I've ever met one,' I say.

'Well, it looks like tonight is your lucky night, Kitty, because I'm about to show you just how good this boy can be.'

Jesus fucking Christ, there is nothing I hate more than when grown men refer to themselves as boys. If there was any doubt that I was going to eliminate this man, those words have sealed his fate. I let him get closer to me. I let his lips touch my neck. Even though I have to suppress a shudder of disgust. Even though I'm already mentally in the shower at home, washing his sleaze off my body.

'Does your wife think you're a good boy?' I ask. I feel him stiffen next to me.

'We have an understanding,' he says. 'So you really don't need to worry about her.'

'Does she know about this understanding?' I ask, innocently. He pulls back this time and looks at me. 'It's just I've met married men before who have told me their wives know everything and it's not been true. You wouldn't lie to me, would you, Max? Not if we're going to be working together. It would be super awkward.'

He sighs, frustrated, and shifts in his seat a little, trying to readjust his trousers. 'Kitty. I promise you, she knows everything. She likes the lifestyle I provide for her and, let's just say, she turns a blind eye to anything I get up to out of hours. So really, there's nothing to worry about.' He leans back in and I can smell the lies on his breath as his mouth moves back to my throat, his fingers making their way up my thigh again. I shuffle away from him.

'So she's okay with you doing this?' I can feel him trying not to roll his eyes.

'Yes, Kitty. She's absolutely fine with it.'

'She's absolutely fine with you using your power to seduce and fuck young women who look up to you?'

He pulls back again, annoyed this time. 'What the fuck is this? Is this some sort of sting? Are you a reporter or something? Because this is fucking entrapment and I've already told you, there's nothing here. My wife knows everything. And any girls, *women*, I've been with have all consented.'

That's the lie I needed to hear. That pushes me past the point of no return. I pull the syringe out of my pocket and stab him in the neck with it.

'What the fuck?' He grabs at his neck and then at me, but I'm quicker than he is and I'm on my feet before he can make contact. 'What the fuck did you just do to me?'

'I'll fill you in when you wake up,' I say, watching his eyelids flutter as he fights to keep them open. I count down from ten in my head and when I reach one, he's out cold. I look at the clock on the wall. The hands are a pair of women's legs. I hate him even more. I've got about an hour before he comes round. Fuck it, I think I will have that glass of wine after all.

Max Macintyre is heavier than he looks. Visceral fat probably. It takes some time and some sweat to get his wrists and ankles bound with the cable ties. I manage to manoeuvre him into a sitting position on the leather sofa by the time he starts waking up. This is another one of my favourite parts. The part when I get to tell them why I'm here and what I'm about to do to them. I'm not sure they enjoy it as much as me though.

He's groggy when his eyes open but he hasn't forgotten who I am.

'What the fuck is this?' he says, his voice thick. I bet he'd really like some water right now. I go to the kitchen and fill a glass. Then I go back to him and throw it in his face.

'There you go,' I say. 'You looked like you needed to freshen up a bit.'

He coughs. 'There's something wrong with you.'

'No. There's something wrong with a world that lets men like you get away with all the shit you do. Did you think there wouldn't be any consequences?'

He sighs, like he's over me and my bullshit. He probably is. 'I've already told you. My wife knows and all my relationships have been consensual.'

'Have they? Do you even know the meaning of the word consensual? Or do you need a producer in your earpiece to explain it to you?'

'Of course I fucking know. Whatever you're accusing me of, you've got it wrong. Who have you been speaking to? Who put you up to this?'

I pick up my phone and open the Safari app, heading to the Cambridge Dictionary.

'*Consent*,' I read, '*to agree to do something, or to allow someone to do something.* Are you sure you don't want to change your story?'

'I've never done anything without consent. Never. I'm not one of those men. I'm not.' He's moved from anger to denial. There are stages of trying to grovel for your life, apparently.

'Okay. Would all the women, the girls, say the same? Do you remember a girl called Scarlett? She did work experience with you a few months ago. Eighteen, blonde, about to head off to university to do a Broadcast degree? Ring any bells?'

He stares at me. 'I remember Scarlett. What has she said? Nothing even happened with her. She just wasn't very good. I told her the placement wasn't working out. If she's said I did anything to her, it's because she's salty about that. You can't believe her.' The lies spill out like I've punctured him.

'So you're saying you didn't assault her in a pub toilet? That's what you're telling me? Am I getting this right? You're saying she's made it up because you ended her work experience placement? Think carefully before you answer because lying to me is going to make this a whole lot worse for you. I hate men who lie, Max. They make me very angry. I'll give you a minute.'

I go back through to the kitchenette. I pour myself another glass of wine – it's actually pretty nice – and have a look in the drawers. There's not much of interest. I'm pleased to find a roll of refuse sacks though. I peel two off and fashion them into a makeshift apron. It's not ideal but this dress *is* Comme des Garçons and I'd rather not ruin it. Plus I can hardly walk out of here and back to my car with blood spatter on me. I also spot a rather attractive knife block standing proudly on one of the marble counters. On closer inspection, I'm delighted to see a nice block of Dick knives – fitting – and pull one out. I tap the point with my index finger and feel a frisson of excitement when the tiniest freckle of blood appears like a miniature ruby, twinkling in the kitchen spotlights. This isn't what I need though. I need something that will cut through bone. I pull out a cleaver. An F Dick eight-inch butcher's cleaver, if I'm not wrong. My monthly subscription to *Know Your Knives* is not wasted.

Taking the knife with me, I make a quick stop at the bookshelf. You can tell a lot about a person from what they read. I'm disappointed but not surprised to see the usual male reading fodder on Max's shelves – Dan Brown, Lee Child. The spines are still disappointingly intact.

'Have you thought about what I asked you?' I say to Max as I walk back over to the sofa. He's struggling against his restraints now and probably has been since I walked away. 'You won't get out of those,' I say. 'They're grade-A cable ties. You'll just hurt yourself. You need a knife. Like this one.' His eyes widen as I show him the Dick I found in his kitchen.

'There may have been some misunderstanding,' he says, quietly.

'Like she said *no* and you misunderstood her and thought she said *yes*? Is that right?'

'She was all over me. She came for a drink with me. Why would she have come for a drink with me if she didn't want something to happen?'

Wow.

'Maybe because she was in awe of someone on her TV *every night* showing interest in her and her career?' I say. 'Maybe because of the fact you're twenty years older than her and she didn't want to offend you? Maybe because she wanted to have a *fucking drink*.' I'm starting to lose my cool and I stalk over to Max, pointing the knife at his groin. He flinches.

'I didn't rape her!'

'Don't worry. I'm not going to cut your dick off. That's so passé.' He lets out a sigh of relief. 'No, I'm going to cut your hands off instead. I think that's a fitting punishment, isn't it? You touched her with them, didn't you? When she'd explicitly said *no* to you.' I inch closer to him and can feel him trembling as I lift his bound hands out of his lap.

'Oh God, please no, please God.'

'God won't help you,' I say. 'He sent me as karma.' I pull his hands onto a coffee table next to the sofa and he cries out as I slam the cleaver down, onto his wrists. A delicious howl of pain and regret.

It's been such a long time since my last kill, I'd almost forgotten what it feels like. The slight resistance of the flesh at first touch with the knife. The release when it punctures the skin. The way the best knives will cut through muscle and tissue like they're butter. The blood. The red, red blood. The colour of luxury and sex and passion. I cut Max Macintyre's groping, greedy hands off in four pretty clean swipes.

He screams the whole time.

'I'm sorry, I'm sorry,' he wails and, honestly, this man really hasn't got any chat unless he's reading it off an autocue. Once his hands are gone, he realises that the cable ties have slipped off his wrists and makes a useless lunge at me. It makes quite a lot of mess and I'm not totally sure how he thinks he's going to catch me without any fingers or opposable thumbs.

'You're not sorry,' I say to him as I step out of the way of his furious, flailing stumps. 'You're a predator. You're a snake. You're a serpent. And I've actually had enough of you at this point.' And with this I swipe the knife across his throat, a beautiful spray of maroon spurts from the gash, raining blood onto the white floor.

I've missed this. I don't care how much I shouldn't have, but I have. I've missed it so much. The way the eyes go all dreamy and glassy in the split second before the life slips out of them. The way my pulse quickens at the very moment theirs begins to slow. The way it feels like stopping time as they slip, slip, slip into the unknown. It's a beautifully choreographed waltz between life and death.

I love it.

I feel powerful again.

I feel like me.

While this pathetic, dying man disgusts me to my absolute core, I have a lot to thank him for too. Thank him for bringing me back from the brink. He's given my life meaning again. His crimes are appalling, unspeakable. They go back a long way and he should never have got this far into his life. He should've been stopped earlier. But, let's face it, that's not the world we live in, is it? We live in a world where monsters are praised and applauded. Where they're promoted and enabled. Where they're given even more opportunities with every vile action. Where they're given slots on primetime television and OBEs and don't even have to go through the public ballot for Wimbledon tickets. It's hardly surprising that men like this hit the roof when they're told *no*. They're not used to it. It's simply not in their vocabulary. So while *this* man is the culprit, *this* man did the things, he's the tip of the iceberg. He's a product of a system that breeds men like him. That celebrates them.

He's not the only one. Not by a long shot. And, no he should never have got this far, but he has. And I can't help but feel like there is something like fate at play here. Like our paths were destined to cross.

I look at his body now as it slips between this existence and the next. He's bloated from too many expensive dinners. Losing his hair and his looks as he hovers on the brink of middle age. But, even in death, there's still a confidence about him. It seems like privileged white men don't even have a fear of mortality. Imagine living an entire life without feeling afraid. It's inconceivable to me. A woman. A surge of anger rips through me at this thought and I can't help but lash out and slice my knife through his throat again, even though he's already pretty fucking dead. The new cut makes me angrier though. It looks like a smug smile. And I've just spent the best part of an hour wiping the first one off his stupid face. I look around the room to see if there's anything I can use to just smash his head in. It'll be a nightmare to clean up, but that is a problem future me can deal with. Right now I just need to not be looking at him. To not have that smile taunt me. I can't see anything that will do the job though, which surprises me. Surely a man with this level of vanity would have a kettle bell or two lying around? I sigh and turn back to him, resisting the urge to spit in his face. Don't want to take any risks with DNA, even though I'll be feeding this sorry carcass through the mincers in a short while.

Before I start the clean-up job I take a meditative moment where I just enjoy it all. The smell, the dampness of his blood on my skin, the feeling of something stretching out inside me. Yes, as much as I hate this man and have taken great pleasure in ending his life, a part of me will forever be grateful to him.

I lean forward and softly press my lips against his waxy cheek.

'Thank you,' I whisper into his dead ear. 'Thank you for bringing me back.'

It's a beautiful moment.

One that is fucking spoiled by my phone blaring out 'Bad Blood' which is my genius ringtone of the moment. But really, I don't even want Taylor Swift ruining this for me.

I need to start turning this thing on silent.

I reject the call without even looking at who it is.

After checking Max's vital signs – zero, yay – I pad back out to the kitchen and have a longer root through the drawers.

There is everything I need here. The black bin bags and meat cleaver. All I have to do is line the floor and chop his body into small enough pieces for me to take to my car, which is parked near the studio. Then I see his phone. I might as well take a look at that while I'm here. See if there's anything I need to know. I pick it up and am surprised to see that it's an older model of iPhone. Clearly *not* his main phone then. Probably the one he uses to conduct his consensually grey liaisons on. I tap the home button but it's locked. It's actually so old, it's asking for a thumbprint to unlock it. This makes me laugh. Fortunately I have the exact tool for this job. I pick up one of his severed hands and use the thumb to unlock the phone.

Bingo.

I was right. The phone is a catalogue of appalling behaviour. Texts and calls to women and only women. I tap into the photos app and find more misery there. Selfies that are not of Macintyre's face, pics sent to him by girls, fans, who all look very *very* young. I scroll through to the settings and turn the lock off. When they come looking for him, they'll find this. Good. It will stop his wife and kid from missing him too much.

My own phone buzzes again.

It's a message from Charlie.

Where are you? Emergency at home.

What? What's he going on about? I try to think what the emergency at home could possibly be, but come up with precisely nothing.

What's happened? I write back.

Please just come back asap, Charlie replies. *I need you.*

A million thoughts cross my mind. Has he had an accident? Is he lying on the floor, unable to move? Has someone broken into the apartment? I swallow, hard. Is he in danger? My heart pangs with concern but also tugs with annoyance. Why now? I can't leave *now*. I haven't even begun to dismember Max Macintyre, let alone clean up the crime scene. My fingerprints and DNA will be everywhere. I can't leave the body here. It's not possible. He needs to go missing. Well, what he really needs is to disappear without a trace into one of my meat grinders and eventually become a sausage roll.

I don't know what to do.

I text Charlie back and ask him again what's happened but he doesn't reply and my annoyance turns into a cold panic. I imagine him slipping in the shower and cracking his head. The home is the most dangerous place in the world; I'm sure I've read that somewhere. I mean, just look how dangerous it was for Max. Or maybe there's an intruder and he's being held at knife point at this moment. Maybe Charlie's being kidnapped this very second. Whatever is going on, I need to get home. I can't leave Charlie alone to deal with it. He wouldn't ask me to go back if it wasn't urgent. I'll have to go home, handle the emergency, and come back here later to clear up. I don't really have a choice. And I should have a good few hours before anyone starts wondering where Max is. I look around the apartment again. I mean, he clearly does this sort of thing often enough to need a specific place to do it.

Mind made up, I go over to Max's body and root around in his pockets until I find his keys. I drop them into my bag. Hopefully I'll be able to get home and back before anyone finds Max Macintyre's dead, handless corpse.

It's hard being a woman.

We're expected to do everything.

I rip off my bin bag overalls, turn the lights off and head out of the door, locking it behind me.

Then I hurry along the dark streets until I get to my car and, after taking some deep, calming breaths and trying to forget there's a dead body I really need to deal with, I begin my drive home to face whatever horror awaits me there.

17

KITTY AND CHARLIE'S APARTMENT, CHELSEA

The horror is even more horrific than I imagined.

When I get to my apartment block, none of our concierges are at the front desk so I quickly take the lift up to the penthouse. But there is absolutely no sign of life here either. When I get inside, the flat is dark and the fears about Charlie being kidnapped flood into my brain again. Even worse is the thought that I could be next. Is there some mystery assailant waiting for me behind the sofa or ready to jump out of one of the bedrooms? My heart is pounding in my ears as I switch the lights on, terrified of what I might see. I brace myself, preparing for blood, smashed furniture or even Charlie's body. I think of the gory scene I left back at Max's place and wonder if a mirror image is going to greet me when I turn on the lights.

I click them on.

The reality is even worse.

'SURPRISE!'

No.

No.

Please, no.

I fucking hate surprise parties.

A crowd of faces smile at me expectantly. Even Maisie and Tor who have known me since school and know exactly how I feel about surprise parties. The turncoats. Hmm. I can forgive Charlie – just about – because we've only known each other a year and we're still learning things about each other. But those two *should* and do know better. How could they betray me like this? I don't know how Charlie put this guest list together because I don't even like most of the people here. There are a couple of The Extras – girls who are permanently on the periphery of my life but whom I don't actually class as friends. I stare back at the twenty or so people in my flat and, finally, smile back when all I want to do is scream. I've got a corpse waiting for me in the next borough. I haven't got time for this shit.

'Oh my God!' I say, hoping I'm hiding my frustration and sounding delighted. 'I'm so surprised!' Although shocked would be a better word really. Traumatised, if we're going for it.

Charlie is a beaming beacon of joy as he bounds over to me. He pushes a glass of champagne into my hand and kisses me on the cheek.

'Happy thirtieth birthday,' he says.

Ugh.

'But we already celebrated my birthday,' I say, still smiling so hard my face hurts. I'd made it quite clear that I didn't want a fuss, that I wanted to do something lovely, just the two of us. That was all I wanted. All I needed. Not this spectacle. I look around the room and can see that Charlie has really gone to town with this. There's a cake with fucking *tiers* and balloons. Big foil monstrosities in the shape of a '3' and an '0'. And someone is filming on their phone so there is no doubt that this absolute *nightmare* is currently being broadcast live on someone's Insta or TikTok.

'I know,' Charlie is saying. 'But it's a special birthday. And you're a special woman. And I knew you'd never get round to organising something like this with your friends yourself. So we did it for you!'

They really did. I look around again.

Fucking balloons. I hate balloons.

'You really shouldn't have,' I say and mean it.

Charlie holds up his glass. 'To Kitty,' he says.

'To Kitty,' everyone echoes. I want to cry. Just not in the way happy, surprised people usually do at these things.

'There's another surprise too,' Charlie's saying now and oh God, please no. I can't, I really can't. There's a surprise and a body and I need to go but the next thing I know, I'm being swept into a hug and a cloud of perfume that takes me back to my childhood. And that is *not* a place I want to go back to.

'Kitty, my darling. Happy birthday.' And I'm not dreaming because my mother is here, right here in my apartment, looking like Monica Bellucci and smelling like the past and I think I'm going to pass out. I have to lean on my mother for support and take some deep, calming breaths while Charlie, smiles away at me in treacherous delight.

I want to kill him. Not really. Maybe a bit.

'What are you doing here?' I ask my mother and the words surprise me because they are not the ones I want to say. I'm impressed that I haven't managed to scream at Charlie for bringing my mother into our sanctuary and scream at my mother for being here.

Here.

In London.

After all this time.

'I thought that would have been quite obvious, darling,' she's saying as she holds me at arm's length and takes me in. 'I'm here to see my beautiful only child celebrate her special day.'

'My special day was almost a week ago,' I say and am annoyed that I sound like a petulant child. She's always had this effect on me.

'I know that.' Her laugh is tinkling bells and fairy wings. 'It's not really a day I'm likely to forget in a hurry.' She turns to Charlie rolling her eyes dramatically. 'Thirty hours in labour and they just chopped her out anyway. She never did like doing things in a conventional way.' That laugh again, and fury sparks inside me. But then her arm is around me and she says, 'The one thing I'll never really forget though is the first time I held her in my arms. She wasn't like some of those mucky, wrinkled babies you see on reality shows. You know when they pull them out and they're all slimy with funny-shaped heads? She was just so perfect and beautiful immediately. Like a doll. And she didn't cry like the other babies I'd been listening to for hours and hours. She just made this funny mewling noise. Like a kitten. That's why I called her Kitty.' My mother strokes my cheek softly just like she did when I was a little girl. Just like I can imagine her doing in those first few minutes when we were new to each other.

And I'm suddenly not angry anymore. All thoughts of Max Macintyre and his body and his blood are flushed from my mind and I'm glad she's here, my mum.

I've missed her.

I've missed her so much.

It's been about five years since I last saw her and that was only a fleeting visit when she came over to check that the meat factories were all running properly. It was like we couldn't face each other after that horrible night with my dad. And it was only with hindsight that I could see he'd been hurting her for a long time. Only as an adult did the signs become clear. The bandaged nose which she laughed off as a tiny nose job. *Just a tweak*, she'd said. There were also dark glasses and weeks-long visits to 'retreats'. The guilt that I hadn't realised and hadn't saved her ate me up every time I saw her. When I *did* finally protect her, it was too much. I hit him too hard. And too many times. I really should have stopped when there was no bone left and I was just pummelling soft, pulpy flesh. It was beyond just saving my mother, it was a maelstrom of rage and fury that I didn't know existed. We would never have been able to have argued self-defence. Not really. That's the sad truth of it. Because I hit and hit and hit. I couldn't stop. And then, once we'd cleaned everything up and my mother had told the police that Dad was gone, missing, she couldn't look at me anymore. She was terrified of me. We tried to see each other once a year, usually at Christmas. But five years ago she stopped coming. She invited me to her new home; our hearts just weren't really in it. But now she's here and she's cooing over me like I'm still that fifteen-year-old girl, suddenly alone in the world.

'Look how beautiful you are,' she's saying as Charlie – my own personal Judas – disappears off to grab more champagne. 'And you're wearing your necklace. It looks stunning on you, darling.' She reaches out and touches the pendant gently. 'Look at you, my darling girl.' Her voice is tender and honeyed and I feel six years old again. 'You look exactly like I did twenty years ago. What's that on your face?' She licks the tip of her thumb, quickly, and rubs it across my cheek like I'm a toddler. 'All gone.'

'It's good to see you,' I say. And I'm surprised to find, despite all my conflicting emotions, that I mean it. 'It's been a long time.'

'Yes,' says my mother, looking thoughtfully at her thumb. Then she smiles and looks back at my face. 'I don't know why you haven't been out to see the house and meet Gabriel. You'd love it. The house. I'll let you make your own mind up about Gabriel, but he's really quite lovely.'

'He's not here then?' I say looking around.

'No, he thought I should see you alone after such a long time. He's seeing some friends in town. He'll meet us back in France.'

Us?

Must be a slip of the tongue.

'He really is very special,' she's saying now. 'And very handsome.'

'And that's exactly what you deserve.' I don't need to end the sentence. We both know I mean after what happened with my father. I want her to be happy. She deserves the fairy tale. But part of me just can't deal with the fact that she could be making the same mistake again. Choosing my father ruined my mother's life. I couldn't bear to watch her repeat that mistake. She has bad judgement. I would be constantly on edge, watching for signs that there was something wrong in her relationship. That's partly why I keep my distance. We became different people after that night. And I didn't recognise either of them.

Charlie is back over now, holding a bottle of Taittinger and topping up both my glass and my mother's like a wonderful potential son-in-law.

'Have you asked her yet?' he says to my mother.

Ominous. I don't like ominous.

'Asked me what?'

My mother flicks a fallen strand of hair away from her face and it's then that I catch sight of it. The sparkling rock on her left hand. About the size of a baby's fist. Glinting like a knife.

'You know I'm getting married,' she says, touching the ring self-consciously.

'Yes, I got the invite. Congratulations.'

'I would really love you to be there, Kits. I want you to give me away.' That's why she's here. Not for my birthday at all but for her. Her wedding.

'You came all this way to ask me?' I say.

'It's very easy to ignore a piece of paper.'

'So you decided to ambush me instead?' I turn to Charlie, resplendent in his treachery. 'You knew about this?'

He can tell from my tone that I'm not exactly delighted to have been railroaded into agreeing I'll go to my mother's wedding. He's smart enough to look sheepish about it.

'Yes,' he says. 'I thought it would be a good opportunity for you and your mum to chat.'

'How long are you over for?' I ask her. 'And when is the wedding?'

She looks down at her feet. 'We fly out tomorrow morning.'

Wait. We?

'Who's we?' I ask. I see my mother and Charlie exchange the quickest of glances. 'The three of us – me and you and Charlie.'

What the fuck?

'You've booked flights?' I say to Charlie. 'But I can't go!'

'Why not?' he says and I can't exactly tell him that it's because I've just murdered one of the country's best-loved TV stars and I need to dispose of his body before his *live* show tomorrow night. I feel cold with panic.

'I just can't,' I say. I don't look directly at my mother but I can feel the disappointment radiating from her. It makes me feel horrible. Sad and guilty.

I can't bear it.

But. If I can get out of this party, there's a chance I can get everything sorted at Max Macintyre's shag pad and be back here in time to catch the flight.

I look around the room again. How can I slip out when I'm the guest of honour? When everyone is looking at me?

'I just need to pop to the bedroom,' I say. I need some space to think, to work out what I'm going to do, how I'm going to get out of here without raising suspicion. 'I'll be right back.'

I walk through to my bedroom, my smile a rictus grin on my face. I close the door behind me, take a few deep breaths and then gulp down the contents of the glass I've carried through. Then I fall onto the bed, trying to work out how I'm going to get out of here and clean up the mess I've left behind.

There's a knock at the door.

'I'll be out in a sec—' I start to say but the door bursts open and Tor storms in. She's not happy. 'Hi!'

'Don't you *hi* me, Kitty Collins,' she fumes, hands on hips. Three guesses as to what this is about. 'Fucking hell, Kitty. Of all the fucking ridiculous things you could have done. Who the hell do you think you are exactly?'

'He told you then?'

She glares at me. 'Of *course* he fucking told me. What did you think he was going to do? Not mention that my best friend *tricked* her way into his private clinic to sound out his intentions for me? I mean, even for you, this is a whole entire new level of fucking fucked-up-ness.' She continues to glare. 'Well? Haven't you got anything to say for yourself? Because I'd really like to hear your justification for this.'

I slump down against the pillows, hoping that Tor sits down next to me. But she doesn't. She stands there, looking down at me and I feel like a little kid getting a huge talking to. She clearly doesn't see that I was acting in her best interests.

'Look, I'm sorry,' I say, 'but I was worried about you. He's your therapist for fuck's sake. And you're vulnerable.'

'No. He *was* my therapist. He isn't anymore. As I fucking explained to you when I fucking told you about this. When I thought there was a chance that you could be fucking happy for me.' I don't think I've ever heard Tor swear so much in such a short space of time and her swear ratio is pretty high. 'Why don't you want me to be happy, Kits? Do you like being my white saviour too much? Is that it?'

'What the fuck? No. You know it's nothing like that. Jesus Christ. I was seriously worried about you, Tor. You *know* this man is abusing his position. You know that. He can't just start dating his patients. Even if they're not his patients anymore. I don't know how you don't see this. You might not even be the only one he's done this to. Have you even thought about that? I needed to see for myself that he isn't going to hurt you.'

Tor turns her back on me and storms over to the door. 'I'm getting myself a wine,' she says. 'Do you want one? And don't even think about going anywhere. We're not done.'

'Yes, please.' The wine will calm her down and maybe I can use this opportunity to get out of this horror show and back over to the one that really needs my attention right now. Tor and her anger will have to wait. After she closes the door, I count slowly to ten, get off the bed and open it myself. I look down the hallway but the coast seems to be clear. I could possibly make it out of the front door without anyone seeing me leave. I take two cautious steps.

'I told you, I'm not done, get back in that room, Kitty.'

I turn back around and Tor is standing there holding two glasses of wine. I sigh and head back to the bedroom, Tor so close behind me that I can hear her breathing.

Inside the bedroom she angrily bangs my glass down onto my dressing table. I watch as she necks almost half of hers in one go.

'This doesn't mean I'm not still furious with you,' she says. 'I seriously cannot believe you falsified a mental health emergency to get access to him. I would've just introduced you if you'd asked me.' I think she's mellowing a bit with me. I reach for my own wine and take a long sip, leaving a silence for her to fill. 'There might have been someone who needed that appointment. Did you even consider that? Honestly, Kits, that's really intense behaviour.'

'I know,' I say. 'And I'm truly, truly sorry. It was a silly thing to do. But I needed to know what he was like—'

'I *told* you what he was like. Why couldn't you just believe me?'

'I needed to know what he was like for myself,' I say. 'Look, Tor, I know you think it was a full-on thing to do, but remember I was *there* in Mykonos. I *saw* how you were after those men . . . I was here with you when we got back and you couldn't even leave your house. It was horrible.' She's looking into her wine glass now and I can sense the anger dissipating. 'The thought that someone could possibly be using that against you, even if there was the tiniest chance of it, made me so furious. And I know you think you've healed and stuff but you're still vulnerable, Tor. I couldn't risk him hurting you.'

She's silent for a few moments before she looks back up at me. 'And? Did he set your mind at ease?'

I take another sip of my wine before I say, 'Yes actually. He did. He seems nice and genuine and I'm sorry I was so sneaky. But I will never ever apologise for trying to protect you.'

She shakes her head but then looks up and smiles at me. 'I tell you what, I'm glad you're on my team, Kits. Not sure I'd like to be on the other side of your crazy.'

'He told me that you've both decided to take things super slowly. Physically, I mean?'

Tor nods. 'Yes. It wasn't even my idea. It was totally his. We've only kissed. He's barely even laid a hand on me, you know. I've never been with a guy who hasn't got his brain in his pants to some degree. I think this could be something really special.'

'Then I'm pleased for you. You deserve someone like that. He didn't even look at me when I pulled out some of my moves.'

Tor's face morphs into something harder. 'Wait . . . what? What do you mean "moves"? Did you go in there to seduce him?'

Oh fuck. 'No, Tor! Not to seduce him. I'd never do that to you. Or Charlie.'

'Right, but you set out to see if he would? Is that why you went to his clinic? So you could get him alone and suss him out? Fucking hell. There really is something wrong with you.' She's livid again.

'No, no. It wasn't like that, Tor!' It totally was. 'And he didn't even look at me so it doesn't matter.'

'Oh it doesn't matter because he passed your little test? Jesus Christ, Kitty, that isn't the point at all! You're not some sort of avenging fucking honey trap. And this might be a shock to you, but not every man thinks you're irresistible either.' She's on her feet again now and I know this isn't a good thing. 'I'm an adult woman, Kitty. And I know you're my friend and you *think* you're looking out for me but you need to stop. What if Aidan was less understanding and dumped me because of what you did? Did you think about that?' She slams her wine glass down on the dresser so hard I'm surprised the stem doesn't snap. 'I think we need a break from each other,' she says.

'What? Tor . . . no! I'm sorry. I'm really sorry. I'll apologise to Aidan as well. I'll go and see him. Please don't be like this.'

'No, Kitty. You can't anyway. He's gone away for a few days.' She exhales heavily. 'I'm going back out to tell Carmella I'm not coming to the wedding. I need some space from you. I feel like you're suffocating me sometimes. Jesus Christ. You're like a controlling boyfriend. This behaviour isn't normal, Kitty.'

'Tor, I'm sorry. I really am. Please don't do this. I don't want to lose you.'

'Then respect my wishes, Kits. I need some space.' She turns to go. 'And don't even think about going and seeing Aidan again. I swear I will never speak to you again if you do.' She takes a deep breath. 'This behaviour is not okay, Kitty. It's really not. It's obsessive. If I had a woman at the centre telling me that she had a partner treating her like this, I'd tell her to run. Fast.'

And with that she storms out of the room even angrier than when she arrived.

I sit alone on my bed for a few more minutes, finishing my wine and trying to block out everything Tor just said to me. I can't think about her now. I need to get out of here and back to Max. But just as I'm getting ready to stand and make my escape there's another knock at the door.

For fuck's sake, why is everyone so obsessed with me tonight?

It opens a crack and Charlie pokes his head round. 'Can I come in?'

'Sure,' I say. I mean, what else *can* I say? *It's not a great time, darling, I've got to nip out and get rid of the body of a primetime TV presenter I just killed.* He comes inside, holding another glass of wine which he hands to me.

'I thought you could use this,' he says.

More than you can ever understand.

'I just saw Tor,' he continues. 'She looked really angry. She told Carmella she's not coming to the wedding? Have you had an argument?'

I swallow more wine. 'Yes,' I say, meekly. 'I fucked up, Charlie.'

'How? What happened? I've never known you two to fight?'

'It was my fault,' I say. 'I didn't trust her. She told me she's been dating her therapist and I freaked out.'

'Right. Well, I think that's understandable,' Charlie says, stroking my arm. 'I think most people would have a strong reaction if someone they care about told them that. I don't think you're in the wrong.'

'I went to see him. I pretended to be a patient.'

'Oh. Well . . . oh.' He leans back and looks at me intently. 'I mean, that's not ideal. But. It's because you care. She'll calm down. She's angry now, but Tor loves you and she'll understand why you did it when she's cooled off a bit. She's important to you. I know your heart was in the right place.' This man. I can literally do no wrong in his eyes. He always sees the best in me. I wish I could be as good as he thinks I am.

'It was,' I say. 'It really was. I wanted to make sure for myself.'

Charlie pulls me into his body and I feel myself melt into his warmth. I look up at him, taking in that face I love so much, his freckles, his dimples, the little lines around his eyes that appear when he looks at me the way he is now.

'Stop looking at me,' he says, with a laugh.

'I can't,' I say. 'I like you.'

He pulls me tighter into him. 'I like you too, Kitty Collins. Very much.'

'Will you promise me something?'

He looks down at me. 'Of course, anything.'

'Please don't ever throw a surprise party for me again.'

Charlie laughs and promises and tickles me until I fall back against the pillows and he falls down next to me, tucking my head under his chin, wrapping his arms around me. We stay like that for a little while, not saying anything, just holding each other. I close my eyes, feeling happy.

Feeling safe.

18

Fuckfuckfuckfuckfuckfuckfuck.

I fell asleep.

It's the morning.

I'm flying to France in about two hours; there's a dead body, a ton of my DNA and a whole murder scene I need to sort out. And I fell asleep. My heart is beating so fast, too fast. This can't be good.

I go through to the lounge where I find Charlie filling the dishwasher, there is no sign of the party at all, apart from the balloons which are still floating around in a corner like naughty ghosts.

'Morning, sleepyhead,' he says, standing up and coming over to me. He wraps his arms around me and I breathe him in. It calms me. 'I didn't have the heart to wake you up last night after you crashed out. I should've known you didn't want a party. I told everyone to go home. I'm sorry.'

'You did that? Were they okay about it?'

He chuckles. 'Yeah, I let them take the booze with them. They all went away happy as Larry. Anyway, you'd better

129

have some coffee. Carmella's picking us up in a car in about half an hour. We can have breakfast in the airport lounge.'

My head spins.

'Half an hour?' I say. 'But I need to go out!' My voice is a squeak.

'I'm sure whatever it is can wait?'

It really fucking cannot.

'No . . . I don't think it can. I really need to go.' I can feel myself descending into panic and have to clutch the kitchen counter to hold myself up.

'Are you okay, Kits?' Charlie asks. 'You've gone really pale. Sit down. I'll get you a coffee.'

I can't sit down and have coffee. There is a dead body I need to get rid of and we are getting picked up in an hour and a half.

'No . . . no,' I say. 'I need to go out, Charlie.' But when I step away from the counter and try to make my way to the door, my legs buckle underneath me. Charlie sees me stumble and rushes over.

'Kits. What's wrong? You're really worrying me.' He guides me into the lounge area and onto the sofa.

I can't sit down. I need to get to Max's flat. Even if I haven't got time to move the body, I need to clean up. I need to get any trace of my DNA out of that flat. I need to double check there's no CCTV at his apartment block.

'Kitty, breathe,' Charlie is saying now and I try but I can't. My breaths are getting stuck in my throat. I feel like I'm choking on them. 'You're having a panic attack, Kits. You need to breathe. Let's do it together.' He reaches for my hands which have become cold and clammy. 'In. Out. In. Out. That's it. You're okay. You're safe.'

Only I'm not, am I? I'm not safe at all because I fucking killed someone and didn't clear up the fucking scene. My DNA will be everywhere when Max Macintyre's body is discovered and people will have seen me with him at the pub, asking for him at the studio. And then I'll go to prison. My lovely boyfriend will find out that I'm a murderer, a *serial* murderer, and he'll leave me. How could I have been so careless?

'Maybe this holiday has come at a good time?' Charlie says when he's happy enough that my breathing has returned to normal and the panic attack is abating. 'Maybe some time away from everything is just what you need?'

He's right.

I need to get the fuck out of here.

As quickly as possible.

If I can't get back to the scene of the crime then I need to get really fucking far away from it.

Half an hour later, Rehan at the front desk calls up to let us know my mother is here to collect us.

'Tell her we're on our way,' I say as Charlie grabs our cases and drags them to the lift. I look around my beautiful apartment, wondering if this is going to be the last time I see it, wondering if I'm going to have to go on the run once I'm in France. I really don't want to go on the run. It seems like such a hassle. Where would I get my eyebrows done, for a start? I check the news app on my phone but there's nothing about Max Macintyre and his mutilated hands being found. Right. I need to breathe. If I can get out of the country before he's found, that's something. That's a good something.

My mother is waiting in the car downstairs; she's sitting in the back which means Charlie has to sit in the front with the driver. I slide in next to her.

'Morning, darling,' she says, leaning over to kiss me. 'Are you feeling better after your sleep? Poor thing. You must've had a stressful day.' She takes her oversized sunglasses off so she can look at me.

'Yeah, a bit,' I say. 'Are you okay? You look tired.' I'm not just saying it to be spiteful. She really does look tired. There are shadows underneath her eyes and her normally immaculate face looks sort of off, like it's been smudged. The last time I saw someone looking this rough was when Maisie announced her pregnancy. I quickly do some mental arithmetic and am relieved that I can rule that out. Something else occurs to me. 'Are you sick?'

She laughs. 'There's nothing like your own child to lift your self-esteem. I'm fine, darling. Just very tired. I didn't sleep well last night. I don't like being away from my own bed.'

I frown as I study her face. My mother goes on several holidays a year and then some. She has no problem sleeping in a bed that's not her own.

When we've checked in the bags and settled into our first-class seats, I take my phone to turn on airplane mode. I decide to have a tiny check of Instagram before we take off and suddenly feel a vine of fear twine around my insides.

Blaze Bundy posted two hours ago.

It's a photo of the view out of an airplane window. The white surface of the wing is visible, along with blue skies and the cotton wool carpet of cloud. But the words turn my bones to glass.

Disciples, I'm going on holiday. I can't reveal my exact destination to you but let's see who I might bump into in France 🐱 🔪 *à bientôt!*

Blaze Bundy is going to France.

And, if I'm reading his not-so-subtle clues correctly, he's coming to kill me.

19

HÔTEL DU CHIEN NOIR, CANNES

It's hard to pretend to be excited about anything now I know there is a misogynistic psychopath trailing me across the Channel to kill me. But at least it's given me something to think about besides the mess I left back in London. Funny how a dead body is the least of my problems now that someone is threatening to make *me* one. So now I have to work out who Blaze Bundy is and get to him before he gets to me. Easier said than done when he knows exactly who I am while all I've got to go on is a black bandana and a major attitude problem.

The good thing is that while I'm being forced to be a dutiful daughter, the itinerary for the next few days consists of spending *a lot* of time with my mother – and with Charlie here too – Blaze Bundy will struggle to get me alone to murder me. For all his women-hating and toxic posturing, he's totally underestimated how hard it is to come between a bride and her big day. On the way to the hotel alone, my mother has almost sent me into a coma with all her talk about florists and dress fittings and cake tastings. If Blaze needs any tips on how to kill me, I could suggest he bores me to death with wedding chat.

The hotel is pretty much what I was expecting from Carmella. Slightly farther along the Croisette from The Carlton, it's equally as luxurious. Our car takes us right to the entrance and a monsieur in a hefty suit that must be unbearable in the heat opens our doors and greets us like we're friends of old. He kisses Carmella on each cheek and she flushes slightly, batting him away playfully. She must spend a lot of time here.

The foyer is the white marble of expensive hotels and it's reassuringly cool. I'm pleasantly surprised at how bright and opulent the place is, I wasn't sure what to expect from a hotel named after depression. In my mind, it had been huge and gothic and tucked away in the Esterel mountains, even though this would not be in keeping with my mother at all. Charlie raises an eyebrow at me as we take in the grandeur and I know he was having the same thoughts.

Carmella is already checked in so she leaves us in the capable, manicured hands of a polished young lady behind the desk who gives us our key cards and tells us our suite is on the seventh floor.

'Well, this is very nice,' Charlie says, throwing his hand luggage onto the bed and looking around the suite. And it is. It's lovely. Not that I'd ever expect anything else from my mother. The suite is off-the-scale luxurious. Everything is so white that it's like being inside a cloud. But, you know, when you've seen one mega opulent five-star hotel, you've seen them all really. Charlie is taking a proper look round though, opening all the cupboards. He whistles when he locates the minibar. He's very impressed. Charlie hardly grew up in poverty – his dad is some sort of financial wizard – but perhaps he's spent too much time hanging around refugee camps for work because he's acting like a lottery winner on their first post-win trip abroad. It's irritating me because, as nice as this hotel is, it's not as nice as my apartment and he actually *lives* there. 'Look at the marble in here, Kits,' he calls out from the bathroom and I feel something start to throb in my temple. This isn't good. For the past year Charlie's voice has made other places throb and I'm really not ready for that to change. I take a deep breath and consciously check in with myself. It's not Charlie that I'm worried about, I know this. It's the fact that I've had to leave a kill scene without cleaning it up. Anxiety grabs me and I take a deep breath and try to put it out of my mind. The blood. My DNA every-fucking-where. All because of my mother and her wedding. Max Macintyre's body is probably being discovered by a cleaner as we speak. And it's only a matter of time before all roads lead to me. When someone who was in that pub remembers us drinking together. I'll probably never be able to go back to London again. I'll have to fuck off to a country that doesn't have an extradition pact with the UK. What countries even are those? Like Libya or somewhere? Somewhere without Net-a-Porter. Somewhere without fucking wifi probably. Fuck, I feel so sick that my legs threaten to buckle from underneath me so I sit down on the bed just as Charlie walks back through from the bathroom.

'Kits?' he says. 'What's wrong? You've gone white as a ghost.' He rushes over to me and puts his hand to my head. 'Are you coming down with something?'

Yes. A serious case of I'm-about-to-be-caught-for-murder, actually.

'Let me get you some water,' he says. 'Stay there. Put your

head between your knees or something.' He brings me a cold bottle of water from the minibar and I gulp it down. It does actually make me feel momentarily better.

'Sorry,' I say to Charlie and wonder how I could've been so irritated with him just moments ago. He's the kindest man I've ever met and he loves me despite constantly causing him stress. 'I think I'm just a bit tired and hungover.'

'You don't need to say sorry,' he says. 'Do you want me to leave you alone for a bit so you can get some rest? I haven't been to Cannes in ages so I wouldn't mind a wander around. And I won't drag you with me if you're not feeling great?'

'Would you mind?' I say. 'I think I'll feel so much better when I've had a sleep and a shower. We can get some food when I wake up? Take a walk over to Chemin des étoiles together seeing as you won't stop yapping on about it.' He chewed my ear off all the way over here about spotting the handprints of random actors and directors I've never even heard of in the Cannes version of the Hollywood Walk of Fame. He was going on about it so much I had to put my AirPods in and turn the noise cancellation right up. I give him a weak smile.

'Of course I don't mind. You get some rest and I'll get some steps in. Do you need me to bring you anything back?'

'No thank you.'

'Okay, I'll see you in a couple of hours.' He gives me a lingering kiss on the lips, which can't be very nice for him because my mouth feels like a pub floor, grabs his bag and closes the door gently behind him as I pretend to go to sleep.

As soon as the door clicks shut I sit up and grab my phone, opening the internet browser and type in Max Macintyre. But there's still nothing. Not yet. But surely people will start to wonder when he fails to show up for his show tonight. I check the time. A few hours. That's all I've got left. I was an idiot to come here. Surely I could've easily come up with a reason I couldn't fly today. And now what? I just wait for them to find the body? A sitting duck. Maybe I could just get a flight home, clear up the mess and fly back? But I wouldn't be able to get there in time, would I? The fucking shag pad will be the first place they look for him and even if I got a plane now, best-case scenario is I'd be caught up to my elbows in entrails, cleaning the fucker up. Fuck. I've really let my game slip. Then I head to some forums where Bundy disciples speculate about who could be hiding behind the bandana. But there is absolutely nothing useful to me. The only suggested name I've even heard of is Peter Andre and I highly doubt he's taking time out of his busy schedule to come and murder me. Anxiety bubbles in my stomach and I haven't even got any drugs with me that will help me relax. I stand up and shuffle to the minibar where I take out two miniature bottles of vodka and down them both. Then I unpack a few things and jump in the shower. Maybe I can wash this feeling of impending doom away with some of the Acqua di Parma body products the hotel has kindly supplied.

It does help, a little, even though I have to give up on showering in favour of lying in the bath because every time I think about Blaze Bundy, and Max Macintyre and his stupid handless corpse lying in that fucking fuck pad, my legs feel like they're going to give way.

Afterwards, I get changed into a bikini and a crochet beach dress and decide to take a little walk myself. Not far, of course, that would be a crazy thing to do with a killer on my trail. Maybe the sun on my skin and the smell of the sea will have a healing effect on me. There must be a reason the meditation tracks on Spotify are always full of sounds of the ocean and crap like that. Hopefully I'll bump into Charlie and we can go and have some food and look at the stupid famous handprints he wants to see so badly.

I take the lift down and walk through the deliciously air-conditioned lobby, smiling politely as members of staff greet me and wish me a *bon après-midi*. And then I step outside where the heat feels like a hairdryer.

It's late afternoon and the beach is actually quite empty; it's got that sleepy feeling when the sun has moved so high in the sky that most of the sun loungers are now in the shade. There's plenty of evidence that this little section of beach has been well used today. There are footprints in the sand and deep rivets where kids have dug moats for their castles. There are empty plastic glasses on the little tables next to the plush loungers and a few sarongs, sunhats and sticky bottles of expensive sun lotion that have been forgotten. It's that time of day when parents are ushering their offspring up to the rooms so they can get them washed and in bed before they take advantage of the hotel's rather excellent babysitting service and come back down to the bar. The couples will have snuck away to shower and have some lazy holiday sex before they come back down for dinner and drinks. There are a few bronzed and bronzing bodies scattered around but no more than half a dozen or so. I slip my Prada flip-flops off and feel the softness of the sand on my feet and between my toes as I walk down towards the sea. I'm a little tipsy from my raid of the minibar. And probably the two glasses of champs I had on the plane. And the two glasses I had in the airport lounge. Or was it three? Okay, so I'm actually probably more than just a little bit tipsy which would explain why I almost fall flat on my face on the beach. And it's only *almost* because someone manages to grab my arm before I hit the deck.

'Woah there,' says a deep voice. A deep manly voice. 'A little too much refreshment this afternoon, was it?'

'It's sunstroke,' I say as I look up into the deepest, darkest eyes I've ever seen in my life. Honestly, they're like pools of— What's really dark? Coal? Can you have pools of coal? Anyway, that's how dark we're talking.

'Sure, sunstroke,' the owner of the eyes is saying with a tiny smirk teasing the corners of his mouth. And what a mouth it is. Plump lips but not so lush that they look feminine and even if they did, the smattering of unkempt stubble around that mouth and jawline would immediately cancel it out. I think this might be the most attractive face I've ever seen in real life. Am I hallucinating? He helps me properly back up to my feet and I decide that I can't be hallucinating because I'm pretty sure that hallucinations can't touch you. And what a touch it is. I don't want it to stop. 'I think I've also been guilty of overindulging in sunstroke myself a few times.' He laughs, showing off perfect white teeth, lets go of my arm and runs a hand through his hair, which is a sort of dishevelled mass of dark curls.

I can't speak.

'You okay there?' he's saying, looking at me with concern. 'Look, sit down and I'll go and grab you a glass of water.'

'No, no, I'm fine,' I say, plonking inelegantly onto a sun lounger.

'Shh. I insist,' he says. 'Water really is the best thing for . . . sunstroke.' I swear I hear him chuckle to himself as he strides purposefully towards the beach bar to get me a drink. Look at that. We've already got a little private joke. I watch as he walks to the bar, having to make a conscious effort to pick my jaw up off the sand. He's wearing dark-coloured shorts and a flimsy white beach shirt, but I can tell that underneath that is the body of an Adonis. I shake my head. What's wrong with me? I'm basically objectifying this man like some sort of beach-letch. And I've got a boyfriend. A lovely, sexy, handsome boyfriend who is kindly giving me some space because I've been acting like a little bitch all day.

I must be ovulating.

The man comes back over with a glass of water full of ice.

'Here you go,' he says. 'You feeling okay now? Not going to swoon again?'

I can't promise this as there is every chance I might swoon if I try to stand up. I nod, gulping down the water, and say, 'Thank you, I'm fine.'

That smirk again. 'Glad to hear it. I'll see you around.'

20

Cannes in summer only comes second to London in summer, I decide. And that's purely because of the unwavering loyalty I have to my hometown. Unlike other European coastal resorts – I'm looking at you, Puerto Banús – it still sparkles with money and luxe, rather than vomit spatter from inebriated tourists. The gleam from the rows and rows of white superyachts in the port is almost as dazzling as the sun. And the shops! Oh my goodness, the whole experience of shopping here. As much as my heart belongs on King's Road and Sloane Square, there's something to be said about popping into Hermès with the twinkling Med waiting for you when you step back out.

The place is teeming with young women; they're practically an infestation. The beaches, the beach bars, the hotel bars are always full to the brim with tanned and toned girls fluttering prettily around, no doubt trying to catch the eye of one of the many Russian millionaires who summer here in packs. Cannes is *not* a city for wives. The husbands pack them off to nearby places like Antibes or Juan-les-Pins. Cannes is a city for lovers, be it the illicit kind or the kind like Charlie and me – newly in love, still besotted with each other, an infatuationship.

Even the Palais des Festivals, which hosts the film festival and the handprints Charlie has been obsessing over, feels special despite being the biggest tourist trap in the whole place. Maybe I'm just a red-carpet whore after all.

'This is so exciting!' Charlie is buzzing like a sugared-up toddler on Christmas morning. I've honestly never seen someone get so excited about some handprints. It's cute. A little irritating because it's still hot and all I really want to do is sit down with an Aperol Spritz or nine. But mostly cute. We've had a wander along the Croisette already, picking up some tourist tat including an 'I Heart Cannes' canvas beach bag with a rope handle. I have zero intention of wrecking my two-thousand-pound LV Neverfull with sand and leaky sun lotion. 'Look! Here's David Lynch!' He takes about five thousand photos of the handprints of David Lynch, whoever-he-is, in the concrete floor. They will join the several billion he's already taken of Angelina Jolie's, Natalie Portman's, Quentin Tarantino's and fuck knows who else. 'Is there anyone you'd like to see, Kits?'

The bartender at the hotel.

Actually, any bartender anywhere.

Blaze Bundy, without his mask and with a knife in his throat.

'Not really, darling.' I sidle over to him and slip my arm through his. 'I'm just happy watching you get so excited over some fingerprints.'

He laughs. 'Ha. Maybe I missed my calling and should have been in the police.'

Er. No, definitely don't do that.

He hands me his phone. 'Can you take a picture of me with this one please?' He squats down next to the handprints and does a double thumbs-up. Total tourist cringe. It's so cheesy and I feel a huge rush of love for this man.

'I love you, Charlie Chambers,' I say.

He gives me a puzzled look in response. 'What's not to love? I'm clearly the coolest man you've ever met.'

'Clearly.'

He stands up and walks over to me, wrapping his arms around me and pulling me into him. 'I love you back, Kitty Collins. Very much.'

See. This is love. This is what love feels like. Safe and comforting and like drinking an Old Fashioned. Charlie is my future and I love him more than I've ever loved anyone. I need to do everything I can to keep him and stay alive. And out of jail. This is home. This man who loves me and would do anything for me. Who loves me for exactly who I am. More or less.

'Shall we go and have supper somewhere nice?' Charlie says into my hair. 'There are some places that look lovely over the road.'

'I've got a better idea,' I say. 'Let's go back to the hotel. I think I'd quite like to show you exactly how much I love you.'

'Oh, really?' Charlie pulls me in even closer. 'How can I say no to that?'

I need to sweeten him up anyway. We're having supper with my mother and Gabriel tonight. I haven't told Charlie yet. And I need to prepare myself for my first meeting with my soon-to-be stepdad. An hour or so in bed with my boyfriend will get rid of any anxiety I'm feeling.

21

It does indeed do the job. An hour and a half later, after showing Charlie how much I love him three times, I'm feeling calmer. There's a lot to be said for the restorative power of orgasms. And this is despite the fact that there's still no word on Max Macintyre's brutal murder, even though his show is airing in the UK right now. I've done a quick scan of social media and celebrity gossip sites and the only thing that's been said is that Max isn't hosting tonight due to 'personal reasons'. There's nothing on his page. Or his wife, Lauren's. I feel a niggle of anxiety again and shove my phone under my pillow. Out of sight, out of mind.

'Do I need to wear a tie?' Charlie's asking. We're getting ready to meet my mother and Gabriel in a restaurant downstairs and he's stressing so much about the dress code.

'No tie,' I say. 'It's not like super formal or anything. It's just a beach restaurant.'

'Do you think Gabriel will be wearing a suit?' he says as if I hadn't said anything. Bless him. He's nervous.

'No, I do not think he will be wearing a suit when it is

still twenty-nine degrees outside. Stop stressing. Just wear something you're comfortable in. Why are you more nervous than me? This is *my* stepfather-to-be we're meeting.'

Charlie is throwing clothes out of his suitcase and around the room in a way that's very much not like him at all. 'But he's French and will look casually and naturally smart and I don't want to look like a British lout.' He turns to me with such a sweet and earnest look on his face that I can't help but kiss him all over it. I had no idea that men worried about this kind of thing as well.

'You look gorgeous whatever you wear,' I say. 'And you could never look like a lout. Now, please, just put on any clothes that fit and aren't swimwear and hurry up.'

He smiles and the dimple I love so much appears in his cheek. As always I have to resist the urge to stick my finger in it. 'Okay. Sorry.'

I look at myself in the full-length mirror and like what I see. I'm wearing a yellow Chloé dress with a pair of Jimmy Choo sandals. I don't look like I just murdered someone and didn't clean up.

Eventually Charlie is ready, dressed casually in a pair of chino shorts and a linen shirt with the sleeves rolled up. I feel bad for men sometimes. They really get the short straw when it comes to clothes. But I suppose it's more than made up for with all the other privileges they get. Being able to go out alone without the constant threat of assault. That kind of thing. I grab his hand and we make our way down to the ground floor to Moulins, the restaurant where we're meeting my mother and Gabriel. I hope my mother's taste in men has improved since she married my dad.

A host who looks like they've stepped straight from a Paris Fashion Week catwalk greets us and shows us to our table, which is outside with a beautiful view of the Mediterranean Sea. We're the first ones there and I order a bottle of Sancerre and some water for the table while we wait. Charlie checks out the menu and I taste the wine and tell the server that it's delicious. Because it is.

'The food looks incredible,' Charlie says, still scanning the options. 'There's quite a few vegan choices too.'

To be honest, food is the last thing on my mind at the moment. I just want to get this first meeting out of the way.

'That's nice,' I say. And then I catch a glimpse of Carmella sashaying her way through the inside section of the restaurant, towards the table, a huge smile on her face and a well-dressed man on her arm. She looks like the cat that got the cream and, honestly, it suits her. She's glowing in a way I've never seen before. Maybe my fears about her and her choices are totally unfounded.

She wraps me in a huge hug when she gets to our table, and once again the smell of her takes me back to childhood. When she's finally let go of me and moved on to Charlie, I see Gabriel has already sat down and I have to do a double-take because he is absolutely not what I expect.

He's younger than I was expecting.

He's got a headful of unruly black curls.

And now he's removed his aviator shades, I can see two dark coal pools where his eyes should be.

It's the man from the beach. And he's got that smirk on his face again. My heart is thudding so hard I wouldn't be surprised if everyone could see it through my dress.

'Kitty, Charlie. This is Gabriel.' My mother is delirious and sounds like a smitten schoolgirl.

He stands up and holds his hand out to Charlie and they do that man-thing where they shake hands and clap each other on the back. 'Nice to meet you, mate,' Gabriel says. He turns to me. 'I've actually already met Kitty.'

My mother turns to him. 'What? When? When did this happen and why didn't you say anything?' She's smiling but I can tell this new information has thrown her off her game a little.

'Well, I didn't actually know it was her at the time,' he says, still smirking. 'She almost fell onto my lap because of her sunstroke.'

'Sunstroke?' Charlie the traitor is saying. He turns to me. 'But we only got here this afternoon.'

'I thought you were marrying a Frenchman?' I say accusingly to my mother, who promptly bursts into laughter. 'You're not French!' I say accusingly to Gabriel.

'Oh, Kits, you're so funny. Why did you think he was French?'

'That's what you told me,' I say, crossly.

'I didn't, darling,' she replies. 'I definitely never told you that he was French. Why would I do that?'

'I think the fact you've been calling him *Gabriele* really heavily suggested he might be French!' My voice is quite high now. Charlie puts a soothing hand on my arm but I shake it off. I don't want to be calmed right now. I feel embarrassed and annoyed.

'You can always call me Daddy, if that's better for you?' Gabriel says with a wink and my mother almost falls over from laughing.

I don't say anything.

'I'm sorry if you feel mislead,' Gabriel is saying as he sits back down. 'That definitely wasn't Carmella's intention. Or mine.' He puts his hands together in a prayer position and does a tiny bow with his head. His hair isn't even thinning on top. How young *is* he?

'Can we just all sit down and have a nice meal?' my mother says, looking pleadingly at me and then at Charlie. 'I'm sorry if you got the wrong end of the stick, Kits. But really, if you'd have come out sooner you'd have met Gabriel and known right away that I wasn't dating a French cliché.' She sits down and smiles. 'Did you expect him to be wearing a Breton shirt with a string of garlic around his neck?'

Gabriel laughs and claps his hands together. 'Come on. Let's have a few drinks and some lovely food and get to know each other properly.' He's wearing a white silk shirt, one that I know is by The Row and costs over two thousand pounds because I was wondering if I should buy one for Charlie. Gabriel has rolled the sleeves up, almost like he deliberately wants to show off his obscenely tanned forearms. Or perhaps it's to draw attention to the watch that's sparkling away on his wrist. If I'm not mistaken, and I seldom am, it's a Patek Philippe. A distinctive dark blue strap with diamonds and sapphires glittering from the face. Tens of thousand of pounds worth of watch. He turns and gestures to the waiter to bring yet another bottle of wine over and I catch another glimpse of that jawline. That. Jawline. This is the man my mother is marrying? How? No offence to my mother, she's beautiful. She looks great. But she's in her fifties. This man cannot be older than forty. And he's model hot. I may have mentioned that. Why's he marrying my post-menopausal mother?

'I like your watch,' Charlie says to Gabriel.

'This old thing?' He laughs. 'It was an engagement gift from my darling fiancée.' He leans over and kisses Carmella on the cheek. 'She's so generous.'

Ah.

There's my answer.

It's not my mother he's interested in, it's her Coutts Silk card.

'Have you had a chance to have a look at the menu?' my mother asks and I feel furious at her. How could she be naïve enough to fall for him? He's an absolute textbook gold-digger. It's so blindingly obvious.

'It all looks great,' Charlie is saying and I suddenly feel furious with him too for not spotting the gold-digger in our midst. 'Kitty? Do you know what you're having yet?'

'I haven't had a chance to look, have I?' I snap, catching Gabriel's eye as I do.

'How's the sunstroke?' he asks me, all innocence.

'Fine, thank you,' I say, taking another long slurp of wine.

'Kitty, go easy on that,' my mother says. 'Drink some water if you've been feeling unwell. You had quite a lot to drink on the plane too.'

'I'm thirty years old,' I say, sounding like I'm about twelve. 'I think I can decide for myself when I've had enough to drink.'

'Okay, darling. No need to be snippy. I was just saying.'

Charlie leans over and pours out some water into all our glasses. His treachery knows no bounds. I, childishly, top up my glass of wine.

'Congratulations on the wedding,' Charlie says to my mother and Gabriel. I feel his hand on my thigh, squeezing it ever so gently. He's telling me that he's right there, that he's got my back. My behaviour has clearly alarmed him, but he thinks I'm still annoyed that Gabriel is actually Gabriel and not *Gabriele* and not French. He doesn't know that the man my mother is marrying is very obviously after her money. 'We're really looking forward to it, aren't we, Kits?'

No.

I nod mutely and pull the menu higher so it's covering my face and I don't have to look at Gabriel. There really aren't many vegan options actually, despite Charlie's cheerful claim to the contrary. Why does he have to be such a perpetual Pollyanna? The waiter, an elegantly dressed French woman, comes to our table and asks if we're ready to order.

'I'll just have the roast leek,' I say unenthusiastically and Charlie orders the same. My mother chooses something French and fishy. There's no way she'll risk any carbs with a teeny dress to squeeze into in a few days. Gabriel meets my gaze and looks almost defiantly at me as he orders.

'Noix d'entrecôte,' he say. 'Bleu. Merci.' He orders a rare steak. Not only is it the bloodiest thing on the menu, it's also the most expensive. He raises an eyebrow at me. Just a little, it's barely perceptible, but it feels like a challenge. Like he's saying *what are you going to do about it?* Then he pours himself and my mother some more wine, smiling at her now. Looking at her with soft, loving eyes. He's good, I'll give him that, but there's no mistaking the way the hairs on the back of my neck stand on end whenever he looks at me. I know a predator when I see one. My instincts are rarely wrong and I don't like this man.

'So, how did you meet?' Charlie asks just as the server comes back over with a basket of bread that my mother looks at longingly.

'It was Tinder actually,' she says, meeting Gabriel's eyes. 'How does anyone meet anyone these days?'

Tinder. Well, that's just perfect, isn't it? It's a perfect hunting ground for men like Gabriel. Men who are looking for an older, wealthy woman to buy them Patek Philippe watches. Two servers come to our table now and present us with our mains. I'm suddenly not hungry and knowing the French, these veggies have probably been washed in boeuf fat.

'Tinder. Really?' I say. 'How modern of you.'

'Don't sound so shocked, Kitty,' my mother says. 'I know my way around a dating app, believe it or not. I'm not actually a hundred years old.'

'I was only supposed to be passing through Cannes,' Gabriel says. 'But then I met Carmella and decided to stick around.' He takes a long gulp of wine. 'The best decision I ever made.' My mother makes a stupid face and a stupid noise and leans over to kiss his cheek.

'Where are you from?' I ask and I can feel Charlie's eyes boring into me. I know I'm not being very polite.

Gabriel shrugs. 'Here and there,' he says. 'Most recently, Portofino.'

'How lovely to just be able to up and leave like that,' I say, ignoring my mother's glare across the table. 'Did you come here for work? You haven't mentioned what you do for a living.' Gabriel meets my eye and gives me what I'm sure he believes is a winning smile.

'I've got a few irons in the fire,' he says and he and Carmella exchange a look that I can't interpret.

'Shall we order another bottle of this Sancerre?' my mother says in a sing-song voice, desperately trying to defuse the tension.

'Let's get two,' says Gabriel without breaking eye contact with me. 'It's a celebration after all. It's not every day I get to meet my delightful new stepdaughter.'

Of course he'd order two. He's clearly not paying.

My mother is.

I'm so in my head about Gabriel that I'm barely part of the conversation that's going on around me and Charlie has to nudge me a couple of times to remind me where I am.

'Are you okay?' he whispers to me as the server arrives with the extra wine and to check everything is *bon* with our meals. 'You seem like you're on another planet today.'

'Just tired,' I say with a smile I'm not sure is even vaguely convincing. I forgot how physically exhausting a murder can be. I'm not in my twenties anymore.

'That'll be your age,' Charlie says, giving me a wink. 'It'll be your lower back next.' I know he's joking but I can feel my heckles rise as I stab at something I think might be aubergine like it's a body.

'Has your mother shown you what you're to wear yet, Kitty?' Gabriel's voice pierces my thoughts and I look up at him. He's chewing on a piece of his steak that is so rare I can see the bloody juices trickling down his chin leaving a slick trail. His eyes are so wolfish that the whole thing feels obscene. Under the table, I stab my thigh with my fork in an attempt to focus.

'No. What? What do you mean?' I look to my mother who is smiling indulgently at me. 'What's he talking about?'

'I've got you a dress.' She beams and I'm immediately terrified imagining something ridiculous and puffy. I wouldn't put it past my mother to dress me up like I'm still six years old. She hasn't been around for such a huge chunk of my life that there's no possible way for her to know what will suit me now. I cringe at the thought of walking her down the aisle looking like something that should be found on top of the toilet in a pensioner's house. She clearly sees this written all over my face and laughs. 'Don't worry, darling. I'm not going to have you dressed up in a meringue or anything like that. It's nice. Classy. Ralph Lauren. I think you'll like it and you'll look beautiful.'

My eyes have wandered back to Gabriel's though and he's locked me in that intense stare again.

'Yes, beautiful,' he says and there's a loaded pause. He lifts his hand up to sweep it through those curls. That's when I see it. Barely visible but definitely there. On the soft white flesh on the underside of his forearm. Just above the expensive watch paid for by Carmella.

A tattoo.

Two letters.

BB.

Exactly the same as the ones scrawled on that hideous blow-up doll when it was pulled out of the Thames. Without warning I feel my guts twist and I throw up all over the sandy floor of the restaurant.

22

'Honestly, I'm fine,' I tell Charlie back in our room. 'I must've picked up a stomach bug or something on the plane. It's nothing to worry about. Stop fussing.'

That tattoo.

Those letters.

He hands me a glass of water. 'Do you think you're going to be sick again?'

I shake my head. The shock has passed now. Well, the initial hit of it has anyway. That feeling of my blood turning to ice has given way to something else. Something even more insidious.

Gabriel isn't a gold-digger.

Or he isn't just *a gold-digger.*

Gabriel is Blaze Bundy and Blaze Bundy wants to kill me.

That's why Blaze singled me out. Because he wants to get me out of the way so he can marry my mother and take her money. God, he's probably planning on killing her too when I'm out of the way.

It makes sense now. The threats. The promise that he'd see

155

me soon. Of course he'd have been in on the plan to bring me over here for the wedding. But his plans for me are different to my mother's. I think of those blow-up dolls, one water-logged and sad, washed up on the bank of the Thames, the other deflated and empty, punctured.

'Oh shit.' Charlie is looking at his phone with a frown on his face.

'What's wrong?' My heart is in my throat again. It's Max Macintyre. It's got to be. He's been found dead and I'm on the National Crime Agency's most wanted list. Oh God, *les flics* are probably on their way here right now.

Fuckfuckfuckfuckfuck.

'It's Jenna,' he says and my heart drops back into its correct location. Jenna is Charlie's second-in-command at The Refugee Charity and is looking after things while he's here with me. Jenna is blonde and perky and an eco-warrior. She also has the raging horn for my boyfriend.

'What does she want?' I ask. 'Is there a problem?'

He doesn't answer for a moment or two, busy tapping out a reply to Jenna.

'Charlie? What's wrong?'

He looks at me and blinks. 'Right, sorry, yes. Jenna is in Calais at the moment and a gang has turned up at the camp and they're causing trouble.'

'Okay, that's horrible, but she can deal with that?'

'I'm not sure,' he says, still looking at his phone. 'They sound pretty scary. She thinks they might have guns and says they've been hanging around the unaccompanied children.' He looks at me. 'I really don't like the sound of it, to be honest. Not at all.'

'Okay, what does that mean?'

'Well, Jenna is asking if I can drop in. I was thinking that I might hire a car and drive up? I'd only be a day or two. I'd definitely be back for the wedding.'

'You're going to leave me?' He can't leave me. Not when my mother is marrying a potential psychopath who wants me dead. Not when there's a body and a string of evidence linking it to me about to be discovered at any point.

'I'm not leaving you, silly,' he says, pulling me into his arms. 'I'll be gone for like two days, three at most, while I sort this out. And then I'll be back. With you. Where I belong.'

'I didn't even want to come,' I grumble even though I know I'm being unfair. It's not like he *wants* to sort out a dodgy gang who is causing trouble. Sometimes it's hard to be gracious though. 'And now you're abandoning me.' See.

'I'm sorry, Kits,' he says. 'I'm really, really sorry. I'll be there and back as quickly as I can and then we can enjoy ourselves properly.'

I look into his eyes, his kind, kind eyes and think – not for the first time – that I don't deserve a man as good as Charlie. My wonderful philanthropist who is nothing but kind and sweet to me. I don't want him to leave me alone. With him here, there's a chance that I can stay one step ahead of Gabriel/ Blaze. There's a chance that I can stay alive. Gabriel wouldn't do anything to me while Charlie's around. One thing I *do* know about murder is that witnesses are a very bad thing. I want to cling to him and tell him to stay here with me. But that would be deeply unattractive and would probably give him the major ick. So I just shake my head and smile at him.

'Of course you should go,' I say. 'You're clearly needed.

157

Plus, you're always saying that you haven't been hands-on enough since you met me.'

A devilish twinkle appears in Charlie's eyes. 'I think I've definitely not been hands-on enough since I met you.' He leans in to kiss me, which both impresses and slightly repulses me as he watched me hurl my supper onto the restaurant floor less than thirty minutes ago. His hands go to the sides of my face and he pulls me into him, kissing me like a starving man. Which he probably is, to be fair. The French really don't cater for vegans.

'You're an amazing woman, Kitty Collins. I hope you know that.'

As Charlie kisses me all the way down my body, pulling my clothes off as he works lower and lower, my mind moves back to Gabriel/Blaze Bundy. Maybe it's not such a bad thing that Charlie won't be here for a couple of days. I need to get to him before he gets to me. And, as I just said, no one needs a witness when they're plotting a murder.

23

I feel quite tearful the next morning when Charlie is getting ready to leave.

'I won't take tons of stuff,' he says as he looks through the clothes he only unpacked yesterday. 'Hopefully I won't be there long enough to need more than a couple of changes of clothes.'

'Do you have to go?' I whine, feeling vulnerable again.

He comes over to the bed where I am still wrapped up in the sheets and kisses me on the top of my head. 'We've been through this,' he says, kindly. 'I can't leave Jenna to deal with a gang on her own.'

Fucking Jenna, the damsel in distress. There probably isn't even a gang at all. She has probably just made the whole thing up to get Charlie on his own.

'She fancies you,' I say. It's not the first time we've had this conversation.

'You're cute when you're jealous,' he says. 'But you're also wrong. As you well know, Jenna doesn't have any feelings for me and is in a relationship of her own.'

'She still fancies you though.' Because she does. She goes all doe-eyed around him, flicking her stupid hair about and giggling like a simpleton.

'Even if she did, which she doesn't, it doesn't matter,' Charlie is saying now and I can't help but love how patient and gentle he is with me, even when he thinks I'm being unreasonable. Which I'm not. 'Because I'm in a committed relationship with a beautiful woman whom I love very much.'

'Whom is that?' I tease.

'That would be you, Miss Collins.' He kisses me deeply. 'Plus I don't like blondes.'

'Urgh. You're a hair racist. Blonde lives matter.'

Charlie laughs and kisses me again.

'Do you have to leave right now though?' I say, pushing him gently back onto the bed and liberating his cock from his trousers. He sighs as I take him into my mouth and relax my jaw, letting him slip down my throat. If I can't get him to stay then I'll just give him something he can't stay away from. He grabs at my hair and groans and I know that Jenna is the last thing on his mind.

Half an hour later, Charlie is dressed again and ready to pick up his hire car from downstairs.

'I'll be as quick as I can,' he says. 'You won't even notice I've gone.'

'I'll miss you,' I say. 'Message me as soon as you arrive and drive carefully.'

'I promise.'

'I love you.'

'And I love you back.'

Then he's gone.

I feel a huge surge of loneliness but I swallow it down. I need to use this time to figure out what I'm going to do about Gabriel/Blaze and kill him before he kills me. I can't save my mother from this monster if I'm dead.

I slip on a Missoni bikini with a matching kaftan and head down to the beach again. It's not quite lunchtime and I want to keep a clear head so I order an orange juice from the bar and find myself a lounger on the front row. Then I smother myself in SPF – I like a tan but I don't like the idea of cancer or having skin like a second-hand satchel – and cover my face with my sunglasses and an oversized sunhat. Not only does it protect my skin from the sun, it also acts as a very handy shade so I can see the screen on my phone properly.

The first thing I do is check the UK news sites. Still nothing about Max Macintyre. It's Saturday today so he won't be expected to turn up for his show but he'll definitely be expected to turn up at home. I open Instagram and click on Lauren's page and then Max's. There's nothing new on either of them. Strange. Someone should have raised the alarm by now. I quickly open my Twitter app – I will *never* call it fucking X – and have a quick scroll but no one is saying anything about him there either. This is too weird. It's making me uneasy. I go back to Insta and click on Blaze Bundy's profile. There aren't any new posts since I checked last night. But the red circle around his profile picture is lit up, meaning he's uploaded a story. My jaw is tense as I click on it. I really need to do something about all this tension in my body. I'm sure near constant jaw-clenching isn't going to be making me look any younger either. Must remember to google if such thing as jaw Botox exists.

There's no soundtrack to the three or four stories Blaze Bundy/Gabriel has uploaded but they don't really need anything for the effect to chill me completely to the bone. Because every single one of the stories shows more or less the same thing – POV reels from someone who is walking along a beach. And not just any beach either. The beach that I'm sitting on at this very moment. It's easy to recognise with the branded white parasols, the unmistakable shimmer of the Med and the distinctive shape of the Côte d'Azur coastline in the distance. But it's the last story that really catches my attention. As the camera sweeps across the sunbathing bodies, Blaze Bundy's other arm swings into view, the one that isn't holding the phone. It's the tiniest of glimpses but enough for me to catch sight of that arm and more importantly that wrist. Because twinkling away in the French sunlight is a watch. A watch encrusted with blue and white stones. Just like the one Gabriel was wearing at dinner.

I need to find out more about him.

And where better to start than social media.

What's his last name again? Murphy. That's it. Gabriel Murphy.

I search Gabriel Murphy on Instagram first of all. If I could somehow link him to the Blaze Bundy account, that would be a good first step. There are hundreds of men with that name though and I order a white wine from the beach bar and sip it as I scroll through them. But none of them are the man my mother is about to marry.

I do a general Google search next and, again, there are too many Gabriel Murphys to count. I skim through the Facebook profiles and the LinkedIn stuff but none of them are the man

I'm looking for. I glance through articles in local newspapers where Gabriel Murphy, sixty-seven, has won a competition for growing an oversized marrow or Gabriel Murphy, nineteen, has received a suspended sentence after pleading guilty to driving under the influence. I spend a couple of hours scrolling through entries like this, but none of them are the man *I* know as Gabriel Murphy. This is weird too. Who doesn't have any digital footprint at all? A man who is hiding a secret identity as a toxic-masculinity influencer, that's who. I throw my phone down in frustration. I'm not finding anything of any use about Gabriel online. I'm going to have to do my research offline. What I really need to do is get hold of his phone. Because that is where all the answers – and videos – lie.

But before I can work out how I'm going to do this, I'm snapped out of my Blaze daze by a beep from my phone. I set a notification to alert me to news stories about Max Macintyre while we were waiting in the airport lounge yesterday.

Something has happened.

24

TV Star Max Macintyre Missing

Television presenter Max Macintyre has been reported missing, sources close to the star have revealed.

Macintyre, 39, was absent from his nightly show *Tonight with Max Macintyre* on Friday and there has been much speculation on social media as to his location. But the Met has now revealed that there is some concern for Macintyre's whereabouts and welfare.

A police spokesperson said, 'We have received a report that a thirty-nine-year-old man from Berkshire has been missing from home for seventy-two hours. We can confirm that this person is Max Macintyre and urge anyone who has any information on his whereabouts to speak to us as a matter of urgency.'

Macintyre's wife, Lauren Macintyre, 32, posted on Instagram today appealing for anyone who may have seen her husband to come forward.

'It's extremely unusual for Max to go off-grid like this, especially as he has been sober for the past three years. I beg you all to keep your eyes open as I am so desperately worried about him. Anyone who knows my husband knows that, despite his on-screen persona, he's actually a very vulnerable human being.

'Max, if you see this, please come home. It doesn't matter what's happened, we can work through this. Your baby needs you. I need you. Please just come home.'

Back in my suite I read the news article over and over again, confused. How is this a story about Max being missing and not murdered? How can he be missing when he has a second home literally next to the TV studios where he didn't turn up for work? I'm no detective but even I know that that would be one of the first places to look for him. It doesn't make any sense. And sober? What? He certainly didn't look very sober to me when he was knocking back drinks in that pub. And then there was that whisky he seemed so proud of in his shag pad. Had he fallen off the wagon? It's interesting that the pub isn't mentioned in the report. It must've been the last place he was seen. Max was clearly a regular there and he would've been seen there drinking with someone who matches my description, so why is no one saying anything about that? Max Macintyre's camp are clearly keeping certain details out of the press. While that actually benefits me in the short term I need to make a plan because it's only a matter of time before his body is found and the police come for me. Maybe when Charlie gets back I could suggest we go on a road trip through Europe to be on the safe side. Do I need to get fake passports? Do I need plastic surgery?

No, what I need to do is calm down. And keep an eye on social media. That's where news is really broken these days, isn't it? For some reason the net isn't closing in on me. Yet. If anyone starts saying anything about Max drinking with a beautiful young woman that night, that's when I need to panic. Not now.

I call room service and get them to bring a bottle of wine up to my room. I need to distract myself from the whole Max Macintyre thing. There's absolutely nothing I can do about it from here apart from get ready to run if I need to. Besides, I've got someone else who needs my full attention right now. The wine arrives and I pour myself a large glass. I need to get into my mother and Gabriel's suite and see if I can steal his phone somehow. I send Carmella a text.

Hey! Is now a good time to come and have a look at that bridesmaid dress you were talking about?

Carmella replies a minute later. *Yes darling, but I'm just having some brunch on the Croisette. Gabriel's had to dash off. Come and keep me company and then we can walk back to the hotel together.*

She sends me her location. I don't really want to leave the safety of the hotel on my own, but it's unlikely that Gabriel is going to grab me off the street and kill me in the middle of the day with tourists everywhere. I tell my mother that I'll be ten minutes and finish my wine, pulling on a beach dress, oversized sunglasses and a big hat. He *might* not be planning to murder me in plain sight but a bit of a disguise can't hurt, can it?

25

LA CROISETTE, CANNES

Ten minutes later and I'm out on the Croisette, letting the sun warm my skin. The sky is unbroken blue and the palm trees that line the road sway almost imperceptibly in the slight breeze. The whole street is alive with chatter in various languages and the air smells of salt water, garlic and expensive perfumes. I suppose there are worse places to play a cat-and-mouse game with a killer.

The brunch place my mother sent me is just a five-minute walk from the hotel but I still make sure I have my wits about me, keeping my eyes peeled for anyone who resembles Gabriel lurking around. The place is so beautiful though that it's hard to believe anything bad could possibly happen here. I must stay vigilant and not let myself be distracted by sun and designer shops.

Ooh, Chanel. Should I pop in as I'm passing?

But I walk past it because I've just spotted something much more interesting across the street on the beach. It's the hair I see first, the messy mop of dark curls. My eyes track downwards and clock the toned torso, the lightly tanned skin, those arms. I can't see the tattoo from here but there's no doubt that it's Gabriel. He's walking along the sand about two hundred metres from where I am on the promenade. I'm fairly sure my hat and sunglasses combo make me incognito and the mass of bodies around me would make spotting me like some sort of well-dressed Where's Wally. But he's not looking at me. Because he's not alone. He's deep in conversation with someone else. A woman. And it's not my mother. It's someone at least half Carmella's age, possibly even younger than me judging by her perky breasts and gravity-defying bubble butt.

The pair of them are strolling down the beach together. Gabriel looks happy and relaxed, throwing his head back to laugh. Then he places an arm on the woman's bare shoulder.

I'm too far away to hear their conversation but it's their body language I'm interested in. She's tall, almost as tall as Gabriel in her bare feet and she has that willowy-ness of a catwalk model. Her skin is lightly tanned, suggesting she hasn't just arrived here. Perhaps a local? Wherever she's from, they're clearly at ease in each other's company. Gabriel is very tactile with her, a hand on her waist when a rogue volleyball comes rocketing towards them, a hand on her elbow to guide her around two small children who are building a sandcastle and a kiss on her cheek before whispering something in her ear which makes her throw back her head with gleeful laughter. Then they embrace before the woman continues strolling along the beach and Gabriel turns back in the direction of the hotel, while I continue onwards to meet my poor, unsuspecting mother.

26

'Are you feeling better, darling? You weren't yourself at dinner last night,' my mother is saying as I peruse the menu. There's nothing vegan here apart from a side salad. And chips. I'm not eating chips. If I ever get married, I'm spending a month in France beforehand. The enforced starvation from the lack of vegan food would work better than any wedding diet. I order a salad, hoping it comes without the lardons which the French are so fond of adding without being asked.

'Yes,' I say. 'Sorry about that. I had a touch of sunstroke.'

Carmella frowns at me over her own bowl of watery onion soup. 'Again? Are you staying properly hydrated? You need to take better care of yourself, darling.'

The server comes over with my food and places the dish in front of me. It is leaves.

'What's Charlie up to today?' my mother asks when they've gone. I'd totally forgotten that she doesn't know he's left.

'He's gone,' I say and my mother shoots a hand up to her mouth. 'Not like that, don't panic. Some emergency in Calais. He's hired a car to drive up there and sort it out. He says

169

he'll only be gone for two or three days but I think he may have underestimated the drive. He'll be back for the wedding though. So you don't need to worry about your seating plan.' I wince at the hint of meanness in my voice.

'Don't be like that,' Carmella says. 'That's a shame though. He was looking forward to spending some time with you.'

I shrug. 'It's fine.' It's not, obviously. I hate the thought that he's going to be spending the next however long with Jenna and her social conscience and her crush. But I trust him. I do. He loves me. There's a tiny niggling grain of *something* deep in my gut reminding me that I trusted a man before and he left me devastated but I mentally crush it. Charlie isn't Adam. Charlie doesn't want to hurt me.

'And everything else is okay? It's a shame Tor and Maisie couldn't make it over.' She's digging now. She knows full well that Tor and I have argued. I'm guessing Tor told her as much at the party when she said she couldn't make it over.

'Maisie needs to be close to her obstetrician,' I say. 'And Tor and I aren't really talking. I guess she would've found it too awkward to come out.'

Carmella sighs. 'But you two never fall out. I hope it's nothing serious?'

'I don't want to talk about it,' I say, prodding a leaf.

'Any word from Hen?'

For fuck's sake.

'Are you going through a list of everyone I've ever met?' I'm annoyed now.

'No, Kits, I'm just trying to make conversation with you. I'm trying to show an interest in the life you've pushed me out of.'

I sigh. God, she knows how to get me right in the feels. 'I know, sorry. I've just got a lot going on at the moment and I'm trying to work through it. Sorry for being spikey.'

She reaches across the table and puts her hand on top of mine. 'It's all right. Just know I'm here, okay? If you ever need to talk to me about anything. I'm here. We've been through a lot together and, even though you're thirty, you're still my baby.'

'Thank you,' I say, wishing that I actually could unburden myself to her, imagining the relief that telling her everything would bring. 'But I'm fine. I promise. Tell me about Gabriel. What's he up to today?' Apart from hanging out with beautiful younger women and plotting my death?

Carmella smiles coyly. 'I'm not sure. He just said something about wedding admin and that he'd be out for most of the day. It's sweet how hands-on he's being with the whole thing.'

Yes, *hands-on* is right. But. The good news here is that Gabriel won't be in their suite, which gives me a chance to have a look around. Maybe I'll even get lucky and he'll have left his phone.

'I can't wait to see my dress.' I hope I sound as enthusiastic as I'm aiming for. 'Can we go right now?'

27

My mother is fizzing with excitement by the time we've made our way back to her suite.

'I can't wait for you to see it,' she trills as she opens her door. 'You're going to look so beautiful. You'll probably completely upstage me!'

'That's unlikely,' I say. 'Look at you!' She is absolutely glowing, sparkling with love and happy anticipation. It's such a shame it's all based on lies and I'm going to have to kill the man she thinks she's in love with.

'Oh you,' she says, blushing. 'Come on, come in. I'll pour you some champagne and you can try on your dress.' She ushers me inside and, if Charlie was impressed by our suite, he would absolutely lose his mind over this place. Of course, my mother has chosen to stay in the penthouse suite for her wedding. It's so stunning that even I feel a bit emotional as I walk in. Like our suite, everything is hues of white, cream, silver and gold, and there is a breath-taking panoramic view of the sea, but this place is something else.

'Oh darling, look at your face,' my mother says. 'I didn't think you were the sort of person to be impressed by hotel rooms.'

'It's a bit more than a room though, isn't it? It's incredible.'

She laughs. 'Well, you only get married once.' She realises her mistake. 'Twice. *I* only get married twice. Hopefully. Do you want to look around?'

'Erm . . . yes.'

Laughing again, she shows me through to the living room which not only has the stunning view, but a sort of art-deco foosball table too. 'Isn't it fun?' she says. 'I have to say I've become quite good at it, much to Gabriel's annoyance. Come and look at the view from the terrace. There are two actually. One looks out over the beach and the other over the town. But we prefer the beach view. We've taken to having breakfast out here most mornings. Isn't it lovely? I could live here.'

She shows me through to the master bedroom and the bathroom, which has walls entirely made of glass and a tub looking out over the Med. I do a quick scan of the room, the bedside tables and charging points but there's no sign of a phone. Of course he wouldn't have left it here. What was I thinking? Carmella ushers me through to another slightly smaller, although still absolutely huge, bedroom with another bathroom and another sea-facing bath. It too is phoneless.

'And look at this.' She's smiling like a schoolgirl as she shows me through to yet another room. 'It's a sauna!'

'I can see,' I say. I want a sauna in my apartment. I wonder if I'd need planning permission for that. 'It's lovely. I hope Gabriel appreciates it.'

She gives me a funny look. 'Why wouldn't he? Anyway,

let's not talk about him right now. Let's go and see your dress. It's in the second bedroom.'

We walk back to the second bedroom and my mother opens the giant wardrobe with a flourish.

'Gabriel keeps his clothes in here,' she laughs, 'I haven't exactly travelled light so there's no room in ours.' I'm suddenly thrown back to my childhood and memories of my mother's vast walk-in wardrobe in our old family home. I used to sometimes hide myself away amongst her skirts and dresses when she was on one of her 'retreats'. Her clothes always smelled of her perfume and they were the next best thing to being in her arms. I adored her when I was little. I hate how distant we've become. Would it have killed me to have visited her over here?

'Here it is,' Carmella is saying now, bringing me back to the present.

Hanging there, amongst an impressive array of designer men's clothing, is one of the most beautiful dresses I've ever seen. It's a pale blue silk with a ruched bow at one shoulder. It's simple but absolutely stunning. I reach out to touch it.

'It's gorgeous,' I say.

'Just like you,' she says, squeezing my arm in delight. 'I can't wait to see you in it. The blue will look so stunning with your hair. Shall I pour some champagne while you try it on? I spoke to Charlie about sizes so I think it's right.' She disappears back through to the living room. I'm already picturing myself in the gown and the photos I'll post on Instagram, with the beautiful Cannes backdrop. Oh wait, I don't do that anymore. Well, I'll still look stunning in the wedding photos. But I can't be distracted by the dress. I need to use this opportunity to have a look through Gabriel's stuff. There might be some clues in the pockets or something. Maybe even his phone or at least a burner. I start to have a bit of a rummage but everything seems to be either brand-new or newly dry-cleaned. There's not so much as a receipt in any of the starched pockets.

But then I see it.

Poking out of a brown brogue on the floor of the vast wardrobe like a leering tongue.

The unmistakable paisley pattern of a bandana.

A black one.

28

Carmella comes back through with two flutes of champagne.

'I can't try it on now,' I say. 'I'm all sandy and oily from being on the beach earlier. I'd ruin it. Why don't we go and sit on that gorgeous terrace with our drinks instead? I'll come back up later when I'm showered and not trailing sand everywhere.' It will give me the chance to ask her some more questions about Gabriel.

'Oh that's a lovely idea, Kits. Yes let's do that. Honestly, you can see out for miles. You'll love it.'

We walk back through to the terrace that looks out to sea and sit down on a small wicker sofa that has been tastefully decorated with cream cushions. She's right. The view is absolutely breath-taking. Miles and miles of sapphire blue water stretches into the distance. It's so blue it doesn't look real, like it could be an AI-generated vista.

'Has Charlie made it to Calais yet?' my mother asks.

God, Charlie. I've been so busy thinking about Gabriel, then Max, then Gabriel again that I totally forgot about

Charlie. It should take about eleven hours to drive from here to Calais. He left at around six o'clock this morning and it's now 4pm so it's a bit early for him to have got there but I'd have thought he'd text me at least. I check my phone but there aren't any messages or missed calls from him.

'I'll just give him a quick call and see where he's at,' I say, standing up and walking across the terrace. Charlie's phone rings and rings until it goes to voicemail. I don't bother leaving a message, tapping out a quick text instead.

Just checking that you'd made it there in one piece. Let me know asap. Love you xxx

'No answer,' I tell my mother as I sit back down. 'He's probably still driving.'

She nods. 'He seems like a lovely man, Kitty. I'm glad you found someone. He clearly loves you very much.'

'He's great,' I say. 'I wasn't sure if I'd ever be able to trust anyone after everything.'

She reaches for my hand and we sit in silence for a few moments, the weight of our shared past hanging heavy above us. I think back to the immediate aftermath of my dad's 'disappearance'. We were hounded by the papers for weeks. I had reporters and photographers follow me to school. We were doorstepped by journalists, and when they didn't get a story from us, they made them up. Rumours circulated about my father having an affair (true) and my mother killing him out of jealousy (false. But actually a little bit too on the nose for comfort). It was horrible. No wonder my mother fled to France.

'And what about you?' I say, seeing my chance to turn the conversation to Gabriel. 'Tell me about Gabriel. I know almost nothing about him. How did he sweep you off your feet? Are any of his family coming out?'

She doesn't say anything though, just carries on looking out to sea. The silence feels strangely loaded.

'What is it?' I say. 'What's wrong?'

'Family is a bit of a sore point with Gabriel,' she says finally. 'Probably best not to mention it in front of him.'

Okay, this is interesting. 'Why not? What happened?'

'Gabriel doesn't have any family,' she says. Well, that's convenient isn't it. 'His parents both died when he was in his teens. He doesn't have any siblings.'

'That's awful,' I say. 'How did they die?'

'A fire,' my mother says. 'Terrible. Destroyed their entire home and pretty much everything in it. Gabriel was lucky to get out alive.'

'He was there?' I say and she nods.

'Yes, but he really doesn't like talking about it. The house wasn't insured. He lost everything.'

'Gosh,' I say even though I'm thinking that an orphan who lost everything would have a lot to gain by marrying into money. By marrying my mother and murdering both her and the only other beneficiary of her fortune, me. 'What about friends?' I say after a few beats of respectful silence have passed. 'He must have friends coming out? Didn't you say he'd met up with some in London?'

'They were more associates,' she says. 'But we've got some of the friends we've made over here coming. You'll meet them all at the rehearsal dinner tomorrow night. I'm so excited. I don't think I ever stop talking about you.' She reaches across and takes my hand. 'Thank you for coming, Kits. I know seeing me isn't easy for you. So I really do appreciate you being here. I don't think I could get married if you weren't. It wouldn't feel right.'

'I'm happy to be here,' I say and I'm pleasantly surprised to notice I'm not lying.

'And I'm sorry I ambushed you at your party. I was just so worried that you'd ignore the invite.' She looks at me. 'You would have, wouldn't you?'

I sigh. 'Probably.'

My mother looks at me. 'Kitty, Gabriel has been nothing but wonderful to me. He's an amazing man. He's kind. He's gentle. He's nothing like your father.'

I think about the photos on my phone. The blow-up doll in the Thames. The tattoo. The horrible, sickening misogynistic posts.

She's right.

He's nothing like my father.

He's worse.

'What do you think of him?' she asks, coy as a schoolgirl. 'Really?'

'He's very handsome,' I say.

I swear my mother almost swoons. 'Isn't he? I still can't believe he wants to be with a dried-up old bag like me.' She's fishing for more compliments here. I'm more than happy to give them.

'Oh my God!' I say. 'You're so far from being a dried-up old bag. Look at you. You're absolutely beautiful and you are going to be the most stunning bride. He's lucky to have you.

Don't you ever forget that. Please. Don't be grateful to him. He's the one who's won the jackpot.' I bet this is exactly how he sees it too.

My mother playfully bats my arm. 'Oh, Kitty. I've missed you so much.'

'Tell me more about him,' I say. 'Other than the family stuff.'

She smiles, happy to talk about her favourite subject. 'Okay. Well, he's forty-two years old. So a toy boy, but you knew that already. He's originally from London but has been out in France now for about seven years. He was in Paris; he spent some time on the Italian Riviera and now he lives here. With me.'

'But what does he *do*?' I ask.

She laughs. 'Oh darling, what do any of us do when we don't have to work for a living? He enjoys himself. He spends time with me. We take a lot of holidays.'

'Do you pay for it all?'

'Kitty!' She gives me a playful slap on my hand. 'What a thing to ask. You know it's extremely unbecoming to talk about money like that.' Her tone is light but I feel a weight to them too. I know that line of questioning is over.

'Does he know?'

She turns to face me, her eyes now extremely serious. She reaches over and takes my hand in hers. 'No,' she says. 'No, he doesn't. I told you that I would take what happened with your dad to the grave and I meant that. I've never told anyone. Have you? Does Charlie know?'

There have been so many times that I've wanted to come clean to Charlie. Not just about my dad, but about everything, all the others. I believe that relationships should be completely honest and transparent. In theory. But then I think of the look on his face if he found out the truth about me, knew that I was a murderer. Charlie's whole MO is to save and preserve life. He'd hate me. He wouldn't be able to even look at me, let alone love me. I can't bear the thought of his eyes growing cold, of his heart shutting down. I wish I could be honest with him. But it's not a risk I am prepared to take.

'No,' I say truthfully.

'Good.' She pulls me in towards her body and holds me tightly for a moment. 'Let's make sure it stays that way. Now, let's drink this champagne and get delightfully giddy together. I've missed you.'

'I've missed you too.'

'I don't think I could be happier than I am right now.'

And we sit there, in a more comfortable silence now, drinking in the view and the champagne. I hate myself for what I'm about to do to her but at least she's having this moment of pure happiness.

Because I know now what I have to do.

There's only one option now that I've seen that bandana, the watch and that tattoo. Now I know his poor little orphan backstory.

I need to kill Gabriel Murphy.

29

I have to kill Gabriel. There's just no way of avoiding it. It's the only way I can save myself and my mother. Ridding the world of the toxic shit he posts won't hurt either.

The only problem is how I'm going to do it. I'm really out of my murdering comfort zone here. I don't have any of my props with me. I couldn't risk bringing any kind of drug with me on the flight and what would I even do with the body without access to the abattoirs? If I had more time I could find myself a nice Frenchman who works in a slaughterhouse and seduce him into letting me use one. This is France after all. Abattoirs were literally born here. I bet almost every other building is one. Water, water, everywhere et cetera.

But no. I'm going to have to make it look like an accident. And I'm going to have to be creative. Here are my ideas so far.

1. Drowning. It's the most obvious way to kill someone while you're staying in a beach resort and there's also the option of pool or sea. Pool would have to look much more accidental whereas the sea could wash the body away and

get rid of that little problem. It would probably be munched on by fish and all the other weird shit that lives in there if I weighed it down enough. Judging by Gabriel's size though, I can't imagine him not being a strong swimmer. Something I might have to investigate.

2. Fall from a cliff. There's a range of mountains called the Esterel Massif which isn't too far away. If I could somehow get Gabriel to come for a walk there with me, I could push him to his death and then say he fell. Cons – I've never been walking in the mountains. Can you even walk in them? Would I need all that special climbing gear? All in all, feels like too much effort.

3. Tragic bar accident. Something like a metal straw through the eye. Or maybe I could somehow set him on fire with one of those cocktails that come with sparklers in them. I'd need to cover him in some sort of accelerant though and how would I do that? Also could be linked back to me if I like go into town asking around where I can buy some.

4. Jellyfish. I've seen a few signs around that there can be jellyfish in the water and to keep an eye out for them. Perhaps could lure him into water and get jellyfish to sting him to death. Cons – depends on actual appearance of jellyfish and it actually being one of those deadly fuckers. A lot of hassle just to give him a little sting.

5. Death by allergy. Find out if Gabriel has a convenient deadly allergy to anything and then obtain it and poison him with it. A nut allergy would be ideal. Cons – this sort of thing only happens in fiction, surely would not be lucky enough but will ask re allergies pretending I'm thinking about the wedding meal.

6. Impalement. Have noticed that the parasols on the beach have extremely pointy tops and anyone who falls upon one would surely not live. Cons – not sure how I'd get him to fall onto one. They're not anywhere near enough to the balconies and cannot *throw* him like it's a giant ring toss game.

7. Drug and suffocate. Easy to slip drugs into drink and then suffocate him in room. Could even make it look like he'd taken own life. Cons – no drugs.

8. Buried alive. There is so much sand. Could maybe convince him to be buried up to his neck for a 'fun Insta post' and just keep going. Cons – beach is a very public place in the day and surely he's not dumb enough to be tricked into this at night.

9. Amusement park accident. Have found big park nearby with rollercoasters and one of those sling shots that lunatics seem to love losing their guts on. Could suggest visit and tease him until he agrees to go on scariest ride then tamper with restraints causing him to fall to his death. Cons – would have to go on it too. Vomit.

10. Get someone else to do it. Maybe create a scene and say he's attacked me while out at a bar. Big strong man decides to protect my honour and beats him to death. Cons – ridiculous.

11. Get him to come on a day trip to the Lérins Island just off Cannes. Kill him and leave his body in the forest. Would probably never be found. How would I get him to come on a day trip without my mother though? And then, what? Come back and say 'I lost your fiancé'? Silly.

Ugh. None of these are actually very fool proof. Surely I've had enough practice on how to kill a man and get away with it by now. I'm absolutely stumped. The best way would really be to drug him and go from there. But no access to ruddy drugs.

I text Carmella.

Me: Just thinking about taking you and Gabriel out for lunch before the big day. Does Gabriel have any allergies I should know about? Peanuts maybe?

Carmella: Oh darling you're so sweet. Always thinking about the little details. No allergies for Gabriel. He is extremely sturdy. Loves peanuts.

Knew it. Bollocks.

Me: Good to know. Can he swim?

Carmella: That's a weird question, darling. But yes, he can. Swam for his school or something dreary when he was younger. Also has his PADI. Going to sleep now, have blinding headache and need to take something to knock myself out. Don't forget the rehearsal dinner tomorrow. Hope Charlie's okay xx

Fuck's sake. I suppose a deadly allergy would've been a bit too convenient though.

Wait.

What did Carmella just say? I look at her message again. She has drugs with her. Of *course* she has drugs with her. I should know my mother well enough to know that she always carries a small *pharmacie*'s worth of meds wherever she goes. She's always been on an assortment of various uppers, downers and tranqs so strong they'd take down an elephant. I used to help myself to plenty of them when I was a teenager.

All I need to do is get into her bathroom and steal some.

And when would be a better time than tomorrow when they're both tied up with the rehearsal dinner.

I think I have a plan.

30

I still haven't heard from Charlie by the following morning, not even a text to let me know he's arrived. I've called him half a dozen times and sent more texts than I can count but there's been nothing back. They're all delivering so I know he hasn't run out of battery or got stuck in some signal blackspot. I guess that the gang has been even more problematic than he thought and he's been too busy to call me. Still a text wouldn't have hurt. I'm actually getting a bit worried about him though. I don't even know that he's even made it to Calais in one piece.

> *Me: Can you just let me know you're safe please xxx*

I wait for the three dots to appear; it's not like Charlie to leave me hanging like this when I'm anxious, but they don't come. I sit on the bed, chewing the skin around my thumb. *Where is he? What if he's hurt?* No. I shake the thought out of my head. I'd have heard if something had happened to him. He's just busy. And I need to be too or I'll drive myself mad. Or I'll put him off me completely by being so needy.

I go down to the pool. May as well enjoy the surroundings while I wait to get into my mother's suite tonight. I'm safe here too. With all the other guests and hotel staff, not to mention the security cameras, no one would be stupid enough to try to hurt me here. I scroll Instagram for news of Max Macintyre – still missing, no updates – and to see if Blaze Bundy/Gabriel has posted anything new. He hasn't. And then I book myself and Carmella into the hotel spa for the whole day tomorrow.

Only she'll be going alone.

She doesn't know this yet.

It's my pre-wedding treat, I text her.

She replies with a string of heart emojis.

My plotting manages to keep my mind away from Charlie and his radio silence but when it gets to the afternoon and I *still* haven't heard from him, I can feel the anxiety bubbling up inside me again. He *knows* that I'm waiting for him to let me know he's okay. He knows that I'm worried about him turning up and tackling a gang who could literally be anyone from anywhere. It's not like him to leave me to stress out and make up terrible situations in my head. He's my voice of reason, the person who *stops* me from doing that. I call him again. When he doesn't answer, I decide to call Jenna instead. Maybe there's a reason he can't get to his phone. At least she'll be able to tell me if he's arrived or not. I scroll through my phone until I find her number. Her phone rings too but only twice before it cuts out.

Excuse me?

Did she just reject my call?

I try again and the same thing happens. I'm furious, I mean that's just rude, isn't it? I leave her a voicemail saying that I'm trying to get hold of Charlie and could she ask him to give me a call asap. And then I sit looking at my phone, silently fuming. Why would Jenna cancel my call? And why won't Charlie reply? I open WhatsApp. Charlie and I don't tend to use it to message each other but I know he talks to work people on it. I click on the last chat we had on here which was way back at Christmas. I don't bother looking at anything apart from his status though. And there it is.

Last seen today 08.34am

So he's been online. His phone is working.

Why hasn't he called me?

A horrible explanation begins to form in my mind. One involving Jenna.

No.

He wouldn't do that to me. Not Charlie. Not when he knows what I went through with Adam and how it's taken me years to even consider trusting a man enough to let him into my life. I ignore the sick feeling in my stomach, the knot of cold panic warning me that something is wrong.

'It's not intuition,' I tell myself all day.

I'm still telling myself that later as I get ready for this bloody rehearsal dinner. 'It's starvation because I've not had anything substantial to eat since I got here.' Damn this country and its absolute refusal to acknowledge veganism. I feel attacked.

The rehearsal dinner is being held right on the beach, which is where the wedding will take place in a few days' time. The staff has cleared away a large section of sun loungers and parasols and replaced them with a long table draped in white silk. The chairs are also dressed in white silk with huge, elegant bows on the backs of them. The whole area has been lit by lanterns and tea lights which are miraculously not going out every time there's a breeze. I wonder how much extra my mother had to pay for that to happen. To make things even more perfect, the sky is completely clear and there's a nearly full moon shining down on us. It's beautiful and I really wish Charlie was here to see how perfect this looks. No, I can't think about Charlie and what he's probably up to right now. I need to focus on the job in hand and I'm already getting a headache from all the stress. I'll take something for it later.

One of my mother's benzos when I get into her stash.

Speaking of Carmella, she's already here, fussing around the table, looking completely like she's stepped out of a wedding Pinterest board. She's stunning and she looks so fucking happy that I momentarily wonder if I'm doing the right thing.

Gabriel is already seated and looking relaxed in a white button-down that isn't very buttoned down. He's looking at my mother with gooey eyes, one hand on her at all times, like there is nothing else in his world. He's good. I'll give him that. If I didn't know what he's really up to, I'd be convinced that he is completely and absolutely in love with my mother. He looks up for a moment, catches my eye and gives me a wink. Completely inappropriate when his hand is on my mother's arse. She looks up too, sees me and waves me over. I plaster a smile on my face – it's not actually that fake as I'm already looking forward to tomorrow when I get to slice his deceitful throat.

'Kits!' my mother trills as I reach them. 'You look lovely. Caught the sun today. Be careful, you don't want to burn. You're sitting here, with me,' she says, patting the seat next to her.

I sit down and look around. There aren't many faces that I recognise, which isn't surprising considering how my mother left basically everyone she knew behind when she fled the UK. But she seems to have built up a good network of friends over here. Hopefully they'll be on hand to pick up the pieces when Gabriel doesn't show up for the wedding. I feel a presence next to me and turn to see bloody Ben Pemberton has taken the seat to my left. The seat where Charlie should be.

'Hey Kits,' he says, 'your mum's bumped me and Nettie over here because your fella's a no-show.'

Ugh. 'Hi, Ben,' I say, uninterested. Antoinette is to his left and gives me a little wave. She's wearing a gorgeous pale green embellished dress that looks like it could be Jenny Packham. I must ask her later. It's not her fault she's related to one of the worst people I've met.

'So where is Charlie-boy tonight? Weird he's not here. You've not lost another one, have you Kits?'

I roll my eyes. Why is he here again? 'He's in Calais dealing with a work emergency,' I explain although I'm not sure how much of it Ben will take in. He probably switched off at the word 'work'. Having never done a day of it in his life. 'And we're very much together. Thank you.'

He gives me a sly look. 'Shame. You will let me know if that changes and you find yourself in need of a plus one for the wedding, won't you?'

'No,' I say. 'I'd literally rather have a corpse as my plus one than you.' Maybe that could be arranged. Ben seems to think I'm joking though and laughs loudly.

'Always such a joker, Kits,' he says and pours himself a large glass of wine from the table. Antoinette gives me a sympathetic look from around her brother. At least I can ignore him after the wedding. That poor girl is related to him. Maybe I should do her a favour and stick a fork through his eye over the meal.

'Thanks for coming so last minute,' I say brightly. 'It can be such a struggle to find seat fillers.' I turn my back on him and hear a squeak of laughter come from Antoinette. Maybe not everyone in that family is an absolutely appalling human after all.

Gabriel is standing up now. He clinks his glass with a spoon to get everyone's attention. Not that he needs to because everyone is already staring at him, rapt. Including, I realise, me.

'Thank you so much, everyone, for coming tonight,' he says. 'Carmella and I are so delighted to be sharing such a magical evening with you. She's made me the happiest man in the world and I can't wait to make her my wife.' My mother blushes like a virgin bride next to him. Jesus. 'I honestly feel like I've met my soul mate in this beautiful woman. I'll save the other stuff for the actual wedding, but please raise a glass with me to my beautiful bride. To Carmella.'

'To Carmella,' the rest of the party chant, while my mother beams like a Christmas decoration.

Suddenly a man springs up and shouts, 'To the bride and groom.'

I scowl at him under my eyelashes before shooting another look at my entranced mother. Bride and groomed, more like.

31

After the dinner, where I actually got a full vegan meal instead of just leaves and chips, the champagne started flowing and I managed to slip away. Luckily my mother is busy playing the role of the blushing bride so I doubt she'll even notice I'm gone. Or that I swiped her key card out of her bag.

So now I'm here in her suite and ready to have a look at all the goodies in her bathroom. My plan is to find something potent enough to knock Gabriel out, something that I can easily hide in a drink. I pour myself a glass of champagne which my mother seems to have a limitless supply of and take it through to the master bathroom. It really is gorgeous in here. All marble and opulence. I wonder if I've got enough time to have a little soak in the tub. It would be super calming to sink down into some bubbles, looking out at that glorious view. They're going to be busy at the dinner for ages yet so I probably could. But, no. As tempting as it is, I'm here on a mission and I can't be distracted. Plus I'll be able to relax properly when I neck one or two of Carmella's Xanax.

There is a cabinet on each side of the Jack-and-Jill sinks. The first one contains nothing but a razor, a toothbrush and some Tom Ford fragrance. Clearly Gabriel's side. I open the cabinet on the other side of the marble sinks and find what I'm looking for. It's like a pick 'n' mix of drugs. Bottles, boxes, blister packs, tubs and tubes of everything you could imagine. Some things never change, I guess. While my father's first choice for getting fucked up was always alcohol swiftly followed by infidelity and a side of domestic violence, my mother was always more into diazepam in its various forms. There has to be something here that I can slip into Gabriel's drink. I trawl through the labels: co-codamol, zopiclone, tramadol. Jesus, she's got the full set here. I could take a few of those and crush them up into a powder and tip it into a drink. I've taken some of these myself though and know that they can have quite a bitter taste. Not that I think Gabriel would notice when he's on his fifteenth glass of wine. But still. Then my eyes land on a bottle of green liquid. I pull it out of the cabinet and see from the label that it's liquid temazepam. I open it and take a sniff. It smells like peppermint.

Okay, now this is something I can work with.

But just as I'm about to swipe the bottle, I hear something from outside the bathroom. The unmistakable boom of a man's voice talking on the phone.

Fuck.

Gabriel's back.

Fuck. Fuck. Fuck.

32

Shit.

What am I going to do?

What if he comes in here? How can I explain what I'm doing in his bathroom and how I got in here?

Gabriel's voice is getting louder, which means he's getting closer. I look around. There's a dressing room off the bathroom and I run into that, trying not to make a sound as I scuttle across the marble floor. I wish I'd taken my shoes off. The dressing room has a wall of wardrobes, the perfect place to hide. But when I open them I have to swallow down a gasp of dismay. The bottom of the wardrobes contains a small shelving unit that I have to climb onto. I haul myself in, praying that my imposed starvation for the past few days means it will hold my weight. I curl myself into a ball and gently pull the door closed. And then I wait. Holding my breath and hoping that he's not come back to the room for a fucking outfit change.

I listen, trembling, as Gabriel comes into the bathroom, still talking on the phone. I barely breathe.

'Yeah, yeah, I told you it's going fine,' he says before pausing, presumably while the person on the other end of the line speaks. He laughs, a loud boom that makes me jump and the wardrobe door rattle slightly. Shit. I don't think I shut it properly.

And then Gabriel's voice is even louder. He must be in the dressing room. Did he hear the sound I made when I jumped?

'Listen, stop worrying. Everything's going to plan.' A pause. 'No. Not yet. She doesn't suspect a thing. I'm going to tell her. I just need to wait for the right moment.' Another pause, followed by another huge laugh – this time I manage to control myself. 'What did you expect? I told you she was a pig.'

What the fuck? He's actually calling my mother a pig?

I suppress the urge to jump out of the wardrobe right now and beat him to death with one of Carmella's heels. Instead I brace myself because I'm almost certain he's about to open the door and find my hiding spot. After an agonising second which seems to drag out for months, I hear his footsteps fade away.

'Look, I've got to go. Carmella's calling. I only came up here to get some headache pills. I'll call you tomorrow.'

I listen closely as Gabriel opens a cabinet in the bathroom, searches around for something and then closes it again. There's another agonising pause and I hear him pick something else up and put it back down. Then, finally, I hear his footsteps as he walks out of the bathroom and back through the suite.

I count to sixty five times before I let myself out of the wardrobe. My heart is hammering and my hands are trembling. I go back into the bathroom, grab the temazepam bottle from the cabinet and turn to go. I spot a box of something I recognise as laxatives and it gives me an idea so I swipe those too. And some Imodium. But just as I'm about to leave, I see what made Gabriel stop in his tracks before he left the room.

My champagne glass.

With my lipstick on it.

I left it sitting next to the sink.

He knows someone was here.

33

'Oh darling, are you sure you can't make it to the spa today?' my mother asks me just as the laxative I took gets my stomach in another vice grip. I rush into the en suite and make it to the loo just in time. Honestly, I hope she appreciates what I'm putting myself through for her. The laxatives I took last night are working a bit too well. I gingerly reappear a few minutes later and Carmella is looking at me with a mixture of concern and faint disgust. 'You really aren't well, are you? Do you think it was the food?'

'It must be,' I groan.

'How terrible. I'll have to speak to the caterers about the vegan option.'

'I'm so sorry. I was really looking forward to spending today with you,' I say.

'Shall I try to reschedule it?' she asks. 'Although I'm not sure when we'd be able to fit it in . . .'

'No, you should go. It's such a beautiful spa and the perfect way for you to relax before the wedding. Plus I've booked a load of treatments for you. You've got to look your absolute best for the wedding.'

She still looks torn. 'But are you going to be okay by yourself? I hate leaving you like this. And with Charlie away too.' Funny how she didn't have this crisis of confidence when she left me alone in London to fend for myself when I was still a teenager. Anyway, that's not what's important now.

'I'll be fine, I promise. I'm really not going to be doing anything other than running between my bed and the bathroom for the foreseeable future. Please go. It's my wedding treat to you. I've booked you a white caviar facial. You'll look about fifteen years younger for your big day.' Beauty treatments are like crack to my mother.

'Okay, but I'll have my mobile on me and Gabriel will be around if you need anything,' she says after two seconds of soul-searching. That caviar facial sealed the deal. 'I'll get you some fresh water before I go.' She bustles around my room for a few more minutes, refilling a jug of water and placing it beside my bed. 'Have you heard from Charlie yet?' she asks, looking like she's never going to leave. No is the answer. I have fucking not. After seeing that he'd been active on WhatsApp but still hadn't even replied to my increasingly desperate messages, I lay awake all night thinking that the only possible explanation really is that he's fucking Jenna. It has to be that. But I don't want to burden my mother with any of this.

'Yes,' I say. 'He's fine. Just super busy, as I thought.'

'Oh I'm so pleased,' Carmella says. 'I was worried something had happened to him. Is he going to be back in time for the wedding?'

The wedding that isn't going to happen?

'Yes, he should be,' I say. 'Now go, enjoy your day. I need to rest so I'm shipshape to walk you down that aisle.'

My mother frowns at me. What the fuck did I say 'ship-shape' for? I've never fucking said 'shipshape' in my whole life and she damn well knows that.

'I need to rest,' I say again.

'Yes, I think you really do. Okay, darling, just call me or Gabriel if you need anything? I've got a load of meds upstairs.' She goes to give me a kiss on the head but appears to change her mind as she realises I could be contagious. 'Feel better, Kits.' And then she eventually fucks off. I count to two hundred slowly before I reach under my pillow and pull out the pack of Imodium and pop a couple in my mouth.

Half an hour later I feel *shipshape* and order room service. I'm starving after last night's laxative supper and need to keep my strength up. Today is a big day.

After I've eaten, I take a long, luxurious bath and listen to some mindfulness meditations on my phone. It's important that I stay calm and centred over the next few hours. No letting my mind sneak off and think about what Charlie and Jenna are probably getting up to.

When I get out I slip on an Erdem bikini and sarong before heading down to the beach bar where I'll message Gabriel and ask him to join me. That's where I need him for the next part of my plan.

To my surprise, he's already there when I arrive, engrossed in something on his phone and sipping from a bottle of beer even though it's barely past lunchtime. Still, who am I to talk? And this actually makes things easier for me.

'Hey Gabriel,' I say, brightly.

He looks up and fixes me with those intense dark eyes. They're totally expressionless for a split second and remind me of a shark. But then he falls back into his role of step-father-to-be and smiles. He even manages to make it look warm. Like I said, he's good.

'Kitty,' he says. 'Come and join me. How are you feeling?'

I pull out a chair at his table and slip into it.

'Such a shame you couldn't make it to the spa. Carmella was looking forward to it so much.'

'She'll be fine on her own,' I say. 'And I'm feeling much better. Thank you for asking.'

'Carmella said you'd had an upset stomach,' he says. 'I thought we had some Imodium with us. I was certain I'd seen some in the cabinet in our bathroom. But when I went to look for it, it wasn't there. Weird, huh?'

He knows. He knows it was me in there last night.

'Super weird,' I say. 'But no matter. I feel right as rain now. I'm even considering a little drink!'

His eyes narrow ever so slightly. 'An extraordinarily fast recovery.'

'Just as well with the wedding in two days,' I say.

'Indeed. Well, I suppose this gives us a chance to get to know each other a little bit better before the big day,' he says, his amiable demeanour firmly back in place. 'I was actually thinking about a spot of lunch if you'd like to join me?'

'That would be lovely,' I say.

'Great, I'll order us something lovely to drink with lunch. I can recommend the rosé champagne, you said you were contemplating a little drink?'

'Yes please,' I say. 'I honestly feel fine now. I think it was probably a combination of too much heat and the food.'

'Not to mention the amount of champagne you sank last

night.' Oh God, he knows it was me in their room. 'A girl after my own heart.'

A waiter comes to the table and Gabriel orders a bottle of rosé champagne that arrives just moments later with two coupes. 'You know these are shaped to represent Marie Antoinette's breasts?' he says as he pours us each a glass. 'Old Louis was a bit of a perv, don't you think?'

'That's not actually true,' I say, taking a sip. 'The glasses were originally designed by a Benedictine monk in England, over a decade before Louis and his lot got their hands on them.' I smile. I hate it when men try to educate me. We'll see how smart he is when he's off his head on the temazepam I'm going to spike him with.

Gabriel puts his elbows on the table and holds my gaze. 'Beauty *and* brains,' he says. 'The apple hasn't fallen far from the tree at all.'

That's exactly the sort of sexist comment Blaze Bundy would make.

Creep.

'Well, when your education costs as much as mine did it's nice to be able to put mansplainers in their place.' I smile at him as I say this, even though I mean it, so he thinks I'm being sweet and playful.

He laughs and it's so deep it's almost a growl. Yeah, enjoy your last moments *Blaze*.

I know I will.

My plan is to spike him, get him to my room, force a confession out of him and then kill him. I'm going to pretend he tried it on with me and I had to push him away. But he was so drunk that he fell and smashed his head on the marble floor. Oopsy. Once he's dead, I can out him as being the misogynistic 'influencer' Blaze Bundy and my mother will realise that she dodged a huge bullet, that this man isn't who she thought he was.

I feel a smile of anticipation creep across my face and pick up my glass, taking a sip of the champagne to hide it.

Gabriel drinks a lot.

Once we've finished the champagne and ordered a huge salad and some small plates to share, he orders a bottle of Sancerre which he wastes no time in getting stuck into.

'Gotta love the South of France,' he says, after taking a small sip of the wine and confirming that it's acceptable to the waiter. 'This lifestyle, you know. You should come over more. I can't understand why anyone lives in the UK if they have the opportunity to live somewhere else. It's falling apart. I was in London recently and couldn't wait to leave. It's just so dirty and grey. Don't you hate it?'

Of course he was over there recently. He'd need to be to plant a blow-up doll in the Thames.

'No,' I say. 'My friends are there, my whole life is there.' Just to remind him that if he does anything to me, if I *disappear*, it will be noticed. People will be looking for me.

'Yeah, but you don't get this, do you?' He waves his arms around gesturing at everything.

'We're staying in a five-star hotel in Cannes,' I say. 'I'm not sure just anyone could have this sort of lifestyle if they came to France. Most people can't afford to live like this. Even for a short while.'

Gabriel raises an eyebrow and it looks as obnoxious as he is. 'I guess that depends on who you know.'

Okay. I've had enough of him already. It's time to get tough. He might be putting on a good show but he doesn't know that I'm onto him. He's gone to a *lot* of effort to get to me; it's not like he's just going to reveal himself easily. But it's time for his mask to slip. And, luckily, I know just the way. It's amazing what men will confess to when you're holding a knife to their scrotum.

I plant my own elbows on the table and rest my head in my hands, keeping eye contact with Gabriel. 'Do you want to play a game?' I say. Of course he does. Blaze loves games. He's made that quite apparent.

He looks back at me. 'What sort of game?'

I lean back again. 'Cocktail roulette!' I say. 'We take it in turns to pick a drink. The loser is the one who has to bail first.' I clap my hands together, childish and excited.

He tilts his head and takes me in again. 'Shouldn't you join Carmella in the spa if you're feeling this much better?'

I shrug. 'Probably. But I think getting to know my new "Daddy" better is also a good way to spend my time.'

I watch as his brain chews this over for a little while. Eventually he nods.

'I suppose it's as good a way to bond as any. Okay, let's go.' His eyes meet mine again and it's game on.

'You go first,' I say. I mean, it's only polite.

'Are you sure?' he growls. 'I know you've been a bit delicate today. I don't want to hurt you.'

Yes you do, Blaze. Yes. You. Do.

'I'm sure. Do your worst.'

Gabriel shrugs, shoves his chair back and walks over to the bar. This is fine. I just need to drink one of his drinks and then I can go in for the kill. He comes back over carrying two martini glasses with something pink inside. This is fine. This is a small drink. This is nothing.

'Watermelon Sugar,' he says as he places the glass in front of me. 'Apparently it's a Harry Styles track.'

Harry Styles. My brain is immediately thrown back to that night at Orion Studios. And what happened after. I pick up the glass.

'It's tequila, vodka, a splash of sherry and then just fruit,' he says. 'A mild one to start.'

I take a sip. It's not. But it's a fucking lot milder than the cocktail I'm going to give him in a minute. So I down it. And hope for the best.

'That's good!' I say. 'My turn?'

'Yes, but go easy on me. I'm just an old man.' He laughs and I hate him.

Of course I have to be a bit easy on him, I can't just give him a drug-laced cocktail straight up. I need him to be a bit pissed so he doesn't suspect anything. I go to the bar and pick up a cocktail menu.

'What can I get for you? The bartender asks. I'm surprised to hear a London accent.

'Oh, you're English?'

He nods. 'Indeed I am. Best mixologist in London, two years running. Been shipped out specially.' He winks at me. 'So what do you fancy? I can make anything you like for you and the boss.' He points over to Gabriel who's on his phone again. Probably checking his follower-count on his Blaze account or something.

The boss? That's some outdated bro-speak.

'An Espresso Martini please. And one Espresso Delight.'

'You know the Espresso Delight is virgin, yeah? There's no booze in it.'

Which is the exact reason I'm having it.

'I know,' I say. 'We're playing a game. And I want to win.' I put my finger to my lips. 'Our secret?'

He laughs. 'You're a bad one. I like it. Don't worry, your secret is safe with me. Go and sit. I'll bring it over.'

'Should I be concerned?' Gabriel says when I sit back down at the table.

'Not at all. I'm going easy on you this round.'

Gabriel raises his eyebrows and the bartender comes over with the drinks. I'm impressed that he's made them look identical.

'Sir,' he says and puts one of the martini glasses down in front of Gabriel with a flourish. 'Madame. Enjoy.' He is completely deadpan as he serves us. Good boy. He won't give the game away.

'Merci,' I say and take a sip. Delicious and completely alcohol-free. Must remember to give him a huge tip.

'Ah, a classic,' Gabriel is saying. 'Nice choice, Kitty. Santé.'

'Santé.'

'Oh, this is good,' Gabriel says after swallowing down a significant amount of his drink. 'That guy's new, but he seems to know his stuff.'

'I think he's really good,' I say, making eye contact with the bartender and giving him a conspirational smile.

When he brings over Gabriel's next choice which is a Mai Tai, I'm pleased to see that he understands the rules of the game as this one is also completely sans booze. I can't help but think about how predatory this would be if it was Gabriel plying me with alcohol while he sipped on mocktails. It's exactly the sort of thing Blaze would do and then brag about online though so I don't feel any guilt. Live by the creepy predatory sword, die by the creepy predatory sword.

After two more rounds each, I can see that Gabriel is becoming slightly worse for wear. I'm pleasantly surprised because I thought it might take longer. This is a man who can seriously hold his drink.

It's time to pull out the big guns.

I sashay over to the bar, trying to look like I'm a bit unsteady on my feet for Gabriel's benefit.

'You winning your game?' The bartender stops polishing glasses and comes over to me with a big smile on his face. 'His head will be banging by tonight.'

I laugh. 'It will. I have a special request this time. Can you make a Grasshopper?'

'Of course I can.'

'You're a superstar,' I say. 'No need to make mine virgin this time though.' I look over at Gabriel, who is squinting at his phone. 'Maybe some water for the table too? Poor him. I feel mean now.'

The bartender laughs. 'I'll bring it over.'

'I am impressed that you're still standing,' Gabriel says with a slight slur when I return. 'Brava. Well done. I'm feeling pretty drunk.'

'I've had a lot of practice,' I say. 'My liver is like steel.'

The barman comes over with two bright green drinks and Gabriel pales a little.

'Oh Christ,' he says. 'What hell is this? I hate crème de menthe.'

'Are you withdrawing from our competition?' I ask.

'No way. But I think I might need to visit the loos and say a prayer before I attempt this course.' He gets out of his seat and stumbles a little as he makes his way inside the hotel to the toilets.

'I think you definitely win.' The bartender laughs.

'I think I do too.'

When he's back behind the bar, I take my weapon out of my bag. It's a tiny vodka bottle that I got from the minibar. I've removed the vodka – with my mouth – and filled it up with temazepam. I take a quick glance around to make sure none of the other guests are looking at me – they're not, they're either looking at their phones or their reflections in their phones. People are so deliciously predictable. I empty the contents of the bottle into the drink in front of me and then switch it with Gabriel's. I then take a long swig of mine.

'Are you okay?' I ask Gabriel when he comes back to the table. 'Maybe you should have some water or sit this round out?'

He shakes his head vigorously, my subtle undermining of his fragile male ego working a treat. He picks up his glass and knocks it back in one. 'That's a potent one,' he says grimacing.

'You look as green as the drink,' I say with a laugh. 'I assume it doesn't count if it comes back up?'

'It's not going anywhere,' he says, pulling a face and swallowing down half a glass of water.'

I bloody hope not.

After about half an hour I can see his eyes start to glaze over and he begins to slump down in his chair.

'Are you okay, Gabriel?' I say.

'I don't know,' he says. 'Feel a bit wobbly actually.'

'It's probably sunstroke.'

'Huh, yeah.'

'Or maybe you've picked up whatever I had.' He stares at me as if he's trying to work out who I am. 'Let's get you upstairs. I think you need a siesta. Do they have that in France?' I move around to where Gabriel is sitting and hold out my hand to help him up.

'Thank you,' he says. 'I really don't know what's come over me.' He staggers along behind me as I walk into the coolness of the hotel lobby. I call the lift and he leans against the wall, wiping sweat off his brow. I usher him into the lift to my floor and then into my room. He barely even seems to register that this isn't the same suite he's staying in with my mother.

'Here we are,' I say. 'Lie down. I'll get you some water, Blaze.' I peer at his face but he doesn't react. That's okay though, he definitely will when he's got that knife in his crotch.

'Thank you, Carmella,' he murmurs. 'I really don't feel very well.'

'That'll be the temazepam I slipped into your drink,' I say. But I don't think he hears me because when I look back round at the bed he's out cold.

Time to get to work.

I tie Gabriel's wrists and ankles together with the rope from the cheap beach bag I picked up while I was exploring with Charlie on our first – and only – day here together. I have to watch a quick YouTube tutorial on how to tie something called a constrictor knot. Luckily there seems to be an appetite for knots people can't escape from so there are plenty to choose from. I actually find it quite therapeutic. Maybe Charlie will be interested in trying out some shibari with me when we get back to London. The thought creeps in before I remember that Charlie is probably in the middle of a fuckfest with Jenna at this very moment. The pain rushes through me, touching every single nerve.

'Not now, Kitty,' I say out loud. 'You can face that later. Focus.' I grit my teeth and pull the rope even tighter.

Once I'm satisfied the knots will hold, I manoeuvre him into a sitting position which isn't easy, he's not a small man, but I want him upright when he comes round. I want to be able to see each tiny fleck of fear in his eyes.

And then I sit back and wait.

34

It takes approximately half an hour for Gabriel to fully regain consciousness. His head is the first thing I see move as he lifts it and meets my eyes. Sleepily, he smiles at me. I smile back. And wait for him to realise what's going on. It doesn't take long.

'What the fuck?' His usual baritone rises a couple of octaves in panic. 'What's going on?' He struggles and tries to stand up, but obviously cannot. Not with his ankles tied. 'Kitty? What's happened? Were we kidnapped?'

I stand up and his eyes widen as he realises that I can. That I'm not trussed up like he is.

'*We* were not,' I say. 'You are though. Bad luck.'

He stares at me, those brown pools now looking muddy with confusion. 'I—I don't understand. Is this a joke?'

'Like some sort of stag prank?' I ask, standing over him.

His Adam's apple bobs as he gulps. 'Yes?'

I shake my head. 'No. Sorry.'

'Then what? What is this about? I'm marrying your mum in two days.'

'Yeah. About that. That's not happening.'

Gabriel blinks and blinks at me.

'Nothing to say?' I ask.

'What? What's going on? Look, can you just untie me? This isn't very funny, Kitty.'

His eyes are darting around, the panic palpable. I like this part. 'Can we just get this really fucking clear, *Blaze*? I am not joking around. I know exactly who you are and what you're planning. So of course I'm not just going to sit back and let you marry my mother. What sort of daughter would that make me?'

Gabriel snorts, but it's bravado, the fear in his eyes gives him away. 'I'm not sure what sort of daughter getting her stepfather drunk and tying him to a chair makes you.'

'You're not my stepfather,' I say. 'You're Blaze Bundy.'

'Who the fuck is Blaze Bundy?'

Hmm. He's not going to give it up easily then. 'Don't lie to me. I know it's you. I've seen your tattoo. And I found the bandana. Come on, just admit it. The drugs are supposed to loosen your tongue.'

He stares at me. 'You *were* in our suite last night then. I knew it.'

'Busted,' I say, holding my hands up. 'I'm so glad Carmella still brings her entire medicine cabinet with her wherever she goes.'

'You drugged me?'

'I did.'

'Fuck. You're off-the-scale nuts.'

I don't like that. 'No. I'm just smarter than you give me credit for. Blaze.'

He sighs. It's frustration. 'Well, you're clearly not because I have absolutely no idea who this Blaze is or why you think I'm him.'

I pick up my phone and open Instagram, scrolling straight through to Blaze Bundy's page. 'This,' I say, 'is Blaze Bundy. Aka, *you*.' I play him one of Blaze's reels. The one where he brags at having not-quite-consensual sex with a woman called Ruby.

Gabriel watches, still wide-eyed. When it ends he looks up at me. I swear his eyes look wet. He really is good. Proper method acting. 'This isn't me, Kitty. I promise you. This is disgusting. Why the hell would you think that's me? Why would you think I'd say something so. . . *disgusting*?'

'The tattoo gave you away,' I say, pulling up his sleeve and exposing the BB inked on his arm. 'It's exactly the same as the one you scrawled on that blow-up doll. You remember? The one you planted in the Thames when you were in London recently. And the bandana. I found that too. Just admit it. It will make things much easier for you.'

'The what? What are you even talking about?'

'You know. Please stop pretending. I'll have a tiny bit of respect for you if you just admit to what you've done. I might even go a bit easier on you when I torture and kill you.'

'What the fuck? I genuinely have no clue what you're talking about. That *thing* on Instagram is not me.'

'Right. So you're saying you haven't set this persona up? That you haven't been taunting me for weeks? That you haven't been playing with me before you kill me, then marry my mother and steal her money?'

'*What?* No! Wow. No.'

'Why are you marrying her then?'

'Because I love her, Kitty, that's why.'

I snort. 'Love her. That's why I saw you walking down the beach the other day all over some girl?'

'What *girl*? Seriously, if this isn't a joke—'

'It's not. I told you that.'

'Then you're seriously unhinged.'

'The best people are.'

I'm getting tired of his crap now. Time to take things up a notch. I take out the steak knife I swiped from the rehearsal dinner. I've really missed seeing the look on their faces when I whip out a huge, shiny blade. Gabriel doesn't disappoint. His eyes widen even more, his nostrils flare and his Adam's apple bobs around like a fucking lifebuoy as he tries to swallow his fear.

'Who was she then?'

'*Who?*' His voice is getting irritatingly shrill now. I stride over to him and hold the knife to his crotch.

'Keep your fucking voice at a reasonable level or I will stab you in the balls, Gabriel.'

'What *fucking* girl?' he hisses.

'Early twenties, blonde hair, big tits. Surely you remember? You saved her from a rogue volleyball? What a hero.'

Gabriel drops his head to his chest and his shoulders begin to shake. This is it. This is when he finally cracks. The knife to the balls never fails. I didn't expect tears though. That's just the vegan icing on the vegan cake.

But when he looks back up at me he's not crying. He's laughing. Is he hysterical? Is he having a breakdown?

'Becky!' he finally manages to spit out. 'You saw me with Becky!'

214

I want to stab him in the balls. More than I've ever wanted to stab anyone in the balls before. 'I don't see what's funny.'

'Becky is our wedding planner. Fucking hell, Kitty. You should really be putting your imagination to better use. It's incredible.'

'Wedding planner?'

'Yes. I'm not sure if you've noticed but there's a wedding happening in a couple of days. Do you think they just organise themselves? Or do you think it's the bride's job to arrange everything? That's quite sexist of you, Kitty.' He's still smirking. Which is quite bold when an angry woman is holding a knife to your wedding tackle.

'Give me your phone,' I say.

'How can I? I'm a bit tied up. You'll have to get it yourself. It's in my back pocket.'

Keeping the knife between his legs, I reach behind him and wriggle his phone out of his chinos pocket and hold it up to his face. It unlocks. I scroll straight to his photos app. That's where I'll find the evidence.

The videos.

They'll be here.

Except they're not.

There *are* videos, lots of them, but they're mostly of my mother. Carmella saying yes to Gabriel who is on one knee in the sand and holding a ring aloft. A candid reel of Carmella on a yacht, smiling and staring out to sea, her wind whipping around her face, before clocking that she's being filmed and playfully admonishing behind-the-camera Gabriel. A clip of my mother wearing wellington boots and laughing as she chases a pig around a muddy pen. There are no videos of Gabriel, face covered by a bandana, speaking through a voice-changer.

None at all.

'See?' he says, his voice is serious now, sad even. 'It's not me.'

But it has to be.

'You could've deleted them,' I say. 'Or filmed them on a different phone. You've probably got a burner. This proves nothing.' I feel like I've run out of steam though. I was so sure I'd find something incriminating on here. I flick through to his call record. He was definitely talking to someone about my mother last night while I was hiding in the wardrobe. He called her a pig! But the only call logged for the whole of yesterday was an incoming one from a French landline. That tells me nothing. I throw the phone down on the bed. It's useless. 'Well, what about the tattoo then? BB? Blaze Bundy.'

Gabriel smiles but it's not the self-satisfied smirk of earlier. It's softer. 'I had it done over twenty years ago,' he says. 'On my first boy's holiday. In Tenerife. When I was pissed.'

'BB though?' I say. 'What does that stand for if it isn't Blaze Bundy?'

'Bad boy!' He's laughing a bit now. 'It stands for "bad boy" because I was drunk and nineteen and I thought I was a player. God, this is wild. Look, you can see how faded it is. I've started having laser treatments to have it removed. It's really embarrassing actually.' He's cackling away now, like he's inhaled something from a balloon. 'It originally said Bad Boy 4 Life. Go on, have a look.'

I roll up his sleeve and turn his arm over, exposing the delicate white flesh. The tattoo is there, but he's right, it's definitely faded. And I can see the ghost of where the '4 Life' once was.

'See?' Gabriel says. 'All I'm guilty of is extremely poor taste in body art. Will you please untie me now? My head is absolutely throbbing and I need some water.'

But it has to be him. Because if not him, then who?

'What about the bandana then?' I say, keeping the knife pointing at him as I go to the drawer where I stashed it. I pull it out and hold it up triumphantly.

'I wondered where that had got to,' Gabriel says. 'Why did you steal my bandana?'

'I didn't *steal* it. I *gathered* it. As evidence. Because Blaze Bundy uses one to hide his true identity.'

'Well, *I* use it to protect the balding spot on top of my head from sunburn.'

That's a lie. 'You don't have a bald spot!' I've already noted his lack of male-pattern baldness.

'Oh, trust me, I'm definitely thinning on top.' He bows his head forward. 'Look.' I do. I can't see even a hint of scalp.

'You have a full and abundant head of hair,' I say.

'Come closer,' he says like the wolf in every fairy tale. 'Look closer. Really close.' I move even closer and peer at the top of his head. I don't see it at first, but then I do. A spot, the same colour as his black curls, that's hairless and shiny.

'Do you . . . do you *spray colour* your bald spot?'

Gabriel raises his head so his eyes meet mine again. 'L'Oréal Magic Touch Up. Things are not always what they seem. Not when you get close to them and look properly.'

This can't be right. I was so sure.

I need to think.

I slump back down on the bed and pick up my phone, going straight to Blaze Bundy's page on Instagram. There must be something here. Something that proves Gabriel is Blaze.

And then, as I'm looking through the posts trying to find someone, anything, that links Blaze Bundy to Gabriel, something happens. A notification telling me that Blaze Bundy is going live.

But how can that be?

That would mean Gabriel is telling the truth.

I click on the link.

'Good day, disciples,' he's saying in that grotesque distorted voice. 'So glad so many of you are joining me. First of all I want to apologise for being MIA the past few days. I've been taking a bit of time out and getting some much needed R and R abroad.'

'What's that?' Gabriel asks. 'What are you watching?'

'Shh,' I say, annoyed at him, at myself. 'Blaze Bundy is doing a live.'

'Doing a live?' Gabriel repeats. 'So you're seeing, in real time, that this guy cannot be me?'

Why won't he shut up? I need to listen to this. I turn the volume up on my phone.

'If you truly want to win at life,' Blaze is saying now. 'Then travel is vital. But. I'm not talking about like romantic trips with a female in tow. That kind of travel is for low-testosterone, low-income men.'

Gabriel scoffs. 'And you really thought this was me? Seriously. That's incredibly offensive.'

I glare at him.

'Travel is about broadening your horizons. And the best

218

way to do that is to use the opportunity to hook up with a different kind of chick than the females you find yourself surrounded with on the daily. But I don't mean lowering your standards, men. There is a certain type of female that you might encounter while travelling and I think you all know what I'm talking about when I say a low-value chick.' He laughs. 'I'm talking about the type of female that stops being a lady the moment she's on different soil. You've all seen this woman. She's getting drunk every night. She's hooking up with different men every night. And then, she probably goes home to her cuck boyfriend, her body count double what it was when she left.' He pauses for a moment.

I look over at Gabriel who is listening, a look of utter bewilderment on his face. 'This is fucking toxic,' he says in a quiet voice.

'Let's just talk about body count for a minute, shall we?' Blaze is saying now. 'I know it's something we've covered in depth before. Let me just look at some of the people who are watching this live. Let's talk about your body counts. KC, I see you've joined this live. I was hoping you might. Hi babe, what's your body count?'

And then it becomes clear. Gabriel isn't Blaze Bundy and the real Blaze Bundy has been taunting me for a completely different reason. A much more dangerous reason.

He knows.

He fucking knows.

And I have absolutely no idea who he is.

I shut down the app and throw my phone away from me.

'What the fuck was that about?' Gabriel asks.

'I don't know,' I say, even though I do and it's more

important than ever that I stop wasting time with Gabriel and find the real Blaze Bundy.

'It's not me, Kitty.'

'I know.' And I want to cry.

'Not all men are like your dad,' Gabriel says gently.

'She told you?' She promised she wouldn't.

'Carmella told me that your dad was violent. That he hurt her. That him disappearing wasn't the worst thing that had happened to her. I'm not like that. I promise you.' I hate feeling so confused. I hate getting things wrong. 'Can you untie me now?'

I stare at him. 'How can I?' I say miserably. 'You're going to tell my mother and then she'll hate me. I can't let you go.'

'I'm not going to say anything, Kitty. I promise. I love Carmella. I don't want to hurt her. It's the last thing I want to do. Let me go. It's obviously been a misunderstanding.'

And I believe him.

I really do.

So I'm about to untie him and let him go. But then the door to my suite flings open and someone screams.

35

'What the hell is going on?'

It's my mother.

And she has a look on her face that I have never seen before.

It's not a good one.

'Kitty?' She's not happy. Not happy at all. 'Can you explain why my fiancé is in your room, on your *bed*, and why he's tied up?'

My mother was never angry while I was growing up; my dad was furious and aggressive enough for both of them. I've never seen her angry. I don't like it. I suck down the temptation to throw myself into her arms and cry like I'm six years old.

'What the fuck?' she says. I slump down onto the bed, suddenly not trusting my legs to carry my weight.

'I'm sorry,' I murmur. 'I'm really sorry.'

'What for? This had better be good.'

'It's okay,' Gabriel says from the bed. 'It was a misunderstanding. She thought I was a vile misogynistic Instagrammer and that I was only marrying you for your

221

money. But we got to the bottom of it and it's all fine. Or it will be once someone unties me.'

Carmella looks from one of us to the other. 'A *misunderstanding?*' she spits. 'You call this a misunderstanding? She's holding a knife.' She spins round to face me and I drop the knife. 'I came up here to check you were okay. I was so worried about you. Were you just trying to get me out of the way so you could—' She waves in Gabriel's direction.

I nod, sadly. 'I thought he was dangerous. I thought he was going to hurt us.'

'What? Jesus Christ, Kitty. *Why?*'

'She got the wrong end of the stick,' Gabriel says and I have to admire how calm he is considering. 'We all make mistakes. Now, can someone untie me?'

'She was going to kill you!' Carmella says. 'I think that's a bit more than a mistake.'

'No one was going to kill anyone,' Gabriel says. 'Could one of you let me go now?'

'I thought he was going to kill *us*,' I say to my mother. 'I thought he was after your money.'

'My money? Why would Gabriel steal my money? He's got loads of his own.' She stares at me. 'He owns this hotel, for God's sake. And several others.'

'What? Since when?' I look at Gabriel and he nods. I think back to what the bartender said earlier. The boss. It wasn't a throwaway sexist comment. Gabriel literally is the boss.

'Since *forever*,' Carmella is saying. 'So no, he's not after my money.'

'You could've told me,' I grumble. 'You know, when I asked what Gabriel did and you laughed and said, "Oh this and that." Maybe there wouldn't have been a misunderstanding if you'd said something.'

Carmella continues to glare at me. 'Maybe there wouldn't have been a misunderstanding if you'd just trusted me.'

Gabriel coughs. 'Still here. Not getting any less tied up.'

'Yes. Okay. Sorry. I'll let you go.' I hurry over to him but I've tied the knots a bit too well. 'Could you pass me the knife please?' I say to my mother, who widens her eyes in disbelief.

'*I'll* do it,' she says and shoves me out of the way so she can hack through Gabriel's restraints.

'Thank you, baby,' he says and kisses her before standing up and doing some, quite frankly, elaborate and unnecessary stretches, no doubt to make me feel horribly guilty. I wasn't *that* rough with him.

'Would you mind giving Kitty and me a few moments alone? Please? Wait for me upstairs. I won't be long,' my mother says to him.

'Sure,' he says. 'I think I should take this though.' He slips the knife out of her hand. 'Just to be safe.' He kisses her again and leaves us alone in the room.

As soon as he's gone Carmella sighs and sinks down onto the bed. The sigh is long and deep and says far more than any words could. 'Kitty. I'm a grown woman. I've been looking after myself for a very long time. A very long time. You should have trusted me. You should've trusted that I trust Gabriel.'

'I'm sorry.' I sit down next to her. 'I really am.' My mother leans over to me and takes my hand in hers. 'I was so sure Gabriel was Blaze Bundy. He's been sending me weird messages and I think he wants to kill me.'

'Darling, you really need to think about getting some help,' she says quietly. 'I'm sure no one is after you. But not just that. I think you need to talk to someone about your. . . anger issues. I know it's a stupid hashtag but you have to believe that not all men are like your dad. Kits. They're not. Charlie isn't, is he?'

I snort. 'Isn't he?' I wish I could be so sure.

'Kitty? Has something happened with Charlie? Is that why you're acting like this? It's like when Adam. . .' She doesn't need to go on. She might not have been in the country when Adam was attacked. But she knows it happened after I found out he was cheating on me. She may not have said as much but she knows I did it. Of course she does, she's seen first-hand what I'm capable of.

Suddenly it all just feels too much and I slump miserably down onto the bed. 'I don't even know where he is at the moment,' I say. 'He hasn't been in touch.'

'You said you'd heard from him? That he was fine and would be back for the wedding? Is that not true?'

I shake my head before letting it drop to my chest. 'No. His phone just rings and rings. He's read my messages but hasn't replied to them. And I tried to call the woman he works with, who he was going to meet, but she's blocked me. I think he's having an affair. I think he's left me.' I shrug and, as my shoulders sink back down, I feel all the fight, all the energy leave me. I look at my mum. She's frowning. She looks as though she wants to say something but is struggling to find the words. 'What?' I say. 'What is it?'

She looks me dead in the eyes. I always forget how beautiful my mother is. And now I see that of course Gabriel is in love with her. She's beautiful. She's kind. She's gentle and she loves deeply. How could I ever think that she's weak?

'Does he know?' she asks. It's not what I was expecting her to say.

'Know what?' My stomach rolls.

'Know what you do? To men?'

I stare at her. What?

'Don't look at me like that, Kits. I'm your mother. How could you think I don't know.' She takes her hand away and tucks it in her lap with her other one. 'Who do you think cleared up the mess you left? That awful TV presenter?'

What?

My jaw hits the floor.

How does she know about that?

What does she mean *cleared up*?

'Max Macintyre? But how?'

She squeezes my hand. 'There was just something about the way you looked that night. I knew it wasn't just the party. There was something in your eyes that I recognised.' She doesn't need to say exactly what she'd seen. She's seen it before. And she'd cleaned my mess up that time too. 'And you had blood on your face. I wiped it off, remember?'

'But how? How did you know where I'd been?'

She reaches out and touches the necklace, the one she sent me for my birthday. 'There's a tracker in it,' she says. 'I'm sorry. But I've been so worried about you since last year when you went off the rails and ended up in hospital. And you never answer my calls or messages. I just wanted a way to keep an eye on you, to make sure you're safe.'

It's true that I was in hospital briefly last year. Everyone thought I'd tried to take my own life after Charlie finished with me. But it was all a misunderstanding. I'd been feeling terrible after accidentally killing Ruben Reynolds instead of his rapist brother and I'd been self-medicating with drink and drugs. I wasn't actually trying to hurt myself. I mean, come on.

'You put a tracker on me?'

'Just a little one.'

'Oh. Well, that's okay then. As long as it's only tiny.'

'But it's lucky I did, isn't it? Because it meant that I knew where you'd been that night. And that I could go and clear the place up. Because it was obvious you weren't going to be able to.'

My head is spinning.

All this time while I've been waiting for Max's body to be discovered, while I've been waiting for him to go from a missing person to a murdered person, he's been. . . he's been. . . where?

'What did you do with him?' I ask, but I already know the answer, don't I? Because Gabriel was right. The apple hasn't fallen very far at all. And because she's done this before too.

'Abattoir,' she says. 'The one in North Hampshire.'

'Wow,' I say. 'I guess that explains why you looked so tired the next morning.'

She squeezes my hand again. 'It was a long night. You left the place in a total state.'

'Thank you,' I say.

'You don't need to thank me, Kitty. Of course I'm going to do everything I possibly can to keep you safe.' She turns to me, reaches over and strokes my face with her thumb. 'But you need to keep yourself safe too. This could've ended so badly for you. How many others have there been?' I don't answer and she sighs. 'Why would you want to throw everything you have away? Why are you putting yourself in danger?'

'Because no one else is!' I want to scream. 'Because there are monsters like Max Macintyre and Blaze Bundy everywhere you look. And there are even bigger monsters behind the scenes, pulling the strings, enabling the monsters, creating a new generation of monsters. And I can't just sit here and watch it happen. I can't. Not when I've got the means to stop some of it.'

'But, Kits, it's not your fight. You can't take this on single-handedly.'

'No, I know that. But it's like charity, right? Obviously giving three pounds a month isn't going to stop child poverty or whatever, but it's something. It's helping. It's not sitting here on our privilege and pretending it isn't happening. It might not stop all of it, but if it helps even one woman, then it's something.'

'You need to stop, Kits. You need to get help and stop. There's only so much I can do to protect you. And I won't be around forever.'

'I'm not going to stop,' I say releasing something in me. I feel lighter. Because it's the truth. I thought I could stop. I thought loving Charlie and having Charlie love me would make me want to stop. But it hasn't. It quelled it for a bit, but it's still been there really. Deep down. And now I don't have Charlie anyway. I don't have anything to stop for. The future I thought I was going to have with him isn't going to happen. I look at my mother. Her eyes are wet. She looks sadder than I've ever seen her.

'I think you should go back to London,' she says. 'Maybe

we really *do* need that distance between us after all. If you're not even going to try . . .'

'What? What do you mean? You just said how much you love me.'

'And I do. I really do. But I can't watch you do this. You were going to kill the man I love!'

'For a good reason—'

'You were wrong!'

We sit in silence for a moment. I don't know what to say.

'You're scared of me,' I finally manage.

'I'm scared of what you're going to do to yourself, Kitty.' She takes a deep breath and stands up. 'I want you to get help. Professional help. I know some people in London. *Discreet* people who can help you. Before you go too far. Like you very nearly did here.'

'What about the wedding?'

'Go home,' she says. 'Please. It's for the best. Think about what I've said. I know that some of your issues with men are my fault and I probably should've taken responsibility for that sooner. We'll fix this. I'll find someone to help you. But the best thing you can do now is go home.' She stands up and kisses me softly on the forehead. 'I love you.'

And then she turns and walks out of my room without looking back.

I sit in shocked silence for a moment or two after she leaves. What the fuck just happened? How have I been exiled from my own mother's wedding? The one I didn't even want to come to in the first place? My eyes grow hot with tears. Tears of anger, sorrow but mostly just solid self-pity. I wipe my hand across my face before they get a chance to run down my cheeks. I grab my phone from the bedside table and call Charlie. Desperate I know but I just need to hear his voice. Even if it's telling me things I don't want to hear. But it rings and rings and finally clicks through to voicemail.

'Charlie,' I say, trying to hide the wobble in my voice. 'Please call me. Please. I don't care what's going on. I just really need to speak to you. Please.'

And then I feel a familiar surge of self-loathing rumble through my body at how pathetic I just sounded. Begging a man to call me. What the fuck? This isn't who I am. Didn't I promise after everything with Adam that I would never let myself stoop to these depths again over a man. I throw my phone down on the bed with a bit more force than I intended and watch as it bounces onto the floor. Then I stalk over to the minibar and pull out all the booze. I open the vodka and tip it down my throat, swiftly followed by a whisky and then a tiny gin. My hollow stomach growls in protest but I don't listen to it and pick out one of the half bottles of wine. I don't bother with a glass for that either. I try Charlie's phone again in a fit of rage this time. But it doesn't even ring now, just clicks straight through to his voicemail. He's switched it off. This is the moment I let myself fully accept that he's gone. That he's left me. After seeing the love Gabriel clearly has for my mother maybe I've been wrong about Charlie this whole time. Maybe I've convinced myself that he loves me because that's what I so desperately wanted. I wanted him to love me to prove that I'm worthy of love, that I'm not a monster. Monsters aren't lovable are they? But if he really loved me, he'd be here. Instead I have no one. No Charlie, no friends and even Carmella doesn't want me here. I'm alone and no one loves me, because I'm a monster. Women lie to ourselves all the time when we don't want to face the truth. *What if he's had an accident? What if he's lost his phone? What if he's not answering my texts because he's dead in a ditch?* The truth is much simpler.

He's not answering because he doesn't want to.

36

I wish more than ever that I could speak to Tor or Maisie. Fuck. I'd even settle for Hen and some of her special brand of insanity right now. But there's no one here.

Instead I turn to the one thing I know will make me feel better and is always there for me. Alcohol. 'You never let me down,' I say as I polish off the last of the booze from the minibar – lager, gross.

I order a bottle of wine from room service and, when it arrives, drink it quickly. It's not long before I'm feeling number. It's better, but it's not enough. I want to feel nothing at all. I want to be obliterated. All I want is for the pain and the constant churning thoughts to stop. Just for one night. And then, tomorrow, I'll do what my mother has asked, go back to London. Maybe find a therapist.

But now. I'm going out.

I clumsily get dressed, finishing off the contents of the minibar as I do so: a red wine and two cans of pre-mixed gin and tonic, for the record. I'm too wobbly for heels so I pair my Missoni minidress with a pair of Gucci flip-flops. My hair is already beachy and wavy in the way it only goes while I'm on holiday so I pull it into a low ponytail. I slick some oil over my lips and I'm ready to go. God, getting ready on holiday is such a dream compared to London. Maybe I should think about moving abroad. Maybe a completely fresh start is exactly what I need. It's not like there's anything left for me in London after all.

Ugh, I need to stop this self-pity. I grab my LV bag, slide my phone into it and head out the door.

'Don't wait up,' I say to no one as I leave.

37

Nighttime Cannes is a different beast to Daytime Cannes. As I stroll along the Croisette looking for somewhere to drink myself into oblivion I'm reminded of nights out in Chelsea with the girls. There is music blaring out of various bars and restaurants and groups of already drunk holiday makers spilling out onto the streets. In between the clusters of men and women are couples, gazing into each other's eyes across the table or walking arm in arm along the promenade. Friends and lovers. I feel desperately out of place on my own. I can't bear it.

I get a few looks as I stumble back the way I just came, but I don't care. Let them stare. I turn my back on the sea and walk away from it, I don't want a bar packed full of happy tourists right now. I need somewhere I can drink in peace. I walk until I eventually find somewhere tucked a few streets back from the lights and fountains and joy of the Croisette. It's dimly lit and doesn't look busy which is exactly what I need right now.

Inside there is a lone bartender and a withered-looking man

and that is it. I order a straight vodka, ignoring the enthusiastic server's attempts to cajole me into trying a cocktail that looks happier than I think I've ever felt in my life.

'Just the vodka,' I say, noticing my words are slurring slightly. 'Make it a double.' In for a euro. Or something. I notice a quick look between the guy behind the bar and the older man who is nursing a pint. 'Is it because I'm a woman drinking alone?' I ask, realising I might be drunker than I thought. 'You wouldn't even think twice if I was a man, would you?' They look at each other again, baffled. The smiley bartender beams at me.

'Je ne parle pas anglais,' he says and cheerfully hands me my drink which I suck back in one before ordering another.

When I've finished that I find myself drifting back out of the bar. Maybe I should just go back to the hotel and get more wine sent to my room. Being out isn't helping my mood at all. I stumble back along the Croisette, purposefully ignoring the lure of the glamorous rooftop bars. What's the point in going to anywhere like that alone? Without my friends?

Instead I make my way down to the beach; I can get to my – Gabriel's – hotel through the beach bar and I get to avoid the depressing party vibes along the main street. The beach is eery in the dark. Most of the bars are closed and the loungers and parasols are away for the night. There are a few people around, but they're mostly drunk couples trying to tick al fresco holiday sex off their bucket lists.

Eventually I spot the twinkling fairy lights of the Chien Noir beach bar and head towards them. I plan to go straight up to my room but I'm stopped when I hear a voice. 'Good evening, mademoiselle!' I turn and it's the bartender from earlier, the one who served Gabriel and me all the cocktails. 'Come have a drink with me?'

I look around. The last thing I want is to bump into my mother and Gabriel right now but I don't think they'd be here. Gabriel will be feeling woozy for a while after that spiked cocktail. And, actually, they probably don't want to run into me either. I'm in luck. They're not here. In fact, it's actually very quiet. The only other person is someone my drunk, blurred vision can't make out, drinking alone at a corner table. I guess it must be later than I realised. The bartender is smiling and beckoning me over. Oh, what the hell. I may as well have one here. Misery loves company, after all.

I head back to the bar and the bartender gives me a smile which is all white teeth and dimples. I'm a sucker for dimples and I am reminded of Charlie, but that's the last thing I want so I order a gin cocktail.

'Virgin?' he asks me, his eyes twinkling.

'Not this time,' I say. 'Thanks for what you did earlier by the way. I didn't realise Gabriel was your actual boss. Wasn't that a bit risky?'

He laughs. 'Nah. Gabe's a great guy. One of the best.' He throws some ice in a cocktail shaker, followed by a good-sized slosh of gin. 'Knows how to have a laugh.' He pours my drink into a tall glass and pops a straw in it. 'Voilà.'

'I'll get this,' another male voice cuts in. Also British. The other lone drinker has come over. But if he thinks he's found a drinking buddy, he is very wrong. I look at him, readying myself to politely tell him that I can get my own drink, but I find myself looking into the bluest eyes I've ever seen – and yes, I know that's a really terrible fucking cliché, but I'm drunk and they are. The face they're attached to isn't bad either. It's tanned, obviously, with a jawline so sharp it almost takes my eye out. There's dark stubble on the jaw and slightly longer dark stubble on the head and I can smell the red flags. They smell like Tom Ford Noir, by the way. Tor's voice suddenly pops into my head.

'The best way to get over a man is to get under another one,' she tells me. It's typical Tor. Well, old Tor. Before Mykonos. It's not a theory I've ever prescribed to myself. Not until now anyway. Why should Charlie have all the fun? And this man is very, very attractive.

So instead of saying no, I'm saying 'thank you' and smiling up at him.

'What is it you're drinking?' he asks me.

'A gin cocktail,' I say.

'Actually, make it two, please mate.' He winks and the bartender nods. 'So what's your name then? And why are you drinking alone?'

'I'm Kitty,' I say.

'Nice to meet you, Kitty,' he says. 'I'm Connor.' He holds out a hand to me and I take the opportunity to check his nails, clean, and forearms, muscular. 'You didn't answer my question, Kitty. What are you doing here alone? No boyfriend?'

I shake my head. I can't quite bring myself to say the words. *Not anymore.*

Connor puts on a mock confused face. 'Hmm. That's a mystery. Okay, friends? Where are they?' I shake my head again and he laughs this time. 'You've got no friends either? Oh dear, Kitty. That is probably the saddest story I've ever heard.' This makes me laugh.

'Sad? Or just pathetic?' I say.

Connor smiles and it makes his eyes twinkle. I mean, of course it doesn't, but it really seems that way and I feel my stomach do a little lurch. It feels like butterflies but it's probably just all those red flags flapping around. I don't care. It's not like I'm here to fall in love with this guy. I'm just thinking about sleeping with him. That's what red-flag guys are for, right?

The bartender places our drinks in front of us, looking at Connor through slightly narrowed eyes.

'Maybe a bit of both?' Connor says with a grin. 'But don't worry, because I find sad and pathetic very, very hot.' He moves a bit closer to me and I can feel the heat from his body on mine. Fuck you, Charlie. I finish my drink in one gulp and even Connor looks surprised. 'I think I'm gonna need to keep an eye on you,' he says.

'Cocktails,' I say. 'It tastes like you're drinking fruit juice and then suddenly your legs are no longer functioning and the room is a carousel.'

He laughs again. 'You're funny. Let me get on that carousel with you.' He orders two more drinks and Connor manoeuvres me onto a barstool. 'Just so you're supported when your legs no longer function.'

We drink our drinks and then some more and talk loudly into each other's ears even though we're the only ones here. Connor tells me that he's here on a family holiday which his mum insists he comes on every year even though he's twenty-seven – a younger man! – and hasn't lived at home for almost a decade. 'Free holiday though,' he says. 'Plus, you just never really know how much time you're going to get with the family.' This makes me think about Charlie again and his dead mum and I don't want to be thinking about Charlie or his dead mum so when Connor suggests we do a shot, I agree enthusiastically. He hands me something clear and I swallow it down in one, barely even registering that it's sambuca until it's burning my throat. He tells me he's from Essex but lives in London with two of his mates. I don't tell him anything about myself apart from my name. We do another shot and the next thing I know, Connor is leaning in towards me and then we're kissing and, honestly, it's a great kiss. It's hungry and almost aggressive. His stubble scratches against my face but I don't care because this is what I need. Something rough and as many physical sensations as possible. Something that stops me from thinking about Charlie and Tor and my mother and the fact I've totally failed to find Blaze Bundy who is still out here and somehow knows everything that I've done. Connor pulls away, smiling.

'That was very nice. What do you say to going down to the beach?' The beach where the drunk, horny couples go.

'I say yes.'

'I knew you would.' He leans in and gently licks my ear lobe. 'You taste of holiday.' It's probably sunscreen but fine. 'Wait here for a sec, okay, I'm just going to the loo and then we'll head off?' He kisses my cheek and then disappears towards the hotel and I lose sight of him quickly because my vision won't focus properly.

Fuck. I really am drunk.

'You okay?'

I look up to find where the voice has come from and it's the bartender. He's looking at me with concern.

'I'm fine,' I say. Or at least that's what I think I say. 'Merci.'

'You sure? Do you know that guy? Is he harassing you?'

I shrug. 'I'm fine.' The shrug almost makes me fall off my stool.

'You want me to walk you up to your room,' he says. 'I don't wanna speak out of line but you seem like you've had quite a lot to drink.'

Is he right? Maybe I'd be much better going upstairs and sleeping this off because I'm going to have one hell of a hangover tomorrow. But then I see Connor winding his way back over to me and he looks so good that my clitoris responds almost violently and why not? Why shouldn't I use a man to take my mind off the shitshow that my life has become.

'I'll be fine,' I say to the barman and I don't turn back to look at him, but I can feel his eyes burning into me as Connor takes my arm to steady me when I dismount from the stool, and guides me away from the bar and along the sand.

38

I know sex on the beach is another fucking cliché and I'm not seventeen, but what else am I going to do? Take him back to the hotel and fuck him in the bed I was supposed to be sharing with Charlie? I might be drunk but I still have some class. Connor doesn't mention going back to his either and I assume it's because of the family thing.

We awkwardly stagger almost down to the water and collapse into the sand laughing. I kick my shoes off and slide onto Connor's lap, straddling him and then we're kissing again. My hands grab at his hair and because Charlie's hair is longer and grabbable, they're confused when they reach Connor's head and there's nothing to hold onto, just slightly overgrown stubble that feels prickly and not as nice as Charlie's lovely soft hair. He always makes this low growling noise when I touch his hair and I miss this too. I almost pull away but then Connor's hands are underneath my dress and my bikini top and he's pulling at the strings to get it off.

'I don't think you need this,' he's saying as he pulls the tiny piece of material away from my body. Then his hands are on my tits and his fingers are squeezing them hard and I'm not thinking about Charlie anymore. Just the delicious pleasure hovering above pain. He slips the straps of my dress over my shoulders and it pools at my waist. Then his tongue is where his hands just were and he's sucking my nipple into his mouth and then he's holding it between his teeth and I feel his hand gently nudge my thighs apart. 'Fucking hell, Kitty,' he says, releasing my breast from his mouth. 'You're so fucking sexy.' He grabs my hand and pulls it down between his legs and I can feel he's hard through his jeans. 'You're a bad girl.'

You have no idea.

'Let's go in the sea,' he says into my ear and I don't say anything which he assumes is a yes. But I don't say anything because I don't know if this is what I really want now. My body misses Charlie. It doesn't want anyone else. But then Connor hoists me up and lifts me and I have to wrap my legs around him so I don't fall, his face still buried in my chest, and then we're in the sea and I'm gasping and somehow my dress is still on the beach and his kisses are rougher now, more like bites, and he's panting about how much he wants me, how much he wants me right now. The sea is cold and the salt on my lips begins to sting where he's been nipping at me. 'This is what you wanted, isn't it?' he says, raising his head to look at me and it suddenly occurs to me how well coordinated he is. Considering how drunk he was a few moments ago, how we had to hold each other upright as we stumbled down the beach, he's now able to lift me and manoeuvre me with ease. I look into his eyes and they don't look like drunk eyes. They look like steel. And I can feel that neither the amount of alcohol he's sunk or the cold water has had any effect on his ability to get an erection.

Not that it's anything to get excited about. I've got bigger heels.

It's not just his sad erection I can feel though. His hands are roaming over my body again, slipping into my bikini bottoms, his fingers trying to nudge their way inside me. But it all feels wrong now. I don't want anyone else's hands on me. In me.

I pull away and gently push him.

This isn't what I want.

This really isn't what I want.

'No,' I say but I don't think he hears me.

'Why are you pushing me away?' he asks, taking a step closer to me and grabbing my arm. He's not slurring anymore and is looking me dead in the eyes. A horrible realisation crawls over me. This isn't a stupidly drunk man. Not by a long shot. The only stupid person here is me. 'What's wrong? You've been all over me.'

I feel suddenly sober. 'I'm sorry,' I say. 'I want to go home. I don't want this. I've got a boyfriend.' Because, until Charlie says anything else, I have. I might be a killer. But I'm not a cheat.

The steel in his eyes becomes obsidian and without warning he raises his right arm and slaps me across the face. I've never been hit by a man before and I'm unprepared for the pain that radiates from my cheek as I stumble for my footing in the water. But before I can fully right myself and make a break back for the shore, he's on me, pulling at my bikini bottoms again, rasping breath in my ear.

'You fucking tease, you fucking whore,' he snarls as he tries to pull my swimsuit down my thighs. 'You're half-naked in the sea with me, you fucking slag.'

I open my mouth to scream but he just laughs.

'Who do you think is going to hear you all the way down here, Kitty?'

And he's right. I know he's right. So I stop struggling. And I even let him slide my bikini bottoms off one leg. He lets out a deep shuddery breath as I reach for him, taking his cock in my hand and squeezing it as hard as I can. I squeeze it and twist it until my hand is a balled fist around it and he's gasping in pain. Then I let go and bring my knee up between his legs. He yelps, stumbles backwards and I make a break for it towards the shore.

We didn't wade out too far and I half run, half swim back as fast as I can. I reach the shore and keep running. But the sand slows me down and I don't get more than a couple of metres before I feel wet hands clamp around my waist and pull me to the ground.

'You fucking little bitch,' he spits at me as he pins me down. 'I will fucking kill you. I'm going to fuck you. Then I'm going to kill you. And then I'm going to fuck you again. And take photos. You cunt.'

His weight is pinning me down and I can't move anything apart from my arms. I scratch at his face, but he easily pushes me away, grabbing again at my bikini bottoms. I scrabble around for something, anything that I can use to hit him with but the sand is unhelpfully smooth. There's not even a stone, let alone a rock, around to help me. There's nothing else I can do. I can't overpower him. There's no one around to hear my screams. He's managed to get my pants down again and I brace myself, closing my eyes and gritting my teeth, still grabbing around me. Then my fingers connect with something. My bag. I pull it closer as Connor fumbles with his wet trousers and grab the one thing in that bag that I know can save me. Something pink and shaped like a vulva. Then, just as he looms over me, ready to rape me, I switch on the laser and point it right at his eyes.

Thank you, Tor.

'What the fuck?' Connor yelps as his hands cover his eyes and he falls onto his back. 'What the fuck have you done? You've blinded me.'

I feel around and find my dress, pulling it over my head. 'Sorry. Was that not what you wanted?' I say as I kick him between the legs again. And then I'm on top of him, with the string bikini top in my hands. I wrap it around his neck and then I pull and pull and pull until I feel him buckle underneath me and collapse back into the sand. I stand up and put my foot on his neck, so that, even if I haven't choked him enough with the bikini string, he won't be able to breathe.

I stay like that for a few moments, until I'm absolutely sure. Then I slip the bikini top back into my bag. I look around but this stretch of beach is still empty. My previous kills have been selfless acts of kindness for women that didn't get the justice, the human compassion they deserved. But this one is fucking personal. More than anything I wish I was at home, near my abattoirs. I'd enjoy every single moment of ripping him limb from limb, cutting into his flesh, torturing him while he's not quite dead.

It's the absolute least he deserves.

But I don't have this option. All I know is that he needs to disappear now and the Med is the perfect place for him to do just that. So I grab him by the ankles and I begin hauling him down the beach towards the sea.

It's not easy, but I'm strong. And right now I feel stronger than ever. Like that superpower you hear about that lets mothers lift cars or whatever to save their kids. I've been harassed before. What woman hasn't? I've been threatened and groped too. But I've never once been this close to actually being raped. And it was terrifying. I've killed men. I've chopped up bodies. I've been questioned by police. But I have never before felt terror like that.

And so I drag and I drag until I get him into the water where, thankfully, he becomes almost weightless. Then I swim with him as far out as I can. I don't know much about body decomposition which is probably an oversight for someone who deals with corpses as often as I have. But I do know that he'll wash up at some point. And he'll wash up naked. Hopefully his death will be recorded. I have to hope for the best. Because people will notice he's missing. And because he's a white male, people will want to know what happened. Hotel CCTV tapes will be checked. And they'll show me talking to him, laughing with him. The bartender will say I was flirting with him. What the tapes won't show is him pretending to be drunk. They won't show him turning on me the moment we were out of sight. They won't show him pulling my clothes off and whispering threats in my ear. He'll be the victim.

He'll be the victim and I have to make sure I've got my story straight before he washes up. But I can think about that later. For now, I just have to hope that the sea carries him far enough away that a shark or something gets to him.

Back on the beach I leave his clothes where he pulled them off, hopefully, it will look like he decided to go for a late night swim that ended badly. Then I slip my shoes back on, pick up my bag and check my phone. Aside from some social media notifications there is nothing. Nothing from my mother and still nothing from Charlie. I try him again, desperate to hear his voice, but it's just his voicemail again. I hadn't even realised I was crying until now. I walk back up the beach and through the bar. The bartender is still there, he's polishing glasses and putting them away. Our eyes meet for the briefest of moments. He gives me a small nod and then looks away.

39

It's late when I wake up the following morning. I can tell because the room is disturbingly bright. I reach over for Charlie and the empty space reminds me that he's not there. And then the horror of the previous night hits me. I pull myself into a sitting position, my knees close to my chest. I stay like this for a very long time, crying and crying.

Eventually I manage to haul myself out of bed and into the shower. I hope it might make me feel better but the water pummels my body like hundreds of fists. I can hardly bear it and get out, gasping. My mouth is so dry I can hardly open it so I drink straight from the tap at the sink before trying to brush the misery away with toothpaste. That's when I catch sight of myself in the art-deco mirror Charlie was so thrilled with. I'm not a pretty sight. My eyes are bloodshot and squinty. My hair still has sand in it, despite my attempt to wash it out. My skin looks sallow rather than tanned. But worst of all, across my cheek, is an angry red mark, snarling back at me. A brutal souvenir from last night when a furious Connor hit me with the back of his hand. An open hand but with all

247

the force of a fist. I gingerly touch my fingers to it. It's hot and tender, a bruise already threatening under the skin. But worse than the physical pain is the burning sting of humiliation. He hit me. He hit me and he tried to have sex with me even though I'd told him no. I watch with a morbid fascination as the fingers I'm still holding against my throbbing cheek begin to tremble again.

'It's okay,' I tell the unrecognisable version of me in the mirror. 'He's gone. He can't get you now.' The words don't soothe mirror-me though and she stares back at me through hurt, haunted eyes.

She doesn't believe me.

She wants her mother.

I take one of the super white hotel washcloths and soak it in cold water. Then I hold it against my pounding cheek.

I hope it helps.

I pull on some clothes; I don't even pay attention to which ones and grab my phone before leaving the room.

I can't bear the thought of being trapped in a lift so I take the stairs to my mother's floor. Each step is agony. My poor body aching with delayed onset muscle soreness from fighting Connor and dragging his body into the water. I make it to her door, knock and wait. But she doesn't answer and neither does Gabriel. I knock again and wait a bit longer but there is still no answer and I feel like crying. I need my mother.

Instead, I make my way to the beach bar. Maybe she's there. I hope the bartender from last night isn't.

I'm so relieved to see my mother and Gabriel already seated when I arrive. They're drinking coffees and Gabriel is pouring over one of the free newspapers. I know I'm not welcome but right now I don't care. I need to tell my mother about last night. Not the killing but what happened to me. I need her to hold me in her arms and stroke my hair and plant little kisses on my head until it doesn't feel like the absolute end of the world anymore. She frowns at me when I approach their table. I can't see her eyes though as they're hidden behind a pair of oversized sunglasses.

'Kitty,' she says. 'I hope you've decided to take my advice. Have you booked a flight home?'

I shake my head.

It hurts.

I say, 'No. Can I talk to you please?'

She sighs and slips her glasses down onto her nose, peering at me over the top of them. 'Oh my God, Kitty, what happened to your face?'

'That's what I want to talk to you about,' I say sliding into one of the seats. 'Something happened. Last night.'

Gabriel looks up at me at this point and I can tell from the horror that flashes across his face that I look every bit as bad as I feared. He folds up his paper and stands. 'I'll give you both a minute.'

My mother tilts her head at me as I slide into the chair Gabriel just left.

'I'm listening,' she says.

But before I get a chance to say anything, an older woman dressed in designer gym wear bustles over to us. Her frantic energy makes me uncomfortable.

'Can you help me?' she asks. 'Please, I need help.'

'We're just—' my mother starts to say but Delululemon doesn't seem to hear her and carries on talking.

'I need help looking for someone,' she continues. 'It's my son. He didn't come back last night. His room hasn't been slept in. We're supposed to be going on an excursion this morning but he didn't turn up. It's not like him. I'm so worried. Something must've happened.'

There's a sinking feeling in the depths of my guts.

'He was staying here with me and his dad, like he does every year.' She thrusts a mobile phone under our noses. 'This is him.' She's showing us a photo. It's him. It's Connor. Everything in front of my eyes swims.

My mother looks at the woman, then at my face, then back to the woman.

'I'm sorry but I'm just talking with my daughter,' she says. 'Can I come and find you shortly?' She reaches out and touches her arm. 'I'm sure he's fine. He's probably drunk somewhere and hasn't realised the time.'

'No, not Connor. He doesn't drink,' the woman says. 'That's why I'm so worried.'

'I'll come and find you in a minute,' my mother says kindly. 'Please try not to worry.'

The woman lets out a sob, nods and shuffles back to a man who must be her husband.

My mother turns to me. 'What happened to your face, Kitty?'

I look around but there is no one in earshot. I'm trembling again. 'I was attacked,' I say. 'Last night. On the beach.' I drop my voice to a barely audible whisper. 'By *her* son.'

My mother sucks in a sharp breath. 'And where is he now?'

I can feel the tears filling up my eyes before I speak. 'In the sea,' I say.

She drops her head into her hands and stays like that for what feels like ages. Eventually she raises it and looks at me before saying, 'You need to go, Kitty. You need to go back to London. Today.'

It's not what I expected to hear and it's certainly not what I want to hear so I just stare at her. 'But. . . I. . . I need—'

'What you need Kitty is to go home. Now.'

'But—'

'No buts, you need to go. I'm sorry this happened to you, Kitty, I really am. And we will talk about it properly later. But please listen to me. Go upstairs, pack your things and get to the airport. Right now, you need to get out of France. Do you understand?'

'Okay,' I say quietly. 'If that's really what you want.'

'It is.' She stares at me for a couple of moments before standing up and walking over to the woman who doesn't know I killed her son last night.

I head back up to my hotel room, unable to stop the tears which are now streaming down my face. I'm not sure what I was expecting from Carmella. But it wasn't this. I needed my mother. I needed her to hold me and comfort me and make it right. But she couldn't. I disgust her so much that she couldn't.

Back in the room, I start throwing my clothes into my suitcase. I have to take a short break to be sick. Then I go back and stare at the clothes Charlie has left behind in the wardrobe. What do I do with these? Is he still planning to come back for them or should I take them back to London with me? I suppose the real question is why do I even care?

He's supposed to love me but he's abandoned me. He left me here alone to be attacked. He hasn't returned a single one of my calls or messages. That's not love.

I'm numb as I continue stuffing my clothes into the suitcase. I decide to leave Charlie's where they are.

Fuck him.

And then I sit on the bed and cry and cry some more. Everything is ruined. I knew I should never have come here. Now Charlie has left me. My mother hates me. I've got nothing to go home to as Tor hates me as well. The thought of Tor makes me feel even worse and I curl up into a ball on the bed and cry some more.

I must have cried myself to sleep because the next thing I know, I'm being jolted awake by my phone beeping, telling me I've got a message. I pull myself up and reach for my phone. I can't believe it.

It's a message from Charlie.

Finally.

My heart thumps wildly as I open the message with shaking fingers.

Kitty. I am so so sorry. I can explain everything. I promise. Please come and meet me so we can talk and I'll tell you everything. Don't hate me. I love you so much.

He drops a pin which shows he's still in the South of France, not far from Nice airport. What does this mean? I thought he was in Calais. What the hell is going on?

I get up and grab my suitcase before heading down to reception.

'Madame, someone would have helped you with that!' the perky French girl tells me. 'You are checking out early?'

'Something's come up at home,' I tell her.

'I am sorry to hear. I hope it is nothing too serious and I hope your stay here was enjoyable.'

'It was lovely, thank you.'

She offers to call me a cab to the airport and I say yes please, but that I need to make a stop on the way.

Twenty minutes later, I'm in an air-conditioned taxi heading towards the address on Charlie's pin drop. Anxiety is racing around my veins with all the stress hormones that will no doubt make my skin break out in the coming days. I don't know what I'm going to say to him. There's very little he can say to me that will make this any better. Even if it turns out he hasn't been with Jenna all this time, there's no excuse for leaving me. There's no excuse for not replying to me or returning my calls. There just isn't. Whatever it is, I would've listened, I would've understood three days ago.

But not now.

It's too late.

I just want to get this over with and go home where I plan to hide in my flat and drink obscene amounts of wine.

'*Nous sommes arrivés*,' the driver says and I realise we've stopped. We've pulled into a driveway of what looks like a very normal residential address. I don't know what I was expecting, but it wasn't something so ordinary. How can I be about to detonate my life in a very average bricks-and-mortar house? '*Ici?*' the driver asks. I check the pin and, yes, this is it.

'*Ici.*' I nod, taking my handbag and asking him to wait for me.

'*Oui, madame,*' he says as if it's nothing and as if my heart isn't actually in my throat. My mind races like that time Maisie and I took her sister's ADHD drugs. Why on earth is Charlie here? What's going on? Has he been in an accident? Did he run the car off the road and has been lying in a ditch for the past three days? Has he lost his memory and is currently living with a woman who has convinced him she's his wife? Probably not that last one but if I've learned anything in my lifetime it's that absolutely anything is possible. Seriously.

I get out of the taxi and spot Charlie's hire car in the driveway. The one I waved him off in just a few days ago. It's all in one piece. There isn't a single mark or bump on it, so that rules the road traffic accident out. Has he been here the whole time?

I stand outside the house for a moment, not really knowing what to do next. I suppose, not really wanting to know what's coming next. What if I find him with someone else? What would I do? Would I hurt him? Would I hurt whoever he's with? Am I capable of that? I don't know why I'm asking myself this. Of course I am.

I almost turn and walk away, but I can't quite bring myself to do it. It's like when you're scrolling through the socials of someone you've been seeing for clues as to why they've gone cold on you. You know that whatever you find isn't going to be good, that it's going to hurt like hell, but you can't stop yourself from doing it anyway. And then I'm walking up the steps that lead to the front door, knowing that whatever lies behind it is going to change my life forever.

There's a doorbell and, as I press it, dreading what I'm going to find. But, after a couple of excruciating moments, the door opens.

'Kitty! You're here! We've been waiting.'

It's Ben.

Ben Pemberton.

I don't understand what's going on. Why is Ben Pemberton answering the door at the address Charlie told me to come to so he could explain why he's been totally AWOL for the last few days.

'Ben?' I say. 'Is Charlie here?'

He's smiling at me and I wonder if he's taken something. That would be very on brand for Ben. 'Yes! He's right inside. Honestly, so glad you're here. Now the party can really get started.'

'Party?' I say, following him inside. What the fuck? Has Charlie been here getting off his face while I've been going out of my mind just a few miles down the road? That doesn't sound right. But it's not impossible. Charlie doesn't touch drugs now but once an addict, always an addict, right? I should know that more than anyone. Has he fallen off the wagon too? 'What's going on, Ben?' I say, hearing the frantic tone in my voice. 'Where's Charlie?'

He laughs. 'You want some Charlie? Well, fret not, young lady. There is plenty of that around. Like I said, it's a party! Come on, put your bag down and come through. Come and have a drink. We've all been waiting for you.'

'No, Ben, I don't want any coke. I mean *my* Charlie. Charlie Chambers.'

'Yes, yes, he's here, follow me.'

He's here. Charlie's here. I feel such astonishing relief and follow Ben into the house and along a cool corridor.

'So what? You guys have been here partying for days?'

'Something like that,' Ben says. 'Come on, everyone's through here.'

I can't believe it. I can't believe that Charlie would do this to me. I know he's an addict and addictions are complicated. But seriously? To go on a huge fucking bender with someone he's always hated, acting as if I don't exist?

I'll wring his fucking neck.

Ben ushers me through to what I assume is the lounge and there he is. There's my boyfriend.

At a table.

Face down in a pile of white powder.

40

'Charlie!' I shout and race over to him, but he doesn't respond. 'Charlie,' I say, more softly this time, but he still doesn't so much as stir, let alone lift his head up. He's completely out cold. 'Oh my God,' I say and then louder. 'Oh my God, Ben, do something, call an ambulance. Do something.'

But Ben just laughs. 'Don't worry, Kits, he's fine. Just sleeping it off.'

I stare at him. 'Ben. He's out cold. He's face down in a pile of coke. It could be his heart. It could be anything. Please. Don't be a dick. Call an ambulance. I don't care whose coke this is, we'll sort that all later, please, we need to help him.'

Ben stops laughing and fixes me with a steely glare that I don't like. 'It's not his heart.'

'Oh, I'm sorry, I completely forgot about you being a fucking doctor. You do such a good job of being a layabout sponging off your dead dad's money. Stop being a prick and call a fucking ambulance, Ben.'

'It's not his heart because he hasn't taken any cocaine,' Ben says simply.

'Then why the fuck is he out cold?'

'It's just the sleeping pills I gave him. Like I said, he'll be fine in a few hours.'

'Why the fuck have you given Charlie sleeping pills?' And then I see it. Around Charlie's ankles is a rope attaching him to the chair. I look at his wrists which are behind his back and I see they're bound together with cable ties.

What. The. Fuck?

Just at that moment, Ben's sister Antoinette comes into the room, holding a tray of drinks.

'Would you like a wine, Kitty?' she says, sweetly. 'It's a rather nice Riesling. We chilled it especially for you.'

As if I would drink a fucking thing in this house. The tap water is probably spiked.

'I need my phone,' I say as I move away from Charlie and towards the door. I dropped my bag in the hallway and my phone is in it. But as I get to the door, Ben pushes me back.

'Sorry, that won't be happening, I'm afraid,' he says. 'Really, you should have a drink. I promise you it's perfectly safe.' He picks a glass off the tray and downs it in one. 'See?'

'I don't want a drink,' I say. 'Move out of the way and let me get my bag.'

'Please have a drink, Kitty,' Antoinette says.

I turn to her. 'I *just* said that I don't want a fucking drink.' I reach out and flip the tray out of her hands. She watches on, startled, as the remaining glasses smash on the tiled floor, their contents spilling into the cracks.

'Oh dear,' says Ben as he looks at the mess too. 'That's a shame.'

I turn to him now. 'What the fuck?'

'We're going to have to do this the hard way.'

I don't see it coming, whatever he hits me with, I just feel it. Searing pain like I've never known, my head feeling like it will explode.

And then.

Darkness.

And a split second where I wish I'd taken a fucking drink.

41

When I come round, the first thing I notice is the blinding headache. And then I realise that I can't move. At first I'm terrified that the blow to the head has left me paralysed. That would be ironic, wouldn't it? After what I did to Adam. But then I see that I've been tied to a chair. It's been positioned so that I'm facing Charlie, who is also awake now. We're alone in the room.

'Hi,' he says and tries for a smile. 'You're awake. Are you hurt?' His voice is croaky and I take a proper look at him. He looks pale, his skin has a greasy sheen over it. He looks like shit to be honest but that face, that lovely, lovely face, is still a sight for my sore eyes.

I want to reach out and touch him but the ties around my wrists won't give a millimetre, let alone an inch.

'What's going on?' I say. 'Why are you here and not in Calais? Did Ben do this?' I'm so woozy and confused and the pounding in my head is not helping.

Charlie's head dips down. 'There wasn't an emergency,' he tells his shoes. 'It was a setup.'

'What do you mean?' My mouth is so dry. I need some water. And some headache pills. And some fucking answers.

Charlie nods towards the door. 'It was them. They set me up. It was Antoinette who messaged me, pretending to be Jenna. They waved me down just up the road from the hotel. I pulled over, they said they were here for the wedding and . . . the next thing I know, I'm here. Tied up. Mostly unconscious, fortunately.'

'But . . . *why*?'

Charlie shrugs sluggishly. 'No idea. None. It's good to see you though. I missed you. How did you know I was here?'

The sound of the door opening makes us stop talking. Ben walks in, followed by Antoinette.

'Sorry to break up this little reunion,' Ben says. 'But we're quite pushed for time now actually. I only have this place till the morning and I reckon there's going to be quite a lot of cleaning up to do.' He turns to face me. 'Have you worked out what's going on yet, Kitty Collins? Go on, you're a clever girl, what's your best guess?'

'My best guess is that you're a fucking psychopath,' I say but I don't think it comes out with the amount of venom that I'm feeling. My head feels thick and foggy. I'm pretty sure it's a concussion.

Ben chuckles. 'I guess it really does take one to know one.'

'Stop fucking around,' I say. 'Tell me why we're here.'

'I will but first I want to show you something.' He turns to his sister. 'Antoinette, get me the bag.'

She disappears out of the room and returns a moment later with a leather backpack.

'I've got some stuff in here that I think you'll be interested in, Kitty. Look.' First of all he pulls out a black bandana which he ties around his face, across his nose, just under his eyes. The next thing he takes from the bag is a pair of sunglasses and then a black baseball cap. He puts them on and the transformation is complete.

'You,' I say. 'You're Blaze Bundy.'

Ben laughs again and reaches back into the bag. This time he pulls out a small black box that looks like a voice recorder. He presses some buttons on it and holds it to his mouth. And then that voice is echoing around the room. That horrible distorted voice that has haunted me.

'But of course,' it says. 'Isn't that a lovely surprise?'

'You're fucking insane,' I shout and frantically try to free myself but it's no use. 'I'm going to fucking kill you,' I scream at Ben.

'Shh now, we'll get to all the killing soon, Kitty. Don't worry about that. But first, I've got something else to show you.' His hands disappear back inside the bag and this time they come out holding an iPad. 'Do you know what this is?'

I don't say anything.

'Come on, Kitty, humour me. I've gone to a lot of effort for you.'

'It's an iPad,' I say. 'And you're a moron.'

'You're funny,' he says without laughing. 'Yes, it is an iPad. But do you know who it belongs to? Or *belonged* to, I should say?'

'No, Ben. How would I know that?'

'Okay, well. I'll start at the beginning then. The beginning being when our sister vanished without a trace.'

Oh.

This is not good. This really isn't good.

'So, obviously both Antoinette and myself have been tearing our hair out about where Hen has vanished to,' he says. 'Yeah, she posted that thing about taking some time out to find herself. But it just didn't ring true for us, did it, Nettie?'

Antoinette shakes her head. 'She missed her thirtieth birthday,' she says, her eyes boring into me. 'There's no way Hen would've missed a chance to have an entire day dedicated to her.'

I fucking knew someone would pick up on that. Why didn't I take her phone when I had the chance? Why? Why? Why?

'I mean, you know Hen better than anyone, Kitty,' Ben is saying. 'Could you really see her going off-grid and living in a commune or something?'

'Grief does strange things to people,' I say.

'Not that strange. Not "give up my weekly facials, beautiful home and lavish lifestyle" strange. Like, really, the thought of Hen running off into the sunset and not taking her extensive footwear collection with her? No. Absolutely not. But we really didn't know what could've happened to her. We didn't have any leads, did we, Nettie?'

Antoinette shakes her head again.

'And our poor mum, out of her mind with grief over our dad, wasn't taking Hen's disappearance very well at all. So you can only imagine my delight when, while going through Hen's place to see if we could find any clue to where she'd got to, Antoinette came across something very interesting. What did you find, Nettie?'

'Hen's iPad,' Antoinette says. She looks at me and gives me a saccharine sweet smile.

'And, rather helpfully I must say, that iPad was still synced to her phone. You know how Hen's phone was basically a part of her anatomy, right, Kitty? Can you guess what we found on there?'

I don't say anything, even though I know full well what he would've found on there. I want to kick myself for not thinking of going to Hen's place to look for something like this. Hen, my lifelong friend, put spyware on my phone because she was a twisted stalker who wanted to freak me out. But she found out a lot more about me than she'd bargained for. My taste for blood. The blood of men who'd hurt women and gotten away with it. And she used her knowledge to blackmail me into killing her dad who she hated. Of course she wasn't going to have all that dirt on me and not have it backed up somewhere. So now Ben and Antoinette know everything too. How could I have been so stupid?

'Come on, Kitty,' Ben says, interrupting my thoughts. 'I'm sure your boyfriend here would love to know what you've been up to behind his back. Wouldn't you, Charlie? I'll give you a hint. There's been other men. A *lot* of other men.'

Ugh. The dickhead.

I glare at him.

'Not like that Charlie, don't listen to him.' I look over at him. He's just sitting there, staring at me. I can't work out what the look in his eyes means. Some mixture of hurt and betrayal. 'He's winding you up. I haven't cheated on you. I promise you, Charlie. I love you.' I swallow down the guilt I feel about what almost happened with Connor.

'That's sweet,' says Ben. 'So why don't you tell Charlie-boy what you've really been up to then? I'm sure you don't want to keep him in suspense. To be honest, Charlie, when you've heard what she's done you'll wish she *had* cheated on you. Come on, Kitty, we're all waiting.'

I still don't say anything.

'Okay, I guess I'm going to have to tell him myself. We need to check out of here tomorrow so I really need to start speeding things along.' He takes a sip from the water bottle next to him. 'She kills people. Men. I've lost track of the number but I'm pretty sure she's into double figures. Is that right, Kitty? She kills them and she gets rid of their bodies in her abattoirs, Charlie. What do you think about that?'

I look at Charlie again just in time to see the colour drain out of his face.

'Charlie. I can explain it all,' I say.

'Is it true?'

'Yes, but it's not like he's making it sound! They were disgusting men. They hurt women. They deserved it!'

'And what about Ruben Reynolds?' Ben says and I *really* want to add him to my body count now. 'Did *he* deserve to die?'

A cold rush of shame swallows me.

'That was an accident,' I say.

Ben leans forward. 'Do you think that would be comforting to Ruben's family if they knew the truth?' he says. 'Because I'm not sure they'd really care that it was actually their *other* son that you intended to murder in cold blood.'

'It was an accident,' I tell Charlie. 'And I felt, *feel* absolutely awful about it. I had a complete breakdown remember?'

I try to stop myself crying as Ben reels off a list of the other men I've murdered.

'And, this is just a guess,' he adds with a flourish, 'but I'm willing to bet that I can add my dad and sister to the list too. Is that right, Kitty? Hen was onto you, wasn't she, so she had to go. Plus her phone's last location was an abattoir in Hampshire according to the Find My Phone app on her iPad. Kind of a giveaway. And my dad was just your type, wasn't he? You might as well confess and get it off your chest because, I'm sure you've worked out by now that you're not getting out of here alive. Either of you.'

'Your dad was a paedophile and a rapist. He deserved to die,' I say. 'And your *sister* was the one who outed him. Because she *wanted* me to kill him.' I see a flicker of pain flash across Ben's face. He clearly doesn't like hearing the truth about his psycho sister. It makes me feel good that I can hurt him even when I'm tied up and he's threatening to kill me. 'You didn't know that, did you?'

He ignores me and carries on with his soliloquy which I'm beginning to suspect he's practised. 'You know, I wasn't going to kill you, that wasn't my original plan. I just wanted to have a bit of fun with you before I handed everything over to the police.'

The police. I swallow hard. I will not let him see my fear.

'You see, we knew you wouldn't be able to ignore a man who *hates* women as much as he does. And I've really enjoyed being Blaze. It's addictive, isn't it, having all those followers hanging onto every word you say? I'm going to keep him going once I've got rid of you. The world needs Blaze Bundy, *men* need Blaze Bundy to educate them about women like you.' He pauses for breath. 'It was actually Antoinette here who came up with the plan to kill you.'

Antoinette smiles. 'It was the wedding invitation from your stupid, benzo-dazed mother that gave me the idea,' she says. 'So much easier and less messy to make you disappear in a different country. Especially now you've had your heart broken by Charlie here. Everyone knows how off the rails you go when your boyfriends upset you. Boo hoo.'

The little cow.

I can't say I'm not shocked. Antoinette has always been such a sweetheart to me. But I guess no one in that family escaped the psychopath gene.

'You don't need to kill Charlie,' I say. 'What's that going to achieve? You could just let him go. You won't say anything, will you, Charlie?'

Charlie doesn't answer though. I can see from the way his jaw is set that he's gritting his teeth, trying to keep himself calm.

'He'll wish he was dead anyway when the truth comes out about you,' Antoinette says. 'Can you imagine what his life will be like? He'd be the boyfriend of the world's most notorious female serial killer. The press will tear him apart. Everyone will wonder if he *knew*. If he was in on it. Trust me, we know exactly what it's like when the press and the public hate you for something someone close to you did.' She gives me a hard stare. The Pemberton family haven't had an easy time since James was outed as an abuser. I'd feel bad for them if they weren't all so absolutely batshit. 'He'd lose everything. He's better off dead.'

I look at Charlie again. I've never seen him so broken. Guilt wraps itself around my guts and squeezes until I can't breathe.

This is my fault.

I did this to him.

'Sorry, Charlie-boy,' Ben is saying now. 'It's nothing personal. You're just collateral damage.'

'I hope you've figured out what you're going to do with us afterwards,' I say to Ben. 'It's hard work, getting away with it. I know I make it look easy. People will notice we're missing. Both my phone and Charlie's can be traced to here. And you're the one who rented this place. I might have messed up with the iPad but I've had a lot more practice than you.'

Ben laughs. 'Ah, the irony of you trying to give me tips on killing. I like that, Kitty.'

'No one knows we're here,' Antoinette says. 'As far as anyone knows we're checked into The Carlton for your mother's wedding,' she says. 'I booked this place under the name of Ben's alter ego. Our phones are burners.'

This is insane. This is the same Ben Pemberton who struggled to get an erection while he and Tor were dating and here he is pulling off something like this. I mean, obviously with the help of his twisted little sidekick, but still. I'd applaud if my hands weren't cable-tied behind my back.

'I have to say, Ben, I'm a little bit impressed. I wouldn't have thought a limp dick like you would have it in you.' I know you're supposed to try to endear yourself to your captors if you ever find yourself in a situation like this, but I can't help it. He flinches, ever so slightly at my words and I feel that rush of power again. I'll never not be amazed at how fragile the male ego is. 'Women talk, Ben. We tell each other everything.'

'Fuck you,' he spits. 'You've always thought you were too good for me. You and those other little sluts you hang around with. Who knows, maybe after I've got rid of you and Charlie, I'll go after Tor and Maisie as well. Wipe out all you whores. I've got some really great tips from Hen's iPad.'

I laugh at him even though the thought of him hurting Tor or Maisie makes my blood boil. 'You're nothing but an incel, Ben. Yeah, you're probably richer than most basement dwellers, but that's what you are. A sad and bitter little man who can't cope with the fact that no woman wants to fuck him. No wonder you enjoyed being Blaze so much. It must've been a relief to be anyone apart from yourself.' I turn to Antoinette. 'I'd be careful if I were you, if he's anything like your father he'll be crawling into your bed at some point.' I see Antoinette grit her teeth. Then she gives Ben a look.

'Shut your mouth,' she says. 'We've heard enough from you.'

'I've got one final surprise in this bag,' Ben is saying. 'Do you want to do the honours, Nettie?' He holds the backpack out to his sister and she reaches both hands inside. When she pulls them back out, each one is wrapped around a shiny black handgun. She hands one to Ben.

'Surprise,' she says and smiles at me. They're both absolute fucking lunatics. Armed lunatics.

I glance over at Charlie who has gone completely white. I guess he's realised, as I have, that there is absolutely no way we're getting out of this. For once, I have no plan.

There's nothing I can do.

I'm not scared of dying, not really, I suppose I always suspected it would come to this. But Charlie doesn't deserve it. I was stupid to think that he wouldn't get hurt. Even if it's not at my hand, it's still my fault. The world is going to lose one of the good men.

'Shall we get this over with then?' Ben says to Antoinette. 'We need to get a move on as we'll need to clear this place up before we head back to Cannes for Carmella's wedding.' He gives me a sly smile.

Antoinette gives a quick nod and walks over to Charlie. I watch in horror as she presses the gun against his temple.

Then Ben comes over to me and presses his hard into my head. He's clearly compensating for his limp dick.

'Any last words, Kitty?'

'Fuck you, you disgusting fucking incel,' I say.

'Oh, well that's not very nice. Okay, Antoinette, like we talked about. On three.' He presses the gun harder into my temple. 'One, two . . .'

But he doesn't get to three.

42

'What the *fuck*, Antoinette?' Ben's on the floor, clutching his right shoulder which is now a mush of blood and shattered bone. I have to hand it to her, the girl's got good aim. I mean, assuming she was *aiming* for her brother, that is. If she was trying to hit Charlie, she's shit.

'Oh sorry, does that *hurt*?' Antoinette stalks over to where Ben is lying and picks up the gun he dropped when he fell. She uses it to prod him in the wound that's gushing with blood and Ben howls in pain. But Antoinette ignores him. She turns to me and I flinch. But, instead of shooting me, she puts both guns down on the floor.

'Sorry about that,' she says, reaching behind me and pulling at the cable ties on my wrists. 'I tried not to do them up too tightly but I had to make it look convincing.' I feel the ties give way and I pull my aching wrists into my lap. She takes my hand gently in her own and turns it over. 'I think you're okay.' Then she reaches down, picks the guns up again and hands one to me.

What in the sibling rivalry is going on?

There's another agonised moan from Ben.

'Are you going to *cry*?' Antoinette says, pointing her gun back at him. 'Go on Ben, have a little bawl, show Kitty exactly how pathetic you are.'

Ben is staring at Antoinette like she's just stamped on his hamster. 'What's going on, Nettie?' he whimpers. 'Why did you shoot me? Did you mean to?'

Antoinette rolls her eyes so dramatically I half expect her to lose her balance and fall over. 'Yes *Ben*, I meant to shoot you, for fuck's sake. Keep up. Or has your brain been totally rotted by spray tans and Taittinger?' She makes a face at me like *what is he like?*

'But why?' he grimaces. 'I don't understand.' Join the club, Benny-boy.

Antoinette, dripping with ennui, lowers herself down to Ben's level. 'Why don't you start by telling Kitty the real reason you hate her and want her dead.'

Ben squirms and tries to stem the blood coming from his shoulder with his other hand. 'I've already told her. She killed Hen.'

'Not *Ben's Version*,' Antoinette says. 'The *real* reason.'

'That is the real reason.' He looks at me, his eyes spitting venom, even through the pain he's clearly in. 'She was my sister.'

Antoinette lets out a short bark of laughter. 'You didn't even like Hen,' she says. 'You thought she was a slut and an imbecile. You told me enough times when she was alive.'

'That's not—'

'Stop.' Antoinette stands back up and waves her gun in Ben's face. 'I quote, "that girl, if she used what's between her ears instead of what's between her legs, she might be halfway bearable." Didn't you say that, Ben? Weren't they your exact words about your *sister*? You hate women. All women, just say it. Say what you are.'

Ben stays silent.

Antoinette gives a frustrated snort and turns to face me. 'Fine. I'll tell her. He doesn't like you because you *rejected* him, Kitty. That's the real reason. That's the driving force behind the whole Blaze Bundy thing. He's completely butthurt because you broke his little heart. Can you believe that?'

I cannot, actually.

When did I ever reject Ben Pemberton? I mean, obviously I *would* have if he'd ever tried anything. But I really can't remember anything.

'I can't. . . *when*?' I say.

Antoinette turns back to Ben. 'She doesn't even remember! You fucking loser. That's how unimportant you are to her. She doesn't remember the moment that made you into this pathetic excuse of a man.' She laughs again and I wonder if I should just shoot her. She's clearly unhinged. But I need to know exactly what's going on here, why she's turned on her brother. 'Tell her,' she's saying to Ben. 'Go on, or I'll shoot your other shoulder out of its socket.' She pushes the barrel of the gun against his left shoulder. That does the trick.

'Okay, okay. Just get that thing away from me.' He winces again as he tries to push himself into a sitting position using his destroyed arm. 'You were about thirteen, I was fifteen,' he says to me, there's no hint of his former bravado in his voice. He obviously hasn't practised this part. 'We were at one of Dad's launch parties.'

273

James Pemberton founded and ran a super successful record label before I strangled him with a Wolford stocking after discovering he'd been using his position to lure young women to hotels, promising glittering careers in the music industry, and raping them. His launch parties were notoriously epic. Huge events in hotels, bars, the homes of some of the famous people he worked with. No expense spared. As a thirteen-year-old whose own dad owned meat factories, it was impossibly glamorous.

'It was a launch party for a singer called Jodi J,' Ben continues.

'I remember Jodi J,' I say. 'She was that twenty-five-year-old your dad was trying to pass off as a teenager.' The party had been held at a now defunct club in Leicester Square. It was the first time I'd been in an actual nightclub and, even though I was only thirteen, no one treated me like a child. Hen, Tor, Maisie and I had a brilliant night and thought we were so grown up when no one asked us for ID when we went to the bar. In hindsight this should've been my first red flag when it came to James. But at the time, it felt incredible being treated like an adult, or how I thought adults were treated. It was the first time I got seriously drunk too. Hangover drunk. *Throwing up in the car home* drunk. I remember all of that, although hazy with both alcohol and time, but I don't remember Ben being there.

'I thought you were the prettiest of Hen's friends,' he's saying now, 'and the least annoying. I tried to kiss you that night, but you pushed me away, went back to my sister, laughing your head off.' He's looking at me with faintly concealed disdain. 'Even back then you thought you were too good for me.'

'She *is* too good for you.' Charlie. My darling Charlie. 'Even after everything you've told me, you're still not worthy of breathing the same air as her.' My heart surges with hope. Maybe this isn't the end for us if we can get out of here. Maybe he can still love me. Maybe we can even love each other more now he knows it all, now my skin has been peeled back and everything inside of me exposed. Maybe.

I look back at Ben, bleeding and pitiful at my feet. 'You did all of this because I laughed at you when I was *thirteen*? Am I getting this right?'

He juts his chin up, trying to look anything other than small. 'Don't flatter yourself, bitch. You just taught me at an early age what women are like.'

Antoinette prods his shoulder again with her gun. 'Don't lie to Kitty. Tell her about the songs you used to write about her.'

Oh God no, please not songs.

Ben isn't forthcoming so Antoinette carries on. 'He used to play these awful *laments* on his guitar. There were dozens of them. What was that really terrible one, Benny? What was it called? Oh yes, Kitty Party. *Oh Kitty, you're just so pretty, why'd you treat me so shitty, what a pity.*' She falls about laughing and I genuinely cannot work out which member of this family is the biggest fucking lunatic. 'I wish there was a guitar here,' she says. 'You could play Kitty her songs.' She looks at his fucked-up arm. 'Maybe not.' She turns back to me. 'He used to play them for James, really thought he'd sign him just because he's his son. Honestly, Kitty, it was fucking hilarious. You'd have *died*.'

I mean, she's right, there's zero chance I wouldn't have found *that* hilarious.

'Even James thought he was a laughing stock though. He was truly terrible. It's so lucky you can't actually *die* from second-hand embarrassment because I'd be a goner.' Antoinette pauses for a moment. 'Did you know that he only dated Tor to make you jealous?'

Urgh.

'But that backfired as well, didn't it, Benny? Because Kitty didn't care at all. And that just made you even more angry. Tell her.' Antoinette wiggles the gun. 'Go on, tell her.'

'I might have thought you were special, when I was younger, that's true,' Ben spits. 'But not anymore. You've hit the wall, Kitty.' He shoots Charlie a look. 'I'm surprised he can even bear to *look* at you now you're past your prime. The tables have turned since the days you looked down your nose at me. So yes, I wanted to make you suffer and that's how Blaze was born.'

Wow.

Just wow. He is so beyond delulu.

'But when I found Hen's iPad and discovered your little hobby, I wanted to hurt you even more. Killing men who hurt women?' He pauses his red-pill monologue to scoff, 'You don't even realise that it's women like you who are the problem. You think you're righting women's wrongs or some shit. That you're smashing the patriarchy. When there's no such thing. Women hold all the power. It's men who suffer. Men like me who are just the butt of jokes with you and your friends.'

'Do you actually believe that?' I say, looking at the feeble, broken body on the floor. At the arms created in gyms with the help of personal trainers and Huel. At the too-white, too-big teeth. At the designer clothes which are nothing but a costume to hide who Ben Pemberton really is, *what* he is. Just another victim of the patriarchy he doesn't believe in. Another white man who is furious that his life didn't deliver what it was supposed to and wants to blame women for it. A white man, one with huge amounts of privilege, who feels he's oppressed. A man who is so scared for his life that he's pissed himself.

I almost feel sorry for him.

Almost.

But not enough to stop me pointing the gun Antoinette gave me at his head and pulling the trigger. She might be a good shot. But I'm better.

43

Ben Pemberton's brain matter looks quite pretty spattered over the white marble flooring. Maybe Maisie's right. Maybe I should think about a career in interior design. I think I have an eye for it.

Antoinette is staring at her brother's busted head and I can't work out the look on her face. Fuck. She's only eighteen. I shouldn't have executed her brother in front of her. I, of all people, know how a trauma like that can fuck you up for the rest of your life. I've probably just given her PTSD and years of extensive therapy.

'Antoinette?' I say softly and she turns to look at me, like I've snapped her out of a trance.

'Oh my God, Kitty. That was amazing.' She's smiling like I've given her a box of puppies, not lifelong trauma. She drops down onto the floor next to Ben and what's left of his face. I blink, stunned, as she fumbles around at his throat for a pulse or any signs of life. 'He's totes dead.' She stands up again and comes over to me. I'm almost convinced she's going to shoot me now. But she doesn't. She pulls me in for a totally awkward hug.

278

What is happening?

'I don't understand,' I say, pulling myself out of her weird embrace. 'Why are you hugging me? I just killed your brother. And I killed your dad. And your sister.'

Antoinette drops back down to her knees and touches the pulse point on Ben's neck again. Then, satisfied that he really is *totes dead*, sits back on her haunches, looking up at me. 'Well. Ben tried to kill you first and Hen was a psycho,' she says. 'And so was James. Plus he wasn't even my real dad. . . so—' she shrugs.

'He wasn't?' I might sound surprised but I'm actually not. It's an incredibly badly kept secret that Antoinette's mother, Laurelle, was as into extramarital sex as her late husband was. Although I'm assuming hers were all consensual and didn't involve minors. She had an affair with my own father. My mind flashes back to a moment when, as a child, I caught the pair of them at it in our house. I was about twelve at the time. Eighteen years ago.

'No,' Antoinette is saying. 'Haven't worked it out yet?'

Eighteen years ago.

Fuck.

Fuck.

'Wait. Are you. . . Was my dad. . . ?'

Antoinette lets out a peal of delighted laughter. 'Yes!' she says nodding enthusiastically. 'I am the love child of Laurelle Pemberton and Michael Collins. Isn't that a hoot! I'm your sister! That and your biggest fan.'

My what now?

'All that stuff Ben was saying about you killing men, I am *so* here for it. Fuck men. Fuck all those men.' She turns to Charlie. 'No offence, Charlie. You seem like a good one.' She turns back to me. 'They deserved every fucking thing they got, Kitty. And I certainly include James Pemberton in that. And my brother. Imagine how growing up in a house with those two has affected me. You're a hero!'

I stare at Antoinette and, yes, I think I can see it. The family resemblance. Her face is much more delicate than either Hen or Ben's. Well, it certainly is now Ben's is mostly smeared across the floor.

'How did you find out?' I know there are some more pressing matters like cleaning up the murder scene and working out what the hell I'm going to do with Ben's body. Oh. And there's probably an awkward conversation I'm going to need to have with Charlie too. But I'm transfixed. How often does someone find out they have a sister? One that has been living right under their nose. My head feels like it might explode. I have so many questions.

'Laurelle told me,' she says. 'Not long after James, you know—' She mimes wrapping some sort of cord around her neck and yanking it. 'I was crying and she was drunk. She shouted at me that I had nothing to be sad about. That he was a predator and not even my real dad anyway.' She chews her lip for a moment. 'I always wondered why I didn't have a stupid rhyming name like those two.'

I'd be lying if I said it hadn't crossed my mind as well.

'Anyway,' she continues, 'I asked her about it when she'd sobered up the next day. She tried to deny it at first, of course. Poor Mummy, imagine *that* coming out as well as everything about James. But eventually she confessed to having an affair with *your* dad. And that's how I came to be.' She does a little jazz hands gesture. 'James didn't know, of course.' She gives a little shudder. 'I think even Mummy was smart enough to not let on that a girl he wasn't related to was right there under his nose.'

'I'm sorry,' I say. 'That must've been a massive shock.' I mean, I'm pretty fucking shocked. A sister.

But Antoinette is shaking her head. 'You'd think so, wouldn't you. But I was absolutely delighted. Honestly, I'd so much rather be Kitty Collins' sister than Hen's. She was the worst and I've always adored you. Even before I knew about your murdery side hustle. So no, I was absolutely thrilled. Best day of my life.'

I think back to all the interactions I've had with Antoinette over the years. I remember eleven-year-old Hen wailing to me about how her mum's new baby was going to be a girl. *It's not fair*, she'd whined. *I don't want another girl. I'm the princess. I'm the special one.* Hen had pretty much resented Antoinette since she was born and made no attempts to hide this. I remember toddler Antoinette trying to play with us when we were about thirteen but Hen was absolutely not interested. To be honest, I felt pretty much the same. We were teenage girls. We were discovering boys and other things we were much too young for in hindsight. We definitely didn't want a crying baby hanging out with us. Sometimes Hen was instructed to babysit while her parents went out but, even then, she didn't pay Antoinette any attention. I remember her crying one night when she should've been asleep. *Shouldn't you at least check on her?* I'd asked Hen who just shrugged her shoulders, her way of saying she couldn't care less. But when Hen snuck off to meet some boy or other in her garden, I'd crept into Antoinette's room and had read her a story. I'd completely forgotten about that.

I look up at Antoinette now. She claps her hands together and does an excited little squeal. 'I've been absolutely dying to tell you, but Mummy said not to. She said to wait a while until everything died down. But then Ben came to me with Hen's fucking iPad and told me what you'd done and how he was planning on killing you. I wasn't going to let that happen, obvs, so I came up with my own plan, to double-cross him and save you! I let Ben think I was on his side. That I'd help him kill you. But really, I was planning on killing him the whole time. He had to go. The mad incel.' She gives me a big smile. 'And ta-da.' Jazz hands again.

Ta-fucking-da, indeed. I don't know if I'm in awe of her or terrified. I don't have time to make a full assessment just yet though as Charlie coughs from where he's still sitting.

'Sorry to interrupt,' he says. 'But is there any chance someone could untie me? It's been three days and I'm really starting to feel it.'

'Oh God, Charlie,' Antoinette says and hurries over to him. She unties his restraints. 'I'm so sorry. We were having a bit of a *Long Lost Family* moment there.'

'I noticed,' he says gruffly, rubbing the corners of his wrists. 'God, that feels good.'

'Are you okay?' I'm next to him now too and reaching out to touch his face but he flinches away from me.

It's like I literally feel my heart crumble.

'I've been better, Kits, I have to say.' He doesn't meet my eye.

What have I done?

Antoinette looks at each of us in turn. 'Why don't you two go through to the kitchen while I make a start on clearing this mess up,' she says looking at Ben's corpse again and pulling a face. 'There's probably quite a lot you need to talk about.'

'Yes. There is.' I turn back to Antoinette. 'You should get some bleach and some bicarb of soda on the bloodstains as soon as possible, by the way. Or they'll be murder to get rid of completely.'

She smiles and gives me a soldier salute.

Christ. She's *enjoying* this.

Charlie and I walk through to the kitchen and the first thing I do is find two glasses in a cupboard and pour us both some water. I gulp mine down, pour another and do the same thing. Concussions certainly dehydrate you.

'Have some water,' I say to Charlie but he just stares at the glass so I put it down on the large marble island in the centre of the room.

'Well, that was a surprise,' I say, pulling out one of the chairs around the island and sitting.

'It really fucking was,' Charlie mutters. His voice sounds croaky.

'Drink it,' I say, gently nudging the water towards him. 'You must be really thirsty.'

He looks at me. 'I don't think I can,' he says. 'I don't think I'd be able to keep it down.'

'Are you feeling sick? Is it the drugs Ben gave you?'

'I am feeling sick,' he says slowly, 'but I think it's more to do with the fact that the woman I've been living with has just confessed to being a serial killer.'

Ah.

Okay, no small talk then.

'I'm glad you're okay,' I say. 'I wish I'd known where you were. I'd have come to find you much sooner.'

He pulls out a chair opposite me and slides into it. 'Where the hell did you think I was?' His voice is still quiet but I can tell he's angry. Confused and angry. I don't know how I can make this better.

'In Calais,' I say. 'You told me you were going to Calais. So that's where I thought you were. But then you didn't call or reply to any of my texts and I thought—'

'What did you think?' He's shaking his head slightly, like he can't bear to hear anything I say. 'When your boyfriend didn't contact you for three days, what did you think?'

'I thought you were with Jenna.' Shame engulfs me.

He lets out a huge sigh. 'You thought I was cheating on you? You really thought that of me?' He looks so very hurt and confused.

'I'm sorry. I just didn't know what to think. You told me you were going to Calais to sort out a problem and then you just went totally off-grid. I was calling and calling and nothing. I even tried calling Jenna but she wouldn't answer me. I'm sorry.'

'I just can't believe you'd think that.' He sounds tired. Tired of me.

'I'm sorry I didn't suspect you'd been kidnapped by a sociopath, hell-bent on revenge,' I say quietly. 'It didn't seem like the obvious explanation.'

Charlie lifts his chin and looks up at the ceiling, blowing out air, like he's just really done with my shit. 'But don't you see that if you didn't just jump to thinking I was cheating on you, then maybe you'd have realised something was wrong?'

He looks at me again and there's a bit of the Charlie I know and love there this time. 'I'd never cheat on you, Kits. We've spoken about this in depth. I thought we were past that. But it was still the first place your mind went to.'

'I'm sorry,' I mumble but he shakes his head.

'Don't. I'm not trying to guilt-trip you, I'm really not. I'm just trying to understand why you thought I was off fucking around when I've promised you I'd never do that. I thought you trusted me.'

'I do—'

'Please, Kits, let me finish.'

I shut my mouth.

'And then I hear all that *really* fucked-up stuff from fucking *Ben* about everything you've done. I can't even begin to start getting my head around that. I just . . . do I even know you?' He pauses, rubs his face.

I can feel the tears on my cheeks but I don't even bother trying to wipe them away. 'Of course you know me, Charlie, everything you know about me is true. I'm not perfect. I spend too much time on social media. I probably drink too much wine with my friends. I don't want a puppy because it would ruin my walls. But I'm kind and I'm caring and when I let someone into my heart, they are there forever. I'm loyal and passionate and I love so fucking hard. All the good things about me, all the things you fell in love with, they're all true. I didn't kill a single one of those men for myself. I did it because the world is better off without them. I didn't *enjoy* it.' The last bit is not strictly true, but I don't think he needs to know that.

'That's not your decision to make, Kitty!' Charlie is usually so amiable that I can count on two fingers the number of times before now that I've seen him so furious. And neither of those times was at me. I don't like it. 'You cannot just appoint yourself to be some sort of avenging angel. We live in a civilised country, Kits. We have a justice system—'

'Which doesn't fucking work! Or hands out the most laughably lenient sentences to these men, while the women they hurt have a life sentence! And they won't stop. Just look at James Pemberton. He was prolific.' I'm on a roll now. 'Can you seriously tell me that the world is not a better place without him stealing fucking oxygen from it? That women and girls aren't that tiny bit safer?'

'That isn't the point!' He rolls his shoulders like they are hurting him and I want, more than anything, to go to him and rub them, to stop his pain. But how can I? When, right now, I'm the root of that pain. 'You can't just go around being this vigilante, no matter how much good you think you're doing. Do you not think that I've wanted to throttle people?'

'Like who?'

'Like the people traffickers who prey on the kids at the refugee camps, the gangs that extort them and risk their lives, the fucking people in charge of our world who put innocent people in these situations in the first place.' He tilts his head and holds my eyes. 'Your ex.'

'You've thought about killing *Adam*?' I ask.

'Yes. Because he hurt you. He made you distrustful. *And he* is why we ended up here.'

Neither of us says anything for a moment.

'So you understand?' Okay. Maybe this isn't as bad as I thought it was.

'Yes. Of course I understand.'

Yay.

'But that doesn't mean I can condone it, Kits.'

Oh.

'I may *think* these things but I'd never actually *do* them. Everything I do, everything I believe in, is about preserving life and seeking justice, real justice, seeing those fuckers properly punished.'

'The justice system doesn't work!'

'But that's not your responsibility. It doesn't mean you can just go out and take things into your own hands. Jesus Christ, what if everyone did that?'

The world would probably be much less fucked up. I don't say this to Charlie, of course.

He sighs again. 'Was I in danger when you thought I was off somewhere with Jenna? Did you think about killing me?'

'No!' I say. 'Of course not. I'd never hurt you, Charlie.'

'But you have,' he says. 'I've spent the last three days thinking I was going to die. And I didn't know why. But it was because of you. Your actions, Kitty. You might not have hurt me directly but just being involved with you nearly cost me my life.'

'I'm sorry,' I whisper. 'I didn't mean for this to happen. I love you.'

He doesn't say it back, just looks at me sadly. 'I don't know who you are.'

We sit in silence again, the air heavy between us and my heart breaking so violently that I'm surprised we can't hear it.

'I'm going to go back to London,' Charlie says eventually. 'And I'm going to move my stuff out of the apartment. This is over. You know that right?'

A fat tear rolls down my face. I don't bother wiping it away.

'Please don't leave me,' I say. 'I need you. I need you to keep me good.'

'Good?' He doesn't quite laugh in disbelief but he may as well have. 'How can you say that when you've killed at least three people since we've been together. Are there any more?'

I nod, feebly. What's the point in lying now? 'Two,' I say.

He drops his head into his hands.

'But one of them was assaulting work experience girls and the other. . . the other. . .' My voice breaks. How do I even begin to tell him about Connor?

Charlie doesn't say anything, he just rubs his hands over his three-day stubble. He looks beyond exhausted. There's no sign of that dimple I love so much.

'When I thought you were with Jenna, I was angry,' I say, feeling the force of the tears that are building up in my eyes. I look up to the ceiling in a bid to keep them where they are. 'I thought about what my friends would tell me to do and I thought I'd feel better if I went out and found someone else too.'

Charlie lets out a sharp puff of breath. It pierces my chest. 'You went on the pull?' I don't recognise his voice. Its edges are jagged glass. There's no warmth in it at all. It cuts through my skin and all my shame pours out.

'I'm sorry.' I don't recognise my voice either. It's a whisper, a ghost. 'But I couldn't go through with it. When his hands were on me, I couldn't. . .' I hold Charlie's eyes and see them wince when I talk about another man's hands on me. 'He wasn't you,' I say. 'And I don't want anyone who isn't you. He felt wrong and I hated myself at that moment.'

I don't know if I'm imagining it but Charlie's face seems to soften. 'Okay,' he says. 'So how did you go from deciding you didn't want this guy to killing him?'

'He wouldn't stop!' The words come out of me like angry insects I've been holding in my mouth since last night. 'I told him to stop, but he wouldn't.' There's no point in trying to hold back the tears now. I give them permission, myself permission, to give in.

Charlie's face is a blur now but he's moving towards me and his arm is around my trembling shoulders. He pulls me into his chest and I bury my face in his T-shirt. I can smell the terror of the last few days on him, but underneath that, I can smell him. 'Did he. . .' He swallows hard. 'Did he rape you?'

I shake my head against his body. 'It didn't get that far.' I pull back and look at Charlie's face. 'But he would have.'

He nods. 'So it was self-defence.'

It was. It really was. I hadn't thought about it like that before. I just thought it was another man I'd killed. Same old Kitty. But it was nothing like the other kills at all. Through all of this, I've killed for other people, other *women*. I've never had to kill for myself.

Charlie pulls me to his chest again. 'I'm sorry that happened to you,' he says into my hair. 'I'm so so sorry.'

'I'm sorry too,' I say, breathing him in. 'I'm so so sorry.'

I let him hold me for a few minutes, knowing that this will be the last time we're this close. Because he's right. I might not have hurt him directly, but what happened to him was because of me. And he deserves better. He deserves someone like the woman I tried and failed to be. Someone good.

'I'm going to leave now,' he says eventually and my heart is ground zero. Every single cell, every atom in my body is screaming out. To beg him to stay. To say that I'll stop, that he's safe, that it's over, properly over. But I can't. So I nod. And I wipe my face. And I let myself melt as he kisses me, knowing that this is the last time. That I'm letting him go to keep him safe.

Because there is a monster in me.

'I do love you, Kitty Collins.' He strokes the side of my face.

'And I love you, Charlie Chambers,' I say and I stick my finger into the dimple in his cheek.

I don't try to stop him when he walks out of the door. I don't watch him go because I know he won't turn back around to look at me. And because I don't want him to. He's right. We can't be together. I take lives while he tries to save them. He says he loves me but how true can that be when I've only ever showed him part of who I truly am. Charlie isn't the type of man who can love my demons and I don't want him to be. Loving me, all of me, would mean changing *him*. And no one should try to change the person they claim to love. So, instead I fall to the floor and when I hear the front door close, I cry and cry. I keep crying and I don't know how long this goes on for but the next thing I know Antoinette is coming in and putting a hand on my shoulder. I want to push it off because I don't want her, I want Charlie and it's partly her fault he's not here. But I don't move. I'm too exhausted. And there's still a fucking dead body that needs to be dealt with.

Antoinette shakes me gently. 'I think you need to come back through. There's been an unexpected development.'

44

What the fuck now?

I follow Antoinette back through to the lounge to find my mother and Gabriel looking at the bloodbath on the floor. Although it's nowhere near as bad as it was, so I have to give Antoinette her dues, she's not bad at cleaning up a crime scene.

'What are you doing here?' I say. 'How are you even here?'

'Is that . . .' My mother tilts her head and squints her eyes to look at the corpse. 'Is that *Ben* Pemberton?'

'Yes. It is,' I say, impressed she could tell with half his face missing. 'But you didn't answer my question. What are you doing here?'

'I always thought he was a bit of a dickhead,' she says.

'Why the hell did you invite him to your *wedding* then?' I ask.

She shrugs. 'I thought he was your friend, darling. Clearly I stand corrected. Anyway, we picked up your bags from that taxi that was waiting and sent it away. The driver was half asleep actually.'

'Right. Well thanks. Now would you mind telling me what the fuck you're doing here, please?'

'There's no need to be snippy, Kitty,' my mother says. 'I'm actually here to apologise. And ask you to please come to the wedding.'

I'd completely forgotten that my last exchange with my mother consisted of her sending me packing after I told her I'd been violently attacked. I stare at her.

'I've got quite a lot going on at the moment,' I say.

'Kitty,' my mother says, 'can we talk in private please?'

I want to say no. I really do. But I swallow the words down because, really, I want my mum. I really want my mum.

'Okay,' I say. 'Let's go through to the kitchen.' It seems like I may as well go and have another difficult conversation in there. I walk back through and my mother follows, leaving Antoinette and Gabriel alone to make awkward small talk. I sit at the island in the same chair Charlie sat in earlier. My mother takes the seat opposite.

'I'm sorry,' she says. 'I am really, really truly sorry, Kitty.'

I don't say anything. I wait.

'You needed me and I didn't handle it very well. And I cannot tell you enough how sorry I am,' she continues. 'I told Gabriel what happened and he insisted that we go to the airport and stop you.'

'But I'm not at the airport,' I say. And then I remember the necklace. I touch the tiny pendant at my throat. 'You tracked me here?'

'Yes, because I needed to say sorry and I needed to tell you that I do want you at the wedding. I want you there more than anything.'

I'm confused. 'But why would you want that when I disgust you so much that when I told you I was attacked, you told me to leave? That you didn't want me at your wedding. That you didn't want me in the country at all!'

'No,' my mother says. 'That isn't what happened. You told me you were attacked. *Then* you told me that you'd killed your attacker. Who happened to be staying in our hotel. I wanted to get you out of the country. To keep you safe!'

Oh.

Well, I suppose that would make sense too.

'I couldn't let you just go off like that. Not when you were in pain. Not when I should've been helping you.' She sighs and reaches across the island for my hands. I let her take them. 'At the moment, that man is still missing. And until he shows up, there's no real reason anyone would think he's dead and not just on a bender. And even if his body turns up, why would anyone think it had anything to do with you? You were with me all night.'

'But—' I'm going to ask her about the CCTV and the bartender who saw us together.

'You were with us. All night.'

Of course. Gabriel owns the hotel.

We sit in silence for a little while.

Finally Carmella says, 'Do you want to tell me what happened? Last night, I mean? There's obviously a whole other story here that I need to hear about too. But one thing at a time. I'll get us some water.'

She fills the glasses I used earlier and sits back down opposite me. And I tell her everything. About how sad and alone I felt. About how I wanted to go out and get completely out of my head and forget about it all. How I thought Charlie was with another woman and how I thought my own mother hated me when I was just trying to protect her. She cries when I tell her about Connor on the beach and how scared I was. She seethes when I tell her about him hitting me and she gently strokes my bruised face. She moves her chair next to mine and pulls me into her body. And she holds me and strokes my hair as I cry it all out. And not just the last few days, the years and years of pain that she's missed out on.

Eventually, the tears stop and I sit up.

'Charlie's gone,' I say. 'I got it all wrong. He wasn't cheating on me at all. Ben Pemberton kidnapped him. Ben was the real Blaze Bundy. And now Charlie knows everything about me and he's gone.'

'Oh darling,' she says. 'I'm so sorry. Are you okay?'

I shake my head. 'No. Not at all. But I'm a monster. And Charlie shouldn't be with a monster.'

'You're being extremely hard on yourself,' Carmella says.

'I'm not. Anyway, I can't think about it now. There's a bit of a situation through there that I need to deal with.'

My mother puts her head against mine. 'A situation *we* need to deal with,' she says.

She takes my hand and we go back through to the lounge where I'm surprised to find Antoinette and Gabriel have already started the process of taking Ben's body apart and wrapping it up in bin bags. Like it's the sort of family activity that people all over the globe are doing.

'Antoinette has filled me in on what happened here,' Gabriel says, sounding remarkably chipper. 'Sounds like you had a close shave there, Kitty.'

My mother looks at him, puzzled.

'I'll tell you everything in the car,' he says to her. 'Right now we need to get this guy cleaned up and in the boot without anyone seeing. And then we need to get to the farmhouse.'

'The farmhouse?' I say.

'Where we live,' says Carmella. 'Which you'd know if you ever bothered visiting.'

'A farmhouse,' I say again. For some reason I always thought my mother lived in some fancy modern villa overlooking the Med. I guess we're both full of surprises.

'What are we going to do about this place?' I say. 'When Ben doesn't come home, this will be the last place he's known to have been.'

'Everything was booked under a fake name,' Antoinette says. 'Ben obviously didn't want anyone to be able to track him after he killed Kits. Sorry, Kits.'

I wave her apology off. 'It's fine. Where was he going to take me?' I ask. 'You know . . . after.'

She points to some suitcases stacked in the corner of the room that I hadn't really noticed. 'He was going to cut you up and put you in those. And then dump you in the sea,' she says.

Right.

Okay.

'It's good to see he was prepared, I suppose.' Is it weird hearing what a sociopath was planning to do with my dead body? I guess on the scale of weird things that have happened to me, it doesn't rank very high.

'He's done a lot of the hard work for us,' Gabriel says and I swear he's enjoying this. 'We should get going though. Kitty, you and I can finish the body. Carmella and Antoinette can clean? Is that okay with everyone? I don't want to take over anything and be *that* guy. I'm actually scared too.'

My mother gives a small laugh and kisses Gabriel on the cheek. 'Yeah. I don't think you'll be stepping out of line any time soon.' She turns to Antoinette. 'I'm assuming your brother stocked up on cleaning products?'

Antoinette nods. 'Oh yes, there are tons under the sink. Gloves too.'

My mother stands up and claps her hands together. 'Time to get down to business.'

Something that I wasn't expecting was to discover how cathartic clearing up a murder scene is when you've just had your heart broken. We're so busy working on Ben's body, wrapping up the parts and packing them into the suitcases that I barely think about Charlie at all. As we work, Antoinette and I fill my mother in on what happened before she arrived. If she's shocked, she doesn't show it. She just nods and listens. Except when Antoinette reaches the big reveal about her paternity.

'I'm sorry, Mrs Collins,' she says. 'I had no idea.'

'You've got nothing to be sorry for,' my mother replies. 'And call me Carmella.'

'You don't seem very shocked,' I say a bit later, when Antoinette and Gabriel are out of earshot, looking for duct tape or something.

'I'm not,' she says. 'I think I always sort of knew. She looks a bit like you. I didn't exactly need a geneticist to work it out.'

'Are you okay?'

She looks at me and smiles. 'Kitty, there is nothing that could come out about your father that would surprise me. I'm absolutely fine. More than fine. I'm glad she was here. I'm glad she saved you.'

*

'I think we're all done,' my mother announces as the sky begins to darken and she puts the final washed coffee cup in the cupboard. 'Time to go home?'

'I'll get the bags and pop them in the car,' says Gabriel.

The bags. Like we've done a big shop.

And then we leave the house, Antoinette puts the keys in the little safe as instructed. 'So cool that most Airbnbs don't even bother checking their guests in,' she says. Then we pile into the car and start our journey to my mother and Gabriel's rural farmhouse.

'What shall I do with this?' Antoinette asks as we set off. She's holding Ben's phone.

I think for a moment. 'Give it to me,' I say. 'I've had an idea.'

45

CARMELLA AND GABRIEL'S HOUSE, GRASSE, FRANCE

It takes about forty minutes to drive to the farmhouse where my mother lives with Gabriel. Antoinette and I use the time to fill them in on Ben's secret double life as Blaze Bundy.

'I still can't believe you thought that was me,' Gabriel says. 'Do I really give off toxic masculinity vibes?'

'No, darling,' my mother says gazing at him so lovingly that it reminds my heart how broken and bruised it is.

Later. I'll indulge it later.

'So what are we going to do with Ben?' I ask as we pull into the gravelly drive of an old-looking stone house. 'Bury him on your land?'

'You'll see,' Gabriel says. 'There are some things I'll show you in a bit. Let's get inside and have a cup of tea first.'

Tea?

I get out of the car and get my first full look at my mother's home. It's definitely not what I imagined. I always thought of her living in something modern, probably made of glass, with a beach view and a pool.

This is nothing like that.

For a start, the only glass is in the windows; the rest of the house is light-coloured stone. It's sprawling rather than neat, a proper farmhouse. And we're nowhere near the beach. Well, not on the coastline as I'd have expected. For some reason, in my head, my mother actually lives somewhere like Gabriel's hotel. I wasn't expecting something rural and rustic. It's beautiful.

'Come on then,' Gabriel says. 'We've got lots to do.' I like the way he says *we*. I feel like part of a family.

'I'll get the kettle on,' my mother says, the minute we're through the front door. 'Plus we need to get rid of the housekeeper. There are certain things I *don't* expect her help with.'

Of course she's got help. There are some things that will never change.

Antoinette and I follow her and Gabriel through to a huge kitchen. A woman with grey hair is shuffling around, mopping the floor and talking in French to a yellow dog that keeps walking over the bits she's just cleaned. The dog stops in its tracks when it hears us come in and then bounds over to my mother and Gabriel, almost knocking them off their feet.

My mother drops down to her knees and starts fussing over the dog, kissing its fur and burying her face in its neck. '*Bonjour Souris. Bonjour. Tu m'as tellement manqué.*'

'This is Souris,' Gabriel tells me as Antoinette joins my mother on the floor with the dog. 'He's supposed to be here for the mice. Really he's here for the fussing.'

'Would you like the grand tour then?' Carmella asks me.

'Yes, please.'

She claps her hands together, like a house-proud wife and not at all like we've got a dead body to dispose of.

'You can go home, Maria,' she says to the housekeeper. 'Take a couple of days off. Full pay, of course.'

'Merci,' says Maria, and my mother turns to me, excited to show me her home. She clearly loves it very much and I soon see why. It's grand but somehow homely at the same time.

It's the outside areas that she's most in love with though. Acres of grass, slightly yellow after weeks of being torched by the early summer sun. There's a pool, around the back, overlooked by olive trees and vines of tomatoes.

'We grow a lot of our own stuff here,' she explains. 'I'll show you the vineyards later.'

'Vineyards? You make wine?'

'A little, don't get too excited.' She gives me a shy smile. 'It's just something we're playing around with. Personally, I think we're rather useless at it, but Gabriel is very enthusiastic. Come on, this way.' She leads me past the pool and over some dried-out grass, a cloud of midges disperses as we walk through them. A breeze wafts a familiar smell into my nose. The smell of my childhood, musky and sour, a combination of straw and hay.

Then I hear the unmistakable sound of snuffling noses.

'Come on, I want to introduce you to someone,' says Carmella. I follow her to a wooden pen which contains six large pigs. They're lazing around, softly snoring, unaware of the two of us staring at them.

'Pigs,' I say, remembering the phone call I overheard while hiding from Gabriel in the wardrobe. He was talking about a literal pig.

'They're a bit of a hobby of mine,' my mother says, giving me another one of those shy smiles. 'I absolutely love them. What do you think?'

'Um . . . nice,' I say and Carmella laughs. 'Why pigs?'

'Oh you know, I think it's probably got something to do with where my money comes from and my part in that. I suppose I'm trying to assuage some of my guilt by looking after these girls and making sure they have a nice life.' She lets out a happy sigh. 'Even Gabriel's come round to them. He wasn't overly keen at first but indulged me. He loves them now.'

'Where do you even get them?' I ask. 'I assume not from Pets at Home.'

'*Animaux à la maison.*' She laughs. 'And no. I take them in from local farms. They're usually runts when they come here. I just can't bear the thought of the little things being killed off because they're small and weak. Just look at them now.' There's nothing small or weak about the pigs in front of me.

'Okay, so you've opened a pig sanctuary in France to live out some sort of *Charlotte's Web* fantasy,' I say and Carmella laughs again. I like the sound. I didn't hear enough of her laughing when I was a child. 'I can't decide if that's more or less fucked up than me being a vegan serial killer.'

'Language, Kitty,' she scolds. Then she adds, 'It's definitely less fucked up. For the record.'

We stare at the pigs for a little while, watching their fat bellies rise and fall as they sleep. Flies buzz around their eyes and rear ends. Occasionally one of them flips its tail like a whip to swat away a fly that's got a bit too close. They're pretty boring and they stink but the look on my mother's face is like she's in a meditative state.

'Do you know what pigs are really useful for?' Carmella says when she eventually snaps out of her porcine reverie.

'Bacon?'

She gives my arm a playful slap. 'Bodies.'

Ah. Of course.

Christ.

'I didn't think that was true,' I mutter. 'Can I touch them?'

'It's absolutely true,' she says, opening the pen gate for me. 'Be careful. A couple of them came to us quite traumatised. They don't trust humans very much.'

'I always knew pigs were smart,' I say as I step into the pen and crouch down beside one snoring beast. I reach out and gently touch it. Its skin is warm and rough, a little bit hairy. I suppose they're not the worst thing in the world. 'They're cute,' I say to my mum.

She watches as I shift over to another snoozing pig.

'Hello, piggy,' I say. 'I hear you're going to help me get out of a tricky situation.' The pig wakes up and stares at me, its beady eyes distrustful. I don't blame it. I reach out to touch it and it suddenly leaps to its feet with a growl. Since when do pigs fucking growl? I jump to my feet and run out of the pen while the pig continues to snort and snarl at me. Carmella lets me back out and is clearly trying not to laugh.

'Maybe they need to get to know you better, Kits.'

'I think we're better off as casual acquaintances,' I say. 'So what? They eat everything?'

'Pretty much,' she says cheerfully. 'We'll have to shave the body and take the teeth out first. Hopefully Marie hasn't been overfeeding them while we've been away. They need to be hungry.'

'I'm not even going to ask how you know all this,' I say.

'Well. I've always been very good at cleaning up other people's messes.'

'We'll wait until after dark before we get the body out of the car,' my mother says as she pours out tea for us when we get back to the house. 'Not that there's any chance of anyone seeing what we're doing but we can't be too careful.' She passes the pot to Antoinette before slicing up a wedge of brie and some grapes. 'I don't mind doing the shaving but I'll leave it to you to remove the teeth.'

'I can do that,' Antoinette says. 'I've been dying to rip those ridiculous Turkey teeth out of his mouth for months.'

'You can stay indoors and watch TV,' I tell her. 'The less involved in this you are, the better.'

Antoinette's bottom lip sticks out. 'I think you've forgotten that I'm the one who planned this whole thing and shot him in the arm,' she mutters, darkly. 'I think I can handle a few teeth.'

'Then tomorrow,' my mother continues, 'we'll all drive back to Cannes for the wedding. The pigs will have made good innings on the body by then and I'll tell Marie they've got flu or something and to stay away from them. She won't argue with swine flu.' She looks around at us. 'Does that sound good to everyone?'

We all nod and sip our tea and nibble our cheese and grapes and I feel like I've slipped into a parallel world.

Once we've finished our drinks and the sun has fully set, Carmella turns to me.

'You ready to do this thing?'

'I guess so,' I say, sneaking a look at Antoinette to check she's okay. I needn't have worried. She looks like she's won a competition.

'Come on then. Let's see what these pigs can do.' I push myself onto my feet and follow Gabriel to the car where we unload the suitcases and wheel them into the house. My mother has lit some candles. 'For the smell,' she says, wrinkling her nose as we start unpacking the parcels containing Ben's body.

I look over at Antoinette again who's watching us intently now, no sign of the earlier bravado. 'Are you okay?'

She nods. 'I'm fine. It's just a bit weird. I can't believe that's really him. That he's really gone.'

I go to her and put my arms around her. He may have been a prize twat who wanted to kill me, but he was still her brother. Half-brother. Whatever. 'You don't have to watch this,' I say. 'You can go and do something else? We'll take care of it.'

Carmella nods in agreement.

But Antoinette shakes her head vehemently. 'No, I want to. He wasn't always very nice to me growing up.'

'I don't mind doing the teeth. I think I'll rather enjoy it seeing as his alter ego almost got me killed.' Gabriel says as he roots through a toolbox on the kitchen island. 'Ah. Here they are.' He pulls out a pair of industrial-looking pliers, opening and closing them a few times. 'Does anyone want to try some of our homemade wine?'

'I'm good, thanks,' I say. This situation is weird enough without adding alcohol to the mix.

'Let's get cracking then.' Gabriel strolls over to where Ben's top half is laid out on the kitchen floor and places the head in his lap. I watch in morbid fascination as Gabriel pulls Ben's jaw open and sticks the pliers inside his mouth. There's a wet sound of tissue disconnecting and then Gabriel holds a shiny white tooth aloft. 'More veneer than actual tooth here,' he says.

'That's my brother for you,' says Antoinette.

It takes about twenty minutes for Gabriel to complete his twisted tooth-fairy task. It would've been quicker but he insisted on examining and commenting on every tooth after extraction before handing them to Antoinette who then pounded them into powder with a mallet. She'd make a pretty good accomplice.

When Gabriel has finished the tooth extraction, it's my turn and I'm pleased to discover he and my mother have an excellent selection of knives in their kitchen. Thanks to the pigs and their insatiable appetites I don't need to worry about doing a tidy job. I really just need to smash some of the bigger bones apart. I run my fingers over a lovely set of Henckels knives. I should get some of these.

'Can I borrow the mallet?' I ask Antoinette who nods and hands it to me. Then she, Gabriel and my mother watch on as I break Ben's legs, arms and torso apart. Gabriel cheerfully slings bits of Ben into a bucket, ready to take to the pigs.

'The family that slays together stays together,' I say as we watch him head to the pig pen with the first bucket of human slops.

Then Carmella shows Antoinette and me to the rooms we can sleep in. 'They both have en suites,' she says. 'Get cleaned up and try to get some rest. Big day tomorrow.'

Before we turn in, it's time for the final part of our plan.

'Are you ready for this?' I ask Gabriel as I aim Ben's phone at him, Instagram ready to go live.

'I should be,' he says from under the black bandana that covers the lower part of his face. 'How do I look? Is it everything you imagined?'

I narrow my eyes at him. 'Save the mockery until after please.' He's never going to let me forget my *petite erruer*. 'Right, three, two, one. . . you're live.'

He raises the voice distorter to his mouth. 'Good evening, disciples,' he says and it's so eerie I can feel my skin breaking out in goose-bumps. 'Or rather, good evening followers. This is going to be my last video. After tonight there will be no more Blaze Bundy. You are not disciples. And I am not a hero. I am not worth your adoration.'

The comments have already begun flooding in. Dismay at what Gabriel is saying, mostly. Disbelief. Someone calls him a pussy.

'I've come to realise that everything I've told you is wrong. Worse than wrong, it's dangerous. I'm nothing but a pathetic man who thought that bringing women down, encouraging others to bring women down, would do something to heal the massive hole in my sad and empty soul. But it did not. If anything, this whole *act* has made me feel more hollow than ever. Women are not the enemy. The patriarchy is.'

The viewers don't like this at all. I see comments from men demanding he take his mask off to reveal himself. Others suggest he's been kidnapped and tell him to blink twice for help.

'The real truth, the *real* red pill, is that the patriarchy serves none of us. It's made you think you're entitled to women's time and bodies. That you should just have these things, regardless of who you are inside. Go out and do the work. Earn their time. Earn their trust. Try *talking* to women and seeing them as people rather than a commodity you should have because you've been born with a penis. Do some internal work. Ask yourself why no woman wants to be with you. Could it be because you're a piece of shit? Has that crossed your mind? Maybe try *not* being a piece of shit. I bet it works better than any phoney advice I've ever come out with. Who knows, you might even end up feeling good about yourself too.

My final words to you are this, get off your computers and get some fucking therapy. Value the women in your lives. Become an ally. Stop being part of the very problem you spend your sad lives complaining about. Go outside. Touch some grass. It's a beautiful world out there. Stop wasting your life being a basement-dwelling prick. Do better.'

I cut the live and delete the Blaze account.

'That okay?' Gabriel asks, untying the bandana.

'Perfect,' I say. 'See. I knew you'd be good at it.'

Later, I shower and crawl into bed, not expecting sleep to come, but it does and I dream that I am getting married. I think it's Charlie as I'm walking up the aisle but when I reach him, he's actually a pig. He turns around and has Ben Pemberton's face.

I really shouldn't chop up a body right before bedtime.

46

Amazingly we make it back to Cannes the next morning, with time to spare.

'We shouldn't have seen each other the night before the wedding, you know,' my mother says to Gabriel in the car as we pull into the hotel.

'We probably shouldn't have spent the night before the wedding clearing up a crime scene, dismantling a body and feeding it to our pigs,' he replies.

My mother nods in agreement. 'I hope that's not a bad omen. Come on, girls, we've got a wedding to get ready for.'

An hour later, Antoinette, my mother and I are sat in Carmella's hotel room while hair and make-up artists fuss around us, making us look like we haven't been up all night. It can't be the easiest of jobs for them.

'Your nails, they are filthy,' one of the MUAs says to me as she scrapes something out from underneath one of my fingernails. It's dried blood. I hope she doesn't realise.

'How are you feeling, Kits?' my mother asks me, handing me a glass of champagne. 'About Charlie?'

It's a good question. But it's not one I can answer right now. Mostly I feel nothing. Not in an 'I don't care' kind of way though. More like my heart has gone completely numb because I just can't handle it right now. I've got to get through this wedding. Then I've got to get back to London and start putting my life back together. I've got to make amends with Tor for a start.

'I'm not sure,' I say. 'I'm trying not to think about it just yet. There's so much other stuff I need to deal with first.'

Carmella nods. 'You'll be okay, sweetie. I know you will.'

'Madame, you are ready to put on your dress now,' one of the women says. She stands up and gives me an excited little squeal before disappearing into the dressing area with yet another one of the Get Ready crew.

Five minutes later she emerges and my breath is completely taken away.

'You look beautiful,' I tell her. And she really does. Her hair is falling in waves over her tanned shoulders and down her back. Her make-up has not only made her look like she's had a full eight-hour sleep, but also like she shimmers. Then there's the dress. It's perfect. I've never been the sort of person to go gushy over wedding dresses which is weird considering how much I really like dresses for every other occasion, but this is something truly special. It's lacy, but not over-the-top lacy, delicate like it's been spun by special spiders. It's tight, like a second skin, so all those extra workouts were absolutely worth it. It splays out at the bottom though, making her look like she's about to pose on the red carpet at the Oscars. I can feel my eyes getting damp and I don't want to be the one that makes someone say that most clichéd of wedding-day lines –

'don't cry, you'll ruin your make-up' – so I look upwards until the tears run back inside my head or wherever they go, saving my lashes and liner. 'You look so beautiful.'

Carmella smiles at me. 'Thank you, my darling. You'd better get your dress on too. I don't want to keep Gabriel waiting. Well, not for too long anyway.' She shuffles out of the dressing room and I go in, slipping off the robe I'm wearing and pulling the silky gown over my head.

My mother was right about this dress. It's perfect on me. Not so perfect that I'll upstage her, but still pretty fucking perfect. The silk swooshes over my body like water and I can't stop staring at myself in the mirror. Charlie is absolutely going to lose his mind when he sees me in this.

And then it hits me.

Properly this time.

And it's like a fist.

He won't see me in this. He won't see me at all. Because he's not here. He's gone back to London and is probably moving his things out of my flat at this exact moment.

He's gone.

I stare at my reflection in the mirror but it's not a young woman in a stunning maid-of-honour dress looking back at me anymore. It's the monster I really am. The monster who kills people. The monster who can't stop. It wouldn't matter if Charlie could see me in the dress because the dress is a veneer. It might as well be made of glass because I can see exactly what's underneath. And it's no wonder he ran. I'd run too. I'd never stop running.

'Kits? Oh my God, Kits!' It's my mother, and suddenly I'm in her arms and she's rocking me like I'm a baby. 'It's okay, darling. It's all going to be okay. I promise you. I'm here. I'm here.'

I hadn't even realised that I was sobbing, also like a baby.

'I'm sorry,' I say snottily into Carmella's shoulder. 'I'm so so sorry.'

'You hush now,' she says. 'There's nothing to be sorry for. Do you need me to postpone this?'

'What? What do you mean?'

'The wedding, do you need me to postpone it?'

'Absolutely not,' I say.

'Are you sure? Because if you can't walk me down the aisle today then I'm not doing it. I'm not doing it without you next to me.'

Amazingly her words actually make me sob more. She lets me cry until I can finally get it together enough to take a deep breath.

'You're not postponing anything,' I say. 'Come on, let's get you married.'

I'm not sure what I'm going to look like when the official photos come back. But for once I don't care because walking my mother down the aisle is one of the happiest moments of my life, despite it being during one of the most heartbreaking.

The whole of the private beach has been closed off for the ceremony and it is breath-taking. There are rows of white chairs adorned with huge white bows all facing the sea, which itself looks like it's dressed in its wedding finery, sparkling and twinkling like a massive blue jewel. There's a long white walkway in lieu of an aisle which I walk Carmella down, both of us barefoot because heels do not do well in sand. At the end of the walkway is a slightly raised podium, also draped in white. Here is where Gabriel is waiting, alongside the celebrant. My mother has a harpist playing a version of 'Ave Maria' rather than the traditional wedding march and when the music starts, Gabriel turns. His face looks like it could explode with joy when he sees us, well, my mother specifically. It's a look I've seen on Charlie's face before. A look that says he just absolutely cannot believe his luck. I wonder if I'll ever see that look again. I sneak a glance at my mother and her face is mirroring Gabriel's exactly. They're both just so damn happy to be marrying each other and, while I'm happy for them, so happy for them, I also feel very very sad for myself.

I spot Antoinette sitting a few rows back from the podium and she gives me an encouraging smile as we make the final few steps towards Gabriel. I hand my mother over to him and he gives me a smile, mouthing the words *thank you* to me. Carmella gives me her bouquet, which is just one oversized white lily, and steps up next to him. And then it begins. All the promises to love and cherish each other through good and bad and everything in between. Words fly around about love and how it can save us and how it's all we need and that it's more than a feeling and I begin to wonder if they wrote their vows while watching *Moulin Rouge*. Stuff about how love lasts forever and is unconditional but that's not true, is it? There are always conditions. Always. Then they're putting rings on each other's fingers and my mother does a very uncharacteristic air punch which I hope someone catches on camera. And then it's time for the bride to be kissed and I have to look away at this point because there is only so much love you can watch while your own heart is shattering silently.

They walk back down the aisle together while everyone whoops and cheers and throws white confetti at them. I follow along behind. Alone. I'm back to being alone. My person is gone.

And then I feel a hand on my arm. I turn around and it's Antoinette, beaming at me.

'You did brilliantly,' she says. 'You're very brave, I know that can't have been easy for you.'

I feel seen.

'Thank you,' I say. 'And no, it was pretty hard to smile through all of that actually. My face hurts.'

She laughs. 'Well, it's over now. Shall we go and get a drink? I think you've definitely earned one.'

So we do.

We drink champagne and toast my mother and Gabriel. Then we drink some more and Antoinette tells me a bit about what it was like growing up with Hen and Ben and James and Laurelle. And I tell her a bit about what it was like growing up as the sole heiress to a slaughter business. She tells me how she always felt different to her siblings and knew there was a reason. I tell her that I always felt different to everyone I was ever around but didn't think about there being a reason. She tells me that she's sad she didn't really get to know her real dad. I tell her not to be because he was a terrible man, maybe not as terrible as the man she grew up thinking was her dad, but still pretty bad. Then we drink to our daddy issues. Carmella shifts some people around at the top table when it's time for the wedding breakfast and Antoinette sits next to me. We giggle together when Gabriel makes his speech which is packed full of the most cringe jokes and we cheer when my mother breaks tradition and makes her own speech where she tells everyone how much she loves me and how proud she is of me. And when the whole thing is over and I crawl into bed, champagne drunk, exhausted but not as sad as I was earlier, in the moments before I fall asleep, I think that maybe, actually, I'm not as alone as I thought I was. I have a sister.

I have a sister.

47

I decide to go back to London the day after the wedding, despite my mother and Gabriel's pleas for me to stay a bit longer.

'I need to go,' I tell them over our last lunch together. 'I need to get back to normality.' What I really mean is that I need to get home and start figuring out who I am now I don't have Charlie. Now I don't have someone to be good for.

'But a few more days won't hurt,' my mother tries to argue.

I smile at her. 'I'll come and see you soon,' I say. 'I promise. Besides, you two have just got married, in case you forgot, this is your honeymoon period. You don't want me hanging around. And, believe me, I don't want to be hanging around you either.'

'You make sure you do come back,' Gabriel says. 'And often.'

'I will.'

They drive me and Antoinette to the airport later that afternoon. We were able to get two last-minute economy seats. Neither of us has flown economy before so it's a bit of an adventure. My mother squeezes me so hard before we go through to Departures, that I don't think she's actually going to let me go.

'I love you, Kitty Collins,' she whispers into my hair as she holds me.

'I love you too, Mrs Murphy,' I say. 'Now go. Go and enjoy your honeymoon.'

'Be careful, won't you? Promise me.'

'I promise,' I say. I have every intention of keeping this promise too.

48

The apartment is empty when I get back. Not just because of Charlie's physical absence. It feels like something else has gone too. Something integral that made it feel like a home. I guess love doesn't live here anymore.

I take my bag into my bedroom and begin unpacking. I don't want to go into the dressing area. I don't want to see Charlie's side empty. So I just chuck everything into the washing basket. I suppose now I can hire another cleaner to do all these things for me.

It's funny, isn't it, all those clichés when a relationship ends, things like how you don't know what you've got till it's gone. I'm feeling them all now. I'm almost at the point of making a heartbreak playlist.

But no, I need to keep myself together. I've been there before and I promised I would never go back. I barely made it out alive the last time. I ignore the impulse to grab a bottle of wine from the wine fridge and crawl into bed, choosing to make myself a herbal tea and watch a movie instead. This is what normal women do when their hearts are broken. I might even have a fucking bath. Although, probably not.

I change into some Victoria's Secret pyjamas, fresh out of the packet so I can't feel sad about Charlie having peeled them off me at some point, and fall into bed. The last thing I do before I close my eyes is message him.

But I don't get that far because there are four missed calls, all from Maisie.

I call her back.

She answers on the first ring. 'Oh, Kitty, thank God, where are you?'

'At home, in bed,' I say.

'You're in London?'

'Yes, I'm in London. What's the matter?'

'Stay there,' she says. 'Stay right there. I'm on my way. I need to see you. Something's happened.'

'What is it? What's happened?'

But she doesn't answer because she's already hung up.

49

Maisie arrives less than twenty minutes later and I'm back out of bed drinking tea.

'Oh Kitty, thank God you're back,' she says and I notice that, like me, her cheeks are streaked with dried tears. She looks paler than ever and there are dark shadows under her eyes. I've seen Maisie heartbroken over men so many times in our lives, but this is a different grief. I'm scared to even ask.

'Maisie? What is it?' I say, ushering her inside. Please don't let it be the babies. *Please don't let it be the babies.* I watch as she flops opposite me on the sofa. Charlie's side. I move so I'm sitting beside her and rub her back gently. 'Is it the babies?' I manage to eventually whisper.

She looks at me, shaking her head sadly.

'Oh fuck, Maisie, I'm so *so* sorry,' I say. 'What can I do? What do you need?'

She shakes her head again, gulping back a sob. 'No, Kits, it's not the babies. The babies are fine.' She places a protective hand on her belly. I'm surprised to see there is a tiny little

319

bump there now. The relief almost floors me before I realise that something else bad has happened.

'Maisie? What is it?'

'It's Tor,' she says. 'She's in hospital.'

50

She looks unrecognisable. Her left eye is barely visible, hidden under a raw, pulpy bruise. Her head is wrapped in a blood-stained bandage. The right side of her face is messed up too. I can't take my eyes off her.

'Tell me I look pretty,' she says, trying a smile but I can see the effort is hurting her. She reaches a hand up and gingerly touches her face. 'Fuck, fractured cheekbones really hurt.'

'Jesus Christ, Tor,' I say. 'What happened?'

'Would you believe me if I told you I walked into a door?' She tries to smile again and winces.

'No.' I slide into the rubber chair next to her bed. 'Stop trying to be funny. This isn't funny.'

'Thank you for coming,' she says. 'I wasn't sure if you would.'

I reach over and take her hand. 'I'd never not come. How are you feeling?'

'Super good. I can't understand why I haven't stayed here before. It's lovely.'

I reach into my bag and pull out a stack of magazines I picked

321

up before coming here. 'I brought you some magazines, like it's 2010. Wasn't sure if you'd have your iPad in here or not.'

'Thank you,' she says. 'That's really kind of you.'

We sit in silence for a few moments.

'So, what's been going on with you?' she asks eventually.

Where to start on that one?

'A lot,' I say, 'but that can wait. I'll fill you in when you're home. You'll definitely need wine and I hear the house white here isn't the best?'

Tor laughs. 'They're definitely watering it down.'

'I'm sorry,' I say. 'I'm sorry we argued. I'm sorry I wasn't here for you.'

She's shaking her head at me even though I can tell it's hurting her. 'There's nothing to be sorry for, Kits.'

'There is. I was out of line. You had boundaries and I overstepped them and I'm so sorry.'

'No, Kits, there's nothing to be sorry for. You were right.'

What?

'What? What do you mean?'

'I mean you were right about Aidan. I should've listened to you.'

'What did he do?'

She moves her head so she's facing me and looks me directly in the eyes. 'It was Aidan. He did this to me.'

I just stare.

She sighs. 'At least say *I told you so* or something.'

But I can't.

If I open my mouth right now, I'll scream.

So we sit in silence until the boiling rage in my veins gentles to a simmer.

'What happened?' I say eventually.

Tor's eyes fill with tears. 'He's not a good man,' she says. 'I really thought, hoped, that he was.' She shakes her head. 'But he's exactly what you told me he was.' She lets out a deep breath.

'Have you told anyone?' I ask but she shakes her head again. 'Then tell me. Tell me everything from the beginning.'

'I feel like *you* might need a wine for this,' she says and tries to smile again but her face is too broken and her eyes are too sad and it just doesn't happen. 'Okay. So up until a week ago, everything was great. It was just as I'd said. Just as he'd said. But he was at my house, I'd made us some food and we were going to watch a movie.' She pauses for a moment and thinks. 'We'd started watching it, I'd made it all romantic, you know, little fairy lights and wine, popcorn. And we were kissing and everything was great. He took my shirt off and I was fine, I was happy for it to happen. I wanted to. But then, he put his hand on my thigh, like high up.' She stops again and puts her own hand at the top of her leg. 'And I just freaked out. I don't know if it was a flashback or something but I suddenly couldn't bear his hands on me. And I pulled away, I said something like *I'm not ready for this* and he just lost his shit.' She stops and takes a deep breath. I can feel her shaking. 'I was scared, Kits. He called me all these names, said he'd been patient with me, that I should be over what happened by now.' Her eyes are full of fear and tears. 'Like that's something I'm ever going to just get over. The next thing I know his fist was in my face and I was screaming at him to stop but he pulled me onto the floor and kicked me in the stomach. I must've blacked out because I can't remember anything after that. The next thing I know I woke up here. I've got three broken ribs too.'

'Have you told the police? The doctors? They must want to know how you ended up like this.'

'I've said I can't remember,' she says quietly.

'But why? Why are you protecting him?'

She drops her eyes to her hands which are now in her lap. 'What's the point though, Kits?'

'The point is, they'll arrest him and charge him with assault! They'll shut him down. They'll put him in prison and he won't be able to do this again.'

She's shaking her head again. 'No, we both know that's not how it works. Don't be naïve, Kits. They'll arrest him and that will make him angry and he'll come after me again. If they even charge him and it even makes it to court, which we know is unlikely, I'll be dragged through a trial. And everything about me will be dragged through the trial. You know they can use my medical notes in court. Everything that I told him about what happened in Mykonos will come out. How those men went missing.' She fixes me with her stare this time. I've often wondered if Tor knows what I did that night. When she came back to our hotel, confused and bleeding, after being drugged and raped at an afterparty on a yacht. How I left her sleeping and went to find the men who hurt her. How I took their boat out into the Aegean Sea and threw their bodies into the water. 'I don't think either of us could withstand that kind of scrutiny,' Tor whispers.

She's right. I've fucked up again. Because of me, my best friend can't get justice for this awful thing that's happened to her. Every time I try to help, I just make things worse.

'So what? He just gets away with it? He continues to practise?'

Tor shrugs and looks up at me again. 'I don't know. Maybe karma will catch up with him as well.'

And in that moment, something passes between us and I know exactly what she's asking me to do. Because she's right. As much as we talk about justice prevailing, it just doesn't, does it?

Not all the time.

Not for everyone.

I know what I have to do.

51

When I get back to the flat, it's cold and empty and I am too. I check Charlie's social media but there's nothing new. I type out a message – *I miss you* – but I don't send it because what's the fucking point? I drink a bottle of expensive Riesling and fall asleep or pass out on the sofa, where I dream about Aidan Ward, pigs and Tor's battered, purple face until I wake up, sweating and trembling.

It's not quite morning but I already know I'm not going to be able to go back to sleep, there's too much whirring around in my mind.

I get up from the sofa and send a message to Will, who I get my drugs from. I ask him for the usual. I don't know if he has any idea what I do with the GHB he gives me but he's never asked. I suppose it's not in his interest to know what I'm doing with it. I also check my knives too. I sharpen them which is something I find soothing while watching episodes of *The Bear* on my sofa. Everything is ready by the time the sun starts to come up and I send a message to Antoinette.

Come over, I've got a project for us.

52

I'm sad that this is the last time I'll see these women, sitting on these plastic chairs and drinking the awful, cheap coffee. But it is what it is. The reason I joined this group was to find an outlet for my anger other than killing and . . . well . . . that hasn't worked out, has it? I haven't told them that I'm leaving but I needed to see them all one last time. I needed to check that I've been able to help them without murder. Well, most of them.

Linda is the first to arrive and I immediately see the change in her.

'Kate!' she says as she walks in, her trademark biscuit tin tucked under her arm. 'We haven't seen you for a while.'

'I've been away,' I say. 'My mother got married. I've been in France.'

'Lovely,' she replies. 'You look well.'

'So do you.' And she does, she really does. I can't put my finger on exactly what it is about her, not at first. Her greying bob is just the same and she's wearing her usual slacks and sweater combo. Why do older women always think this is such a look? I almost wonder if she would've been better off with me hiring her a stylist. But then I see what is different in her. It's her eyes. They don't look sad. They meet mine without glancing at the ground in the moments before. When she smiles at me, her eyes smile too.

'Well,' she says. 'You've missed all the drama. Do you want some tea?'

'I've got a coffee, thank you.' I hold up the Stanley cup I brought from home. That thing I said about missing the cheap coffee? Not true.

'No.' She giggles in a way I've never heard before. It's almost girlish. 'Tea. Gossip. Keira says it all the time. Am I not getting it right?'

'Oh! Of course, my bad.' I don't have the heart to correct her.

'I've left him, Kate! I've finally done it! I've got myself a little flat, quite near Keira actually. I still can't believe it. I'm like a new woman.'

'Wow,' I say, hoping I'm pulling off the right amount of surprised. 'How did that happen? I thought there was no way you could do it?'

'I had an unexpected windfall,' she says, chuckling. 'An email two weeks ago telling me I'd won a contest I don't even remember entering. I know it's vulgar to talk about money, Kate, so I won't disclose the amount. But enough to set me up in a little flat. And enough to support myself for the rest of my days. As long as I'm careful. No living like the Kardashingtons.'

'That's amazing,' I say. 'I'm so pleased for you.' She doesn't need to tell me how much money she'd 'won'. I sent the email congratulating her for being the lucky recipient of £500,000. It was money well spent. 'How did he take it? Freddie?'

'He wasn't happy,' she says, 'but I don't flipping care. I'm free.' She squeezes her hands together and, honestly, looks about ten years younger. 'Do you want a macaroon? To celebrate?'

'Yes, please,' I say, already planning to put it straight into my bag when I get a chance.

Keira is the next to arrive.

'I thought you were going to get a lift in with me?' she gently admonishes Linda when she sees her perched in her plastic chair. 'I've been waiting for you.'

'Oh, I'm sorry, darling, I thought I'd sent you a text message.' She pulls out a brand-new iPhone from her pocket. 'Hmm. Maybe I forgot to press the send button. You'll have to show me again. Anyway, I decided to get the bus. I haven't been on a bus on my own in about ten years! It was an adventure.' She smiles at us both. 'Maybe not one I'd like to go on again, but I did it!'

Keira beams at her.

'That's my girl,' she says. 'Kate, you look super tanned. Have you been away?'

'She's been in France,' Linda says. 'For her mum's wedding.'

'How are you doing, Keira?' I ask her. 'Any news?'

'Funnily enough, yes,' she says. 'You know those guys who attacked me? The ones who got away with it because the police give zero fucks – sorry, Linda – about hate crime? The police had a tip-off and they've all been arrested for drug possession. The police found a huge amount of cocaine in their garden shed. Okay, it's still frustrating that they weren't arrested for what they did to me, but they're off the streets now. I can walk around without looking over my shoulder.' I give her a huge smile. It's helpful having my former supplier on speed dial, especially when he's always happy to help me out. For the right price.

Bea arrives next and fills me in on the super-duper hot-shot family lawyer who slid into her DMs, offering her pro-bono representation.

'It's so crazy,' she says. 'I had totally lost my faith in humans. But she's helping me. I'm really going to get my kids back.'

I don't tell her that the lawyer isn't really working for free. That I'm the one picking up the – pretty fucking hefty – tab. But if anyone needs to believe there is still good in the world, it's Bea.

Cassie comes in next and she too looks more relaxed than I've seen her.

'How's Scarlett doing?' Bea asks her. 'Still thinking about going back to university?'

Cassie nods. 'Yes. She's probably going to stay local, which actually suits me just fine. It's so good to see her coming out of her shell. Even if it's just to take some baby steps.' She looks at me and smiles.

Finally, Melinda sweeps in gushing apologies for being late. Angry Women Anonymous has also had a healthy cash injection – this time from an anonymous donor and Melinda has been in London having meetings with other women who are interested in expanding the AWA community across the country.

'You've missed so much, Kate!' she says.

'I really have.'

We all talk about our weeks and, for the first time, the vibe in the room is completely different. It's less angry and more loving. Although we all acknowledge that our feminist rage is still there and still valid. It's actually emotional when the meeting ends. I give all the women hugs, deeply sad that our journey together will end here. But unfortunately, I don't have a guardian angel who's about to sweep in and get rid of the thing causing my anger.

I have to be my own guardian angel.

Tor's guardian angel.

'See you next week, love,' Linda says to me before hopping into Keira's car. 'We're going to a pub,' she shouts out of the window. 'Wish me luck!'

I'm almost at my car when Cassie catches up with me.

'Kitty!' she says and I turn around. 'We're not going to see you next week, are we?'

'How did you know?'

'Just a sense I got,' she says. 'I'm not sure I'll be back either. It looks like someone took care of the thing that was making me so angry.'

'I'm really pleased to hear that. How's Scarlett?'

'She's doing much better actually.' Cassie smiles and for the first time since I met her it makes it as far as her eyes. 'She's still nervous but she's finally agreed to see a counsellor and is making tiny little steps of progress each day. I'm very proud of her. She feels much safer now.'

My heart sings. 'Oh Cassie, that really, really is just the most wonderful news. Honestly, it's made my week. Thank you.'

'I'm the one who needs to be thanking you really.' Cassie's voice drops to little more than a whisper and she looks around to make sure there is no one in earshot. 'Truly. What you did for Scarlett was amazing. I can never thank you enough.'

'I have no idea what you're talking about,' I say. 'I really should go now though. My sister and I are going away for a little while.'

'Okay,' Cassie says. 'But really and truly, thank you from the bottom of my heart. Scarlett and I will forever be grateful to you. As would the parents of all those girls they found photos of, if they knew.'

'I really have no idea what you're talking about!' I let out a little laugh. 'Take care now.'

'I will,' Cassie says. She gives me a gentle squeeze on my shoulder.

'Do you need a lift?' I ask but she shakes her head.

'You've done more than enough for me,' she says with a smile before wandering off in the direction of the bus stop.

53

'I still don't understand why a therapist is going to LA,' Antoinette says as she sips a glass of wine in the lounge.

'It's the city of broken women,' I say. 'He'll be like a kid in a candy shop.'

Aidan Ward was smart enough to leave the country after attacking Tor. Something Antoinette and I discovered when we dropped into his clinic. His secretary didn't know where he'd gone. I suppose violent men scared of being caught don't tend to leave forwarding addresses.

Aidan Ward was not smart enough to disable his location on his Snapchat though. That's how we discovered he was in LA.

And that's why Antoinette and I are about to get on a flight to LAX under the guise of a yoga retreat.

'I think it's time to board,' Antoinette says, draining her wine. 'Are you ready, Kitty?'

'Oh yes,' I say. 'I have never been readier.'

A Letter from Katy Brent

Thank you so much for choosing to read *I Bet You'd Look Good in a Coffin*. I hope you enjoyed it! If you did and would like to be the first to know about my new releases, sign up to my mailing list.

Sign up here! https://signup.harpercollins.co.uk/join/6n7/signup-hq-katybrent

If you loved *I Bet You'd Look Good in a Coffin* I would be so grateful if you would leave a review. I always love to hear what readers thought, and it helps new readers discover my books too.

Thanks,

Katy

Find out where Kitty's journey began. . .

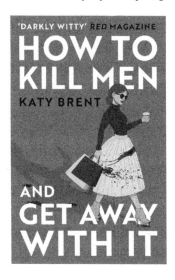

Meet Kitty Collins.
FRIEND. LOVER. KILLER.

He was following me. That guy from the nightclub who wouldn't leave me alone.

I hadn't intended to kill him of course. But I wasn't displeased when I did and, despite the mess I made, I appeared to get away with it.

That's where my addiction started . . .

I've got a taste for revenge and quite frankly, **I'm killing it**.

Available in audio, ebook and paperback.

Something bad happened last night.

I've woken up with the hangover from hell, a stranger in my bed, and I've gone viral for the worst reasons. My best friend Posey is dead. The police think it was a tragic accident.

I know she was murdered.

There's only one thing stopping me from dying of shame. I need to find a killer.

But after last night, I can't remember a thing…

'A whip-smart whodunnit, this will keep you guessing' *Red*

Available in audio, ebook and paperback.

Acknowledgements

Apparently it takes a village to raise a child, well it definitely takes one to publish a book too and I truly believe I am blessed with one of the best villages there is. Five stars. Definitely recommend.

First of all, thank you to everyone at HQ and HarperCollins. My brilliant and insightful editor, Cicely Aspinall, thank you for sprinkling your stardust over my words. Emma Pickard, Komal Patel and Isabel Williams, thank you for being my cheerleaders. A big thank you to Lisa Milton for your unwavering support, cheers boss. Thanks to Caroline Lakeman for always making me the best covers, I love them. Also honorable mentions to Audrey Linton, Seema Mitra, Fliss Porter, Marie Iwobi, Emily Scorer, Georgina Green, Lauren Trabucchi, Hannah Lismore, Jo Rose, Rebecca Fortuin, Ciara, and Francesca Tuzzeo for all your hard work. It means the world.

Euan Thorneycroft, I hit the jackpot when it comes to agents. Thank you for everything.

My writing friends, there are so many of you now and that is really one of the best things about being an author. Book people are the best people. Thank you to Jesse Sutanto, Julie Mae Cohen, Amy Beashel, Brooke Hardwick, Nikki Sheehan, Laurie Elizabeth Flynn, Rowan Coleman, Rob Dinsdale, Nussaibah Younis and everyone else who has been there for me on this journey so far. You might not realise it but each one of you has helped me in some way with this book.

Thanks to my mum, Carla Brent and my stepdad, Keith Tucker for all the love and support. Always. And to my dear sister, Luci Brent, no one makes me laugh like you do, sis.

The biggest thank you of all goes to the readers, booksellers, bloggers and Bookstagrammers. I think I say this every time I write one of these but I LITERALLY wouldn't be doing this without you. You are the very foundations of this village and I appreciate every single one of you. Please never stop recommending my books, posting about my books and messaging me about my books. I truly, TRULY, love hearing from you. Nothing picks me out of a hole like a message telling me what you've loved about my writing.

Last and not least, thank you to my brilliant, funny, kind and generally wonderful children, Seb and Sophia. I love you both more than you could ever know. Always and forever.

Dear Reader,

We hope you enjoyed reading this book. If you did, we'd be so appreciative if you left a review. It really helps us and the author to bring more books like this to you.

Here at HQ Digital we are dedicated to publishing fiction that will keep you turning the pages into the early hours. Don't want to miss a thing? To find out more about our books, promotions, discover exclusive content and enter competitions you can keep in touch in the following ways:

JOIN OUR COMMUNITY:

Sign up to our new email newsletter: http://smarturl.it/SignUpHQ

Read our new blog www.hqstories.co.uk

X https://twitter.com/HQStories

f www.facebook.com/HQStories

BUDDING WRITER?

We're also looking for authors to join the HQ Digital family! Find out more here:

https://www.hqstories.co.uk/want-to-write-for-us/

Thanks for reading, from the HQ Digital team